Lie for Me

CASSANDRA B. ANDREUCCI

TRIGGER WARNINGS

THIS BOOK CONTAINS THE FOLLOWING, BUT IS NOT LIMITED TO:

EXPLICIT SEX SCENES

DEPICTIONS OF VIOLENCE, BLOOD, TORTURE & MURDER

DEPICTIONS OF MANIPULATION & MANIPULATIVE BEHAVIORS

DEPICTIONS OF A TOXIC RELATIONSHIP

ILLEGAL ACTIVITIES, INCLUDING UNLAWFUL MARRIAGE AND UNLAWFUL SURVEILLANCE

DEPICTIONS OF STALKING BEHAVIOR

DUBIOUS CONSENT

KINK-RELATED ACTIVITIES, INCLUDING BUT NOT LIMITED TO:
    BREATH PLAY
    ROUGH/PRIMAL PLAY
    IMPACT PLAY (INVOLVING BRUISES)
    VOYEURISM
    EDGING
    CONSENSUAL NON-CONSENT (WITHOUT EXPLICIT CONVERSATION PRIOR TO THE ACT)

PLEASE READ THIS NOVEL WITH CAUTION

For those who like many variations of messy.
I see you xo.

— C

This is also for Ash & EJ.
You little devils.

PROLOGUE

THE SCREAMS BOUNCING OFF the walls blend with the powerful thumping of my heart in my ears like a macabre symphony. I tip my head back and close my eyes, filling my lungs with the stale air of the basement, reveling in the satisfaction vibrating under my skin.

I needed this. Really fucking needed it.

I let the blood-coated hammer slip from my hand, the message it delivered well received, as the screaming turns into pathetic keening sounds.

"If you don't stop, I will slice through your vocal cords," I drawl as I tilt my head forward and open my eyes.

The useless lump of a man who's strapped to the chair in front of me tries desperately to quieten his cries. His white shirt and light grey slacks are now tatters hanging from his rotund body, patches dark with sweat or discolored from his blood. He's a mess of cuts and bruises, the structure of his face now misshapen from the swelling.

Sweat pours down his forehead and cheeks as he screws his eyes shut and hiccups through his softer cries, snot mixing with the drool pouring over his chin.

My lip curls. Deplorable.

A figure materializes from the shadows at my side. Wade holds out a hand towel to me, his face pinching as he regards our friend in the chair.

"What did you want me to do with...*this?*" Wade spits as I clean my hands.

"Get rid of it," I say with dismissal.

I turn away as the man starts violently thrashing around, begging for his life.

"Just be grateful I didn't take your hands," I call over my shoulder as I step up to the desk in the corner, drop the soiled hand towel on the surface and pick up my suit jacket, sliding it on.

I don't give a shit if Wade lets him live with the promise of death if he says a word, or if he kills him and makes the body disappear. I got what I needed. I fish out my phone from the inner breast pocket and pull up my notes, logging the new information I've acquired, then switch to the tracking program.

I smile at the red dot on the screen—she's at home. Perfect.

An hour later, I pull my car into my usual parking space, climbing out quickly and locking the doors. Anticipation thrums in my veins with each townhouse I pass down the long driveway. Work has kept me from seeing her, and it's made me desperate for proximity.

I make it to the townhouse and use my key to open the front door, then slip in, keeping the lights off and bound up the stairs to the second floor. I cross to the west-facing bedroom and enter, immediately going to the window.

Tension melts from my body as she comes into view next door, the soft light of the room caressing her languid frame.

Christ, she's beautiful.

No matter how many hours I've watched her, she's still the most incandescent creature I've ever encountered. She has this sparkle that shimmers from within that's uniquely hers. A shiny temptation I've wanted to wrap my hands around and tear open, to steal some of that starlight and fill it with the bleakness from my own deranged heart, then put her back together, making her into a perfectly broken doll that's all mine.

I breathe through the sick fantasies playing across my vision and focus back on the scene in front of me. Then I frown.

She's crying.

I pull out my phone and bring up the camera feeds so I have audio. Her soft sniffles fill the room, grating on my resolve. She shouldn't be crying unless *I* make her cry.

Heavy footsteps echo through her house and then the door to her room opens. Fuel gets poured on the rage burning in my chest. Her *boyfriend*.

"Babe, come on," he whines, stepping up to her side. "Don't be like this."

He cups her elbow gently, but she rips her arm from his touch and moves away.

"Get out," she barks, her usually smooth, lyrical voice husky from emotion.

"Babe—"

She whips around. "Don't '*babe*' me. This is *over*, like you just said. Now get the fuck out of my house."

The cancer of a man huffs a "bitch", then spins on his heel and storms off. Continuing to watch her on the cameras as she flings herself onto her bed in a miserable heap, I hear her *ex*-boyfriend slam the door below and stomp a few doors down to his own townhouse.

What a waste of oxygen.

As she lifts her phone and types, I pull out the other phone from my pocket that mirrors hers and watch the messages appear on the screen.

He broke up with me.

What the fuck?! Why?

He's moving and doesn't want me to come.

What a fucking asshole!

Right?

How should we fuck up his life?

He's not worth the energy. It's over. That's punishment enough for him.

Over.

Finally fucking over.

I grin so hard it hurts.

Now it's time for *us*.

I sigh contentedly and take one last, long look at her, before putting both phones in my pocket and leaving the empty townhouse. I purchased it so I could be close to her. But soon, soon it won't be necessary.

Soon, my beloved, we'll be together.

Permanently.

1
PHAEDRA

I **FUCKED UP.**

I've had four too many Slippery Nipple shots, to the point that my *actual* nipples might make an appearance soon. I glance down at the plunging neckline of my dress to make sure they're still tucked away. The heavy beats of the club music pulse through my soul as I cling to the bar top and close my eyes, swaying my body in time with the tempo.

"Hey!" the bartender shouts, jolting my eyes open. "You good?"

"Yes," I shout back as I nod. "Sorry."

She doesn't look convinced as she pulls a glass from a rack, fills it with water, then sets it in front of me.

"Thank you!" I say, taking a sip of the chilled liquid.

"More shots?" Zahra asks from my side.

I burst out laughing. "Fuck, *no,* Zah."

My best friend rolls her eyes. "Lightweight."

"We're on our *eighth* shot *in a row*," I point out. "And we drank a whole bottle of champagne before we got here. I'd like to have a relatively functional liver tomorrow."

She cringes as she scoops up her Tequila Sunrise. "You're saying too many big words for right now."

"Let's go dance," I beg, picking up my glass of water.

Zahra never enjoyed dancing and took the first opportunity to quit classes when we were kids, but it's what I live and breathe, so she indulges me if she's drunk enough.

"No," she whines, then starts sucking down her drink faster. She knows what I'm about to say and knows I'm going to win this argument.

"*Whose* idea was it to come here?" I ask, knowingly.

She holds up a finger for emphasis. "*Technically*, this is work."

Zahra is a journalist that writes on lifestyle, fashion and society gossip pieces for a variety of magazines and websites, which gets her these amazing invites to so many cool parties, clubs and events.

Tonight, we're at a club called *Deux,* a new club in Manhattan that Zahra has been gushing about ever since she got the invite. Especially because the owners offered to cover an all-expenses-paid weekend for her *and* a plus-one.

She often begs me to tag along to these types of opportunities and, most of the time, I decline, my New York days long forgotten. But tonight was different, so we packed her new sedan with our bags for the weekend, drove here from Stamford, Connecticut after I finished teaching my morning class, drank our complimentary bottle of champagne at our fancy hotel while we got ready, and now I want to *dance*.

"*Just* work, huh?" I ask.

Her face softens as she reaches out and gives my elbow a sympathetic squeeze. "I'm sorry, Phae."

I bat her sympathetic hold off me. "None of that. You're the one that said Dylan wouldn't last."

Dylan and I had been dating for just over a year. He moved into a townhouse in the same complex and we met at our mailbox. He had just finished at Harvard and started working in finance—stock trading, something I still don't understand—with his focus on finding work in New York City and moving here from Connecticut.

He knew I didn't want to come back to New York, but I was warming to the idea, which he was fine with until last week when suddenly it was this *huge* deal, so he broke up with me and moved out of the complex the next day.

"It still sucks," Zahra says in a soft tone.

I fight the urge to roll my eyes, taking the opening instead and flashing her a grin. "What would make me feel *so* much better is if you took me to the dancefloor."

She shakes her head incredulously but stretches over the bar with her empty glass and puts it in an empty rack near the sink, then turns toward the crowd.

I turn with my water in hand and immediately crash into a wall. A large, warm wall.

Warm?

The wall produces hands that steady me before I tip backwards on my heels.

I look up, and *up*, my eyes roaming over a light shirt with no tie, smooth dark brown skin on thick, corded neck muscles with a prominent Adam's apple, a short, dark beard covering a strong jaw, plush lips curved into a lopsided grin, and then my eyes finally clash with a dark, penetrating gaze.

My lungs freeze. Holy shit, this man is beautiful. *Dangerously* so.

Long lashes and high cheekbones compliment those dark, dark eyes, along with an artfully tousled mess of dark curls that makes my fingers itch to touch.

The man has the broadest shoulders I've ever seen on someone who isn't a professional bodybuilder, and he's dressed in a very nice suit that's expertly cut to his generously muscled body.

I realize I've been ogling the sliver of exposed flesh at the open collar for *far* too long, so I drag my eyes back to his face, and I continue to lose brain cells while captivated by his perfection.

I say the first string of words that the remaining gray matter in my brain can comprehend. "I'm wet."

Mystery man's lips move into a full-blown grin as I feel the heat of mortification spread over my face and chest.

"Are you?" he says in a voice so low and gravelly that I *feel* it through my body.

I pull my focus from the magnetism of those dark eyes and look down between us. The fairly full glass of water is now a mostly empty glass, and there's a wet patch on both my red dress and his light shirt.

Not looking at Dark Eyes directly finally gets some brain function to start again, and I register his hand wrapped around mine on the glass and feel his steadying grip on my waist.

"I'm so sorry," I rush out, trying to step back, but his hold tightens on my waist.

The move forces me to look into that dark gaze again, and it renders me breathless.

Get a fucking grip, Phae.

"What are you going to do about it?" he asks.

"About what?" I ask wistfully, too distracted by his sinfully curved mouth. His lips are perfectly symmetrical, the envy of women everywhere.

My heartbeat picks up as that tempting mouth moves closer. My eyes flick up to dark pools dripping with heat.

"About how wet you are." His voice, that rumble, the suggestion. Good god.

I pull in a sharp breath, and my eyes almost roll. *Fuck*, he smells incredible—a wickedly sensual fusion of something woodsy, with a hint of citrus. I want to rub myself all over him.

Down, girl.

Blinking away the haze his scent and looks has put me in, I clear my throat and this time step back without resistance. "Your shirt."

"Your dress," he counters with an arch of a thick, neat brow.

I look down at the wet patch again. It has definitely spread. "It's just water."

The glass is suddenly plucked out of my hand, making me look up at Dark Eyes as he moves forward. I instinctively step back until I hit the bar behind me, yelping at the contact.

Dark Eyes doesn't stop until his hard body is pressing into me, his eyes never leaving mine as he leans forward, forcing me to arch my back over the bar.

I'm keenly aware of every part of our bodies touching, every nerve ending buzzing. He's so tall compared to my five-foot-five plus the four-inch heels that my breasts are pressed into the lower part of his expansive chest, and his chin would definitely clear my head if I wasn't in heels. Have I ever known someone so...huge?

He moves his arm past me, which forces one of my legs to shift to between his, my knee pressing into thick, powerful thighs. I try not to focus on that as I realize he's doing what Zahra did; putting my glass on the rack by the sink.

His arm pulls back, but he doesn't move as he regards me with a slight tilt of his head and a ghost of a smile. It's almost like he's watching to see what I'll do.

His pause unlocks the survival part of my brain that I realize has been screaming at me the whole time to run the fuck away. What *am* I doing? This is a beautiful, *giant,* strange man trapping me against a bar.

I tense up my body, ready to shove this man off and get away, when he suddenly steps back, laces his fingers in mine, and then pulls me away from the bar. I have no choice but to follow him, as his grip is firm on my hand. The crowd seemingly parts for him as we move around the dance floor.

I look around the dense crowd. Where the hell is Zahra?

My heart pounds harder with panic as we near the exit, but he leads us past it toward the restrooms. Then he walks *past* the lines and enters a 'No Entry' door that leads into a short hallway with an emergency exit at the end and two other nondescript doors. The door closes to the club behind me and muffles the sound dramatically.

"We can't be in here," I whisper as Dark Eyes opens the first door.

"I know the owner," he says offhandedly as he flicks a switch on the wall and the sconces on the wall illuminate the luxurious marble bathroom in a low, warm glow.

He tugs me into the room and doesn't let go of my hand until the door is closed behind him.

Great, now I'm trapped in a fucking bathroom with him blocking the door and having no idea where my best friend went.

Despite the stupid situation I've put myself in, I can't help but take this quiet moment to study the man again.

His tousled curls are inky black, matching his beard, and the suit he's wearing is navy, the shirt a light blue, which complements his brown skin. I don't dare to get lost in those dark eyes again, instead, focusing on his tempting lips.

This guy has me trapped, and yet I still wonder what those lips would feel like against mine.

"I won't harm you," he says, drawing my attention. He's watching me again.

"I don't know that," I rush out.

He bows his head and holds out his hands placatingly, then tucks them behind him, trapping them between his body and the door he's leaning against. "Better?"

"Not really," I breathe.

He points toward the vanity with his chin. "Last drawer, there's a hairdryer."

I frown. "Why would there be a hairdryer?"

He smiles, and fuck me, why is everything this man does disarming?

"There's also a shower." He jerks his chin to the space above me. "Behind you."

I might be drunk and trapped, but I'm not stupid enough to take my eyes off this guy, so I step back until my back hits what feels like glass.

"It's weird for a club to have a shower in a bathroom," I comment.

"Not when the place used to be an illegal brothel."

I jerk forward. "What?"

Dark Eyes chuckles, the rumbling sound making me shiver. "I'm joking. I don't know why, but where there's a shower, there's a hairdryer."

After a few silent seconds, I'm too aware of the soggy fabric clinging to my skin, so I finally take the bait and step sideways toward the vanity, keeping my eye on Dark Eyes.

When my hip taps the marble, I feel down until I touch the last drawer handle and pull it open. In my periphery, I see the hairdryer and pull it out.

"Socket is this side of the vanity," Dark Eyes informs, continuing to watch me with amusement.

I slide along the surface, and, feeling more secure with the hairdryer as a weapon, finally move my eyes from Dark Eyes briefly to plug in the device. I turn it to low heat and high force, then start waving it back and forth over my dress, my attention returning to Dark Eyes.

He hasn't moved, watching the dryer with rapt attention. Or is he staring at my tits?

"Hey," I bark over the dryer sounds, drawing his gaze up to my face. "Eyes up here."

Slowly, he moves his hands out from behind him, then steps to his right, away from me. He moves slowly around the perimeter of the room until he reaches the toilet opposite me and takes a seat on the closed lid. He goes so far to lift an ankle and rest it on his knee, getting *comfortable*.

"What's your name?" I blurt out and instantly want to smack myself. *Stop engaging with the hot stranger who thinks it's perfectly normal to take women into private bathrooms.*

"Whatever you want it to be," he says.

"'Creepy dude that trapped me in the bathroom' is too long."

He tilts his head in that assessing way again. "You think I'm creepy?"

I take a moment to consider it. "No, but your behavior is concerning."

He nods and moves both feet to the ground, and he stands. "I agree, and I apologize. I shall leave you to it."

"Wait!" I say, jerking forward before he takes a step. "What if the owner catches me here?"

Dark Eyes shrugs, tucking his hands in his pants pocket. "Tell him you know me."

"You still haven't given me your name," I point out.

"Shaw," he provides.

I frown. "Just 'Shaw'?"

He nods. "And you?"

"What about me?"

"Your name."

Panic seizes my lungs. Shit. Phaedra is too easy to remember. My last name, Mills, is common enough, but I don't want to give him that either. A strand of my long hair flies out in front of me, giving me my answer.

"You can call me Lilac."

2
PHAEDRA

"LILAC," SHAW REPEATS, LIKE he's tasting the name on his tongue. "Like your beautiful hair."

"Exactly," I say with a small smile, continuing to dry my dress.

Shaw takes a step toward the door slowly. "Would you like me to leave, Lilac?"

My eyes drop to the damp patch still on his shirt, and the back of my neck prickles with guilt. "You should dry that first."

He dips his head and, changing his angle, walks up to me, keeping a couple feet between us, his hands behind his back again.

"You seem pretty efficient with the dryer," Shaw comments. "Care to provide me with your expertise?"

I roll my eyes, check the state of my dress—it's mostly dry—then turn the warm air toward Shaw and swivel the dryer back and forth over his shirt.

"What brings you here tonight?" he asks.

"Work." It's not *my* truth, but it's *a* truth.

Shaw raises a brow, his dark gaze skating over my sleeveless, skintight red dress and black four-inch stilettos, before returning to my face. "What kind of...*work?*"

"I'm not an escort, if that's what you're asking."

He continues to regard me silently, waiting for my answer.

"I'm a journalist."

"What are you reporting on?" he asks.

I give him a mocking smile. "The history of this place being an illegal brothel."

My answer pulls one of those delicious rumbling chuckles from him, which makes my stomach flutter.

"Why are *you* here?" I ask.

"I came to see someone."

My eyes widen. "Shit, like a date?"

"Doesn't matter," he says, his dark eyes sparkling with intention. "I'm where I want to be."

"In a bathroom with a stranger who poured water all over you?"

Shaw smiles. "Exactly."

I have to drag my gaze from his face which projects *exactly* what he wants—he wants *more*. More with me.

And god knows I will climb this man like a fucking tree if I stare into those pools of sin he calls eyes for much longer.

I focus my attention on the patch of water I'm drying. It's mostly dry but the edges are still damp because his jacket is in the way. Without thinking, I step closer, reach out, and slide my fingers over his shirt, moving his jacket.

Jesus, he's so warm and hard. My fingers venture further across—he has *ridges* of muscle, for fuck's sake.

"Ridiculous," I mumble out loud.

"What is?" Shaw asks, drawing my attention back to his face.

Fuck.

We're way closer than before. The only thing between us is the hairdryer which is still blowing.

"Your body is..." I trail off, my voice hoarse.

"Ridiculous?" Shaw supplies.

My fingers continue to wander up his torso, reveling in his body shuddering under my touch. "Yeah... Ridiculous."

His eyes dip to my mouth, his tongue swiping across his bottom lip. "If you keep touching me, Lilac, I won't be able to restrain myself from returning the favor."

I turn off the dryer, putting it down absently behind me, then put my other hand on Shaw's torso. My fingers barely move before a hand sinks into my hair at the base of my neck, and Shaw crushes his lips to mine.

The world seems to still for half a second, completely, perfectly still for a breath of a moment, and then it bursts around me.

We're clawing hands, tight grips, and warring mouths and tongues as Shaw moves forward until my ass hits the vanity, then picks me up easily and plants me on the top. He pulls his mouth away and I let out a protesting whimper.

Shaw nudges my knees apart, stepping between them and pulling me flush against his chest. He cradles my jaw, forcing me to look into those captivating eyes.

"This isn't usually how I...conduct myself," he pants. "But you...*this*..."

"Yeah," I breathe. I get what he means. There's an almost tangible pull between us that's impossible to ignore.

His eyes search my face. "May I—"

I cut him off by hooking my hand on the back of his neck and pull his mouth to mine while wrapping my legs around his waist. His *impressive* erection presses into my soaked thong; the zipper of his pants is in just the right position for my clit to get delicious friction.

Shaw's grip on my jaw tightens as he pulls back just enough for me to stare into dark, molten pools of lust. I'm already obsessed with his eyes.

"I need to hear it, Lilac," he grits out.

"Less talking, more fucking, Shaw."

My words unleash his restraint as he slams his mouth back to mine. His hold on my jaw slides down my throat and chest until his finger hooks into the neckline of my dress and pushes it aside, exposing my breast and hardened nipple to him. He does it to the other one, then pulls back, admiring my tits.

"Fucking spectacular," he pants before his head dips down and he captures a nipple between his teeth.

I gasp at the slight sting, then shiver as his tongue laves over the stiff peak, sending jolts of electricity directly to my core. My fingers sink into his curls—the thick strands so *fucking* silky—as he nips and licks over my left breast, then my right, making my brain fuzzy and my clit throb.

"Shaw," I groan.

He grazes his teeth along my nipple until he lifts off, those dark eyes clashing with mine again, pulling me into their depth.

"Condom," I say when I find language again in the recesses of my mind.

Shaw nods, reaching over to the top drawer and opening it, pulling out a condom.

"You've done this before?" I ask, amused.

He chuckles. "Not here, no."

Realization suddenly clicks in my mind. "*You're* the owner, aren't you?"

The grin spreading across his lips is breathtaking. "Guilty."

I shake my head incredulously as I loosen my legs around his waist and start unbuckling Shaw's belt while he pulls off his jacket and tosses it onto the vanity next to me.

He pulls his shirt out of the way and my hand slides into his boxer briefs, wrapping around his thick cock, and we both moan. It's the biggest cock I've ever seen or touched, long and girthy, straight with the slightest curve upward. The skin is warm and soft as it pulses under my touch. I pump him teasingly, fascinated by the wetness seeping from the tip.

I lick my lips. I want to taste him.

"Look at me like that and I'll put you on your knees," Shaw growls.

What a fantastic idea. I lift my chin to look at him as I slide off the vanity, then continue to sink to the floor slowly. Shaw sees my intentions, and he grabs my hips, stopping my descent. He spins me abruptly so I face the mirror, my palms meeting cool marble to steady myself.

I catch my reflection. One side of my dress has slid down to my elbow, but both of my breasts are still out, my nipples still hard and now a rosy pink from Shaw's attention. My lips are swollen from kissing, my waist-length lilac hair that was once neat, relaxed curls, now disheveled from his firm grips.

I also realize our size difference a lot more. I've been dancing ballet since I was six, so I'd always been slim with lack of curves, until the last three years after I retired from the East Ballet Company. I still teach ballet and dance recreationally, but now I have some weight on my hips and chest, giving me some soft curves.

But I'm still only a slim, short woman compared to this thick and giant man behind me. Right now, partially obscured because of the low lighting, he's like a foreboding presence watching from the shadows.

A predator in wait, preparing to devour its prey.

That thought spikes the adrenaline in my blood, making my body buzz with anticipation. My heart races as, through the mirror, I watch Shaw trace his fingers from my temple, behind my ear and down the side of my neck, gathering my hair and pulling it to the other side. He leans down and plants a soft kiss at the juncture of my neck and shoulder.

"I need to feel your cunt pulsing around me while I come," he says, his mouth moving over my skin before sinking his teeth into my shoulder.

My knees nearly buckle.

He releases me, runs his tongue flat over the bite, then straightens. He watches me through the mirror as my eyes follow the foil packet in his hand to his mouth, watch as he rips it open with his teeth, then it disappears behind me.

I twist to see Shaw rolling the latex down his straining shaft, and then a hand gathers all of my hair and twists it around a fist. My head then gets jerked back to the mirror. Shaw's dark eyes catch mine in the reflection as he nudges the hand wrapped up in my hair forward, forcing me to bend over the vanity further. My palms slide until my fingers press into the mirror, my breath fogging up the reflective glass.

Shaw pulls his magnetic gaze from me to look down as I feel his free hand slide my dress up, exposing my ass.

"Fuck," he groans, his hand sliding over my bare cheeks reverently. "So perfect."

His fingers hook under the straps of my thong, and I'm expecting him to tear it off my body, but he doesn't, quickly sliding the scrap of fabric over my ass and hips, letting it fall to my ankles. I lift a foot and shake it off, then slide my legs further apart.

"Touch me," I whimper, not giving a single fuck that I sound as desperate as I feel.

Shaw obliges, his touch skirting over my ass cheek again, and then a thick finger glides through my dripping arousal, over my entrance and pressing into my clit. I let out a choked moan as I jerk forward at the rush of sensation, but Shaw follows, pressing firmer, circling over the sensitive spot that makes stars dance across my vision.

"I want to explore every inch of this body," Shaw says in a low tone. "Taste every part of you."

"Later," I rush out, drawing his eyes back to me. "Right now, I need you to f—"

My words cut off as two fingers sink into me. My body clenches around the digits as my eyes roll.

"So tight," Shaw comments as he moves his fingers in and out of me lazily, curving them down to drag across the front walls, completely reorganizing my neural pathways. "And dripping for me."

I just notice through the mind-bending sensations that he's scissoring his fingers out with every other thrust in, stretching me in preparation for his cock.

"Do it," I pant, catching his eye in the mirror. "I can take it."

Shaw narrows his eyes at me, his face suddenly serious. "Are you sure about that, Lilac?"

"*Yes.*"

His fingers pull out of me, his hand grabbing my ass cheek roughly as he spreads me open and then he thrusts his cock to the hilt in one swift move. Stinging pain lances through my body at the sudden stretch, but my lungs freeze and my eyes roll closed at the euphoric rush immediately after.

Shaw lets out a deep, strangled groan that I feel vibrate through my whole body, making me pulse around him.

"*Christ,*" he grits out through clenched teeth.

The grip in my hair tightens as Shaw pulls most of the way out, then slams back in again, and my ability to formulate sentences disintegrates. He repeats the move, slow and measured out, hard and fast in; the decadent pain and waves of pleasure feed the simmering heat gathering in my body, driving it higher and higher to the peak of oblivion.

On his next thrust in, I push back, my hips meeting his and I once again see stars as my body clenches around Shaw's cock. He stalls with a tortured groan, his hand squeezes my ass cheek hard enough that I'm definitely going to have bruises.

I push up from the vanity so I can slide a hand to my clit, but it changes the angle, making Shaw sink in deeper, and I stop breathing.

Shaw twists more hair around his fist and tests out this new angle with a quick thrust and my knees *actually* buckle. The only thing holding me up is his grip on my hair.

"I'm close," I pant.

Shaw looks at me through the mirror and nods in agreement. He's close too. "You ready?"

"Fuck yes," I moan, my fingers finding my clit.

A wicked grin spreads over Shaw's lips, and then he moves. Gone is the controlled rhythm of before, replaced with a hard, frenzied fuck that jerks my body forward with every thrust.

I rub furious circles over my clit and the constant change in pressure from being fucked into the marble of the vanity sends me flying over the edge at such a frantic speed that I scream as I come.

White bursts across my vision as pleasure pours through my entire body. It's like liquid fire in my veins, every part of me pulsing with the most intense orgasm I've ever experienced.

It feels like forever until I finally come back to this plane. My heated, naked chest is pressed into the cool marble as I take short breaths, the grip in my hair gone, and there's an oddly comforting heavy pressure over my lower back.

I blink my vision clear and turn my head—Shaw is leaning over my lower half with his head hanging between his shoulders as he pants heavily.

Seeing him spent like this sends another jolt through me and I throb around him.

He groans, his head snapping up to me. A lazy smile curves those delicious lips. "Ready for round two already?"

Tenderness suddenly rolls through various parts of my body and I wince. "Raincheck?"

He chuckles as he nods. "I need at least ten minutes."

I try not to hiss as Shaw pulls out slowly and takes a step back to give me space to move. I push myself up on shaky arms and tuck my tits away as Shaw moves around behind me. He tosses the condom in a trashcan by the toilet while I clean myself up using paper towel and water, then step back into my panties and fix the hem of my dress.

Shaw comes up to my side and washes his hands as I comb my fingers through my wild lilac curls, taming most of it, and check my makeup. Apart from my lipstick, being well and truly gone, the rest is still intact.

"You're beautiful," Shaw comments as he's drying his hands, watching me through the mirror.

I smile, turning to him. "So are you."

He steps forward, cupping the back of my neck, and presses his lips to mine once more. I melt against him, enjoying the feel of his hard body against me, and fill my lungs with his woods and citrus scent for a moment longer.

This is nothing but a fun, crazy night to add to my memory bank, so I'm going to make sure it's one that would make my future senior home nurses gasp over.

Shaw pulls back too soon, his dark eyes searching my face. "Are you ready?"

My brow furrows in confusion. "For what?"

Something indiscernible flashes in his eyes before it's smothered by amusement. It was just a blip of that *something*, but I notice it.

"To return to society," he says.

"Yeah," I say, still stuck on what it was that I saw, but his words trigger something more pressing than micro expressions. "Oh, fuck, *Zahra*."

"Your brunette friend?"

I nod. "She has my phone. She's probably freaking out."

Shaw pulls his phone from his pants pocket. "She's with my best friend and my sister."

He taps on his phone a couple times, grins, then turns the screen toward me. There's a photo of Zahra wearing someone else's sunglasses and pouring champagne from a giant bottle into the mouth of a suited man on his knees in front of her.

"Well, she's fine," I laugh.

Shaw drops his arm with a smile. "Seems so."

I turn back to the vanity and pick up his suit jacket, then hold it open. Shaw accepts the gesture, hooking his arms into the sleeves and pulling the jacket on before turning back to me.

I smooth down the lapels and fix up his collar, then he pulls me to his side, his arm wrapping around me and his hand resting comfortably on my hip. "Let's take this party elsewhere."

3
ATTICUS

VANILLA AND LILAC.

It's in my nose and on my tongue. I've been dreaming about that combination for so long, and it's more than I thought it'd be.

She's everything I thought she'd be.

Phaedra.

Or Lilac, as she's calling herself tonight.

Fitting, given the thick streams of lilac-purple hair falling in wild waves down to the curve of her perfect ass.

I grin into my glass of gin on the rocks, watching Phaedra drink with her friend and my sister. Her ass will have my marks on it in the morning from my rough grip.

And now that I've finally gotten a taste, she'll have to get used to wearing my marks regularly.

"I can hear your mind scheming from here," Sloane says, just loud enough to be heard over the music.

I finish the rest of my drink and put it down on the low table in front of me. "Let's go."

My best friend raises a brow at me curiously. "We just got here."

"We have business to attend to at the penthouse."

"I think you mean *you* have business," he retorts. "*My* business is right in front of me."

He tilts his head toward the women and fury blurs the edges of my vision.

Phaedra is no one's business but *mine*.

I lock down the temptation to gouge out Sloane's eyes and pull out my phone. "We're bringing your business to mine."

As if that's what he was waiting to hear, a wide grin spreads across his face as he stands, his arms out. "Ladies, it's time for the after-party."

I stand as well, my skin tingling from the feeling of her eyes watching me. Those beautiful bright topaz irises surrounded by long, dark lashes. In the sunlight, they have the slightest tinge of green. She gets her eye color from her father, but her olive skin and naturally dark brown hair from her mother.

I'm much more in favor of the lilac hair.

I finally lift my attention from confirming our pickup with my driver to Phaedra. I see her breath catch, her eyes dilate even in the low lights of my club. Knowing she's just as transfixed by me as I am with her sends electricity shooting down my spine.

I almost laugh; 'transfixed' is a severely insufficient description of the roaring insanity ravaging my body and mind every waking second that Phaedra exists.

Pocketing my phone, I prowl forward, my focus solely on her.

It will *always* be on her.

My Phaedra.
Now to make her mine permanently.

4
PHAEDRA

MUFFLED SOUNDS PULL ME from a deep sleep. It feels like I'm underwater: there's an uncomfortable pressure on my chest and head, and my limbs feel heavy. The muffled sounds get louder and I realize it's someone calling my name.

"Phaedra Mills, you better wake the fuck up before I body slam you."

The only person who would be that incredibly rude to me is Zahra.

"I'm up," I slur, willing myself to break through the fog in my mind. I pry my eyes open and white light burns my retinas immediately, so I fling my arm over my eyes. "What the fuck?"

"That's the sun, cupcake," Zahra chirps, her voice grating on my nerves and making the pounding in my head worse.

"Fucking sun," I mutter as every single movement Zahra makes blasts through my head. "Zah...stop...please."

"Stop what?"

I groan. "Existing."

She laughs, and I want to die.

"I told you those body shots off the stripper was not the way to go," she comments.

I jolt upright in the bed and blink my eyes rapidly. My stomach seizes tightly, saliva flooding my mouth, and I cup both hands over my lips. An empty trashcan with a liner is shoved under my chin just as I heave, then puke my guts up.

"Knew that was coming," Zahra mutters as she continues to move around the room while I empty my life choices into the trashcan I'm now hugging.

Once the gagging subsides and I can breathe again, a washcloth appears at my side. I take the cool, damp cloth and wipe my sweating and leaking face.

"Toss it in the trash," Zahra instructs, and I do as I'm told.

I tie up the liner then Zahra swaps me the trashcan for a box of Tylenol and a bottle of water. I take two pills, guzzle half the water and manage to cap the bottle before falling back down to the mattress. I don't make it to the soft heaven.

"Oh no, you don't," Zahra says as she catches my body and shoves me back into a seated position. "You need to shower so we can leave."

"Leave?" I croak out, and look around. This isn't Zahra's apartment or my condo. It's a large bedroom with French double doors opening to a living space. I turn to see walls of windows showing an impressive view of a ton of high-rise buildings.

"Where are we?" I ask.

Zahra laughs, but when I don't join in, her makeup-free, concerned face comes into view. "Do you really not remember?"

I rack my brain, trying to pull memories of the last few days. My eyes drift to the bedside table; there's a small glass vase with a single stem in its water. A cluster of small purple flowers with a couple of green leaves. They're lilacs.

Lilac.

Like your beautiful hair.

Memories flood back all at once. Zahra convincing me to go to New York. The club. The bathroom. Dark eyes.

Shaw.

"I can see your life flashing before your eyes," Zahra says, amused.

Her comment pulls me from the scrambled replay of the night, that bathroom memory being the star of the show, and I look at her.

Zahra's already dressed in a black sports bra and matching leggings, with most of her dark brown braids gathered up in a teal silk scarf with some strands hanging around her face. Her deep brown skin and eyes are practically glowing like we didn't just spend the whole night chugging liquor and making poor decisions.

"How are you not withering away?" I ask, using sheer will to stay upright.

She smirks. "Hair of the dog."

I balk, my stomach twisting. "How can you stomach alcohol right now?"

She laughs, standing from the bed, and continues to pack both our overnight bags. "I've been up for four hours, and we got back seven hours ago. I picked up where I left off, and now I'm riding it out better than you will."

I groan, dropping my head in my hands and rubbing the bottom of my palms into my eyes. "This is going to *suck*."

"Yeah, I know," Zahra agrees. "But right now, I need you to get your ass in the shower so we can check out."

I take a deep breath before pulling my face out of my hands and crawl out of the bed. Zahra shoves a pile of clothes in my arms, grabs my shoulders, spins me toward the adjoining bathroom, and slaps my ass. "Off you go."

I yelp at the sting, confused as to why that hurt more than usual. My brain supplies the answer by shoving the memory of Shaw gripping my ass cheek, spreading me wider as he thrusts—

I rush toward the bathroom, face and neck hot as I try to squash the memories of the dark stranger from last night.

—— § ——

I'm showered and dressed in twenty minutes, much to Zahra's approval, and then we're out of the hotel room as soon as I've shoved my sleep clothes into my bag. Zahra checks out at the front desk as I drag myself to the café in the hotel lobby and order us food and much-needed coffee.

Once I have the fully loaded bagels and two cold brews with half-and-half in hand, I meet Zahra out the front. We demolish our bagels while we wait for the valet to bring the car around, then pack the trunk.

"You good to drive?" I ask.

"Definitely," she says, pulling out one of the coffees from the tray in my hand. "It's been hours since my last drink."

I nod and round the metallic blue car to the front passenger side with my coffee, and slide onto the soft, cream leather seat as Zahra gets behind the wheel. I take her coffee and put it into the cupholder, do the same with mine, then pick a music playlist and settle back in the seat.

It's an hour to my condo give or take the traffic to get out of Manhattan, and usually I love a road trip no matter the distance, but my brain keeps hitting me with flashes from last night. They aren't in any discernible order, so I take a minute to mentally file them.

Finishing the ballet class I was teaching.

Arriving at the hotel.

Getting room service for dinner and having champagne.

Zahra insisting I wear her red dress.

Getting to the club. *What was it called again?*

Slippery Nipple shots. Way too many of them.

Crashing into someone.

My brain pauses. Shaw. I remember his face in exact detail. Remembering how he bent me over the bar, then in the bathroom. My body pulses at the memory of how hard he fucked me. I'm sore today, but I'd definitely do it again.

Did we do it again?

I remember leaving the bathroom, returning to Zahra and meeting Shaw's stunning sister and charismatic best friend—both their names I've completely forgotten—but I remember nothing after that.

"How did we get back to the hotel?" I ask, turning to Zahra and interrupting her singing to the pop music playing.

Her eyes flick to me for a second, then back to the road. "Seriously?"

"I remember meeting some people in VIP, and then…" I trail off, trying to remember anything after that. A fuzzy memory constructs. "We got in a town car?"

"Wait, you don't remember the penthouse?" Zahra asks, her eyes flicking to me again, then back to the road.

I frown. "*What* penthouse?"

Zahra laughs. "Don't fuck with me, Phae. The penthouse. The one the hottie who had eyes only for you owned."

I dive into the recesses of my brain, but there's nothing about a penthouse.

When I don't answer, Zahra gasps. "Holy shit."

"Tell me everything," I demand, angling my body toward her and turning down the music.

Zahra nods, taking a moment to gather her thoughts as we slow to a crawl in New York afternoon traffic.

"So, it was a limousine we got into, not a town car. We went to hottie's apartment on like the eightieth or ninetieth floor of some fancy building with the craziest views of Central Park. There were other people there. It was a whole party we crashed."

Images unlock in my head: a sea of blurry people, so many windows, and—

"There was someone playing a grand piano," I blurt out. "Tchaikovsky."

Zahra nods. "Yeah, you stood there for so long listening to him play. You even started requesting songs."

My cheeks burn. Of course I did.

"What happened next?" I ask.

"Uh... Oh, I made out with hottie's friend. And maybe also his sister?"

"Do you remember their names?"

She shakes her head. "They told me twice, but you know I'm hopeless with names."

"Did I *really* take body shots off a stripper?" I ask, cringing already. I've done it before.

Zahra barks out a laugh. "I was joking. There weren't any strippers. It was finance bros measuring their figurative dicks by boasting about how much money they earned that day. We were the most entertaining people there. Pretty sure they thought *we* were strippers."

"We're *always* the most entertaining people," I counter with a smirk.

"True," she says, returning my smile. It turns quickly into a frown. "After the piano man and a lot of the other guests left, we kind of lost track of each other."

My heart rate picks up. "What?"

"*You're* the one who wanted to go bang the hottie somewhere in his penthouse," Zahra says defensively. "And I was in an intense game of poker with his friend and the last remaining finance bros."

I roll my eyes. "Did you tell everyone your dad was a card shark again?"

Zahra's wolfish grin is answer enough.

"How long was I gone for?" I ask, still trying to work out what I did after I left Zahra.

"Maybe fifteen minutes?" Zahra supplies. "It was long enough that I'd wiped the floor with the finance bros in poker, but quick enough that I made a comment about hottie not being able to last long." She looks at me again briefly, concern pinching her brows. "You invoked Kevin."

I sit back in my seat. "Shit."

"Kevin" is our code word when we want to leave a situation. It's not necessarily a "call the cops immediately" code; it's like when a first date gets awkward, suddenly my 'Grandpa Kevin' is in the hospital, or if the vibe of the party feels off, Zahra's dog "Kevin" just escaped her apartment.

I close my eyes and breathe slowly, trying to clear the fuzz in my brain and find the memories I'm missing. I start at the piano man, remembering someone giving me more champagne, then I… I'm in a kitchen, maybe it was white? Zahra's doing shots with a man. I can't tell what he looks like. I think I took some shots too. And then…

Nothing. A black spot in my memory from there.

Fuck.

I invoked Kevin. Surely, there was something…

A blurry vision manifests. It's a huge wooden desk. And bookshelves. An office maybe? I remember the feel of the desk under my fingertips, all the papers over it. I think I picked up a pen and twirled it around.

And then there was the feel of the desk under my ass. And warmth between my legs. A body. *Shaw's* body. My legs wrapped around Shaw's warm body.

Did we have sex again?

I shake my head. I know in my gut that we didn't, but I think I tried?

"I think maybe I tried to have sex with hottie again and he rejected me," I say out loud, opening my eyes to look at Zahra. "That's probably why I invoked Kevin."

Zahra nods in agreement. "That would make sense. He didn't come out to send us off. Maybe he was embarrassed?" She suddenly jolts straighter, looking between me and the road rapidly. "Wait. *Again?* You already fucked him? When? *Where?*"

I wince. "Uh—"

She smacks me in the boob. "You asshole. Spill, immediately."

I tell her the watered-down version while I nurse my sore breast.

"You dirty bitch," she says with admiration. "God, I love you."

"I love you, too."

"To end our adventure," Zahra says, picking up her nearly finished coffee and taking a sip. "Kevin was invoked, we got a car service, you sobbed when room service arrived with your sweet potato fries, then after we ate that, we took each other's makeup off and went to bed."

"I didn't say anything else after we left?" I ask.

There's something buzzing in the back of my brain wanting attention, but I can't untangle any more from my brain fog.

Zahra shakes her head as she finishes off the rest of her coffee. "Not that I remember. I asked if you were okay. You said the penthouse was probably not a good idea, and then the conversation moved on."

"Drunk me was probably right," I mutter, picking up my own

coffee and taking a sip.

I was probably embarrassed about being forward with Shaw and him rejecting me, so I invoked Kevin and we booked it out of there.

If there was anything else that happened, I'm sure I'll remember it later and then I'll deal.

I nod to myself, drain the rest of my coffee, turn up the music, and settle into the drive.

5

PHAEDRA

Two Months Later

MY LAST **SATURDAY CLASS**, my teen group, concludes their session and rush off to get their things from the edges of the studio's main floor.

I walk the perimeter of the light-filled space, running my hands across the barre in front of the wall of mirrors, answering last-minute questions from my students before following them out to the small reception and parent waiting area.

I'm rushed by a couple of parents with the usual inquiries to the progression of their child's dancing, which I answer with the same realistic assurances I always give them and then they're politely ushered out by Will, my administration whiz.

He's in his second year of college and was a student of mine before he got into an accident and broke his leg. Though he could have gotten back into ballet, he decided to chase other pursuits.

I offered him a position while he was in recovery to handle the part of this job I despise—paperwork—and he's been with me ever since.

Our arrangement is perfect for him because he works any hours that fit around his classes, plus he gives me a few free hours a week in exchange for private tuition for his sister, who's one of my star students.

"These came for you," he says as he crosses over to his desk and picks up a pile of mail, then turns to me. "Leave any I can sort out for you on my desk."

He knows the ones that are bills just by the envelopes, but Will is very serious about correspondence law, so he waits for me to open them before he does his thing.

"Thanks, Will," I say, taking the pile. "Are you ready for your presentation tomorrow?"

He winces. "Not exactly."

I swat him with the mail. "What are you doing here, then? *Go.*"

Relief softens his face as he rushes to his desk and grabs his messenger bag as I cross to my office.

"Thanks, Phae," Will calls. "I'll lock up."

"Thank you. Good luck!" I call over my shoulder, sifting through the envelopes as I round my desk.

I categorize the letters, making a pile for Will, and sifting through the advertising junk. One envelope piques my attention near the bottom of the pile. It's not a usual one, but it's addressed to my condo complex address—probably from the stack I brought with me on my way here—so I decide to open it.

I unfold the letter. The words "Certificate of Marriage Registration" is printed across the top in blue ink. Shit, I've opened someone else's mail from the complex.

I know most of my neighbors, so I peek at the names, wanting to know who I need to return it to with congratulatory cupcakes.

My heart stops.

This is to certify that **ATTICUS OLIVER SHAW**

and **PHAEDRA DARCY MILLS** (New Surname: **SHAW**)

were married

AUGUST 9TH at **SKY BUILDING, MANHATTAN**

"What...the fuck?" I whisper.

I read it again.

And again.

And *again*.

I drop the paper like it bit me.

This can't be happening.

I check the envelope. It's addressed to me. No, not me, to Phaedra *Shaw*. But that's my address and apartment number.

I look at the certificate again. Blink a few times. Yep, my name is still there. Along with my date of birth and address. Finally, I register other details of the certificate.

It's from the New York City clerk's office. The last time I was in New York was two months ago with Zahra...

On August ninth.

That was the night we went to that club, and I met...

Shaw.

My heart rate skyrockets as adrenaline and fury burst through my body. "What the *fucking* fuck!"

I swipe aside the mail, pick up my phone with shaking hands and call Zahra.

"Hey, girl," she says when she answers.

"I'm going to fucking kill him, Zah," I bark louder than necessary.

"I'll bring the shovel and trash bags, but we shouldn't talk about this on the phone," Zahra says, unfazed by my outburst.

"I can*not* believe this is happening," I pant, suddenly short of breath.

"Deep, slow breaths, baby," Zahra coos. "Then tell me what's going on."

I inhale, hold it, then exhale, slowing my heartbeat. "Remember our New York trip?"

"Of course," she says neutrally.

"And hottie with the penthouse?"

"He gave you chlamydia," Zahra says immediately.

"That would have been easier to handle," I mutter.

She gasps. "You're pregnant."

I rub my temple with my free hand and close my eyes. "At this point, I wish."

"Phae," Zahra says, worry laced in her tone.

"I'm *married*," I blurt out.

Silence on the other end meets me for a long moment.

"Say that again?" Zahra asks, deceptively calm.

"I... *We* are married. Me and hottie. Shaw. His name is Shaw. Well, no, it's *Atticus* Shaw according to this." I'm rambling: a reflection of the absolute disarray my mind is right now.

"According to *what*?" Zahra asks. She still sounds calm, but I know this is her seething internally. She must not be at home, or I'd be hearing a lot more expletives.

I tell her about the marriage license I found in the mail. Again, I'm met with a tense moment of silence.

"Where are you?" Zahra asks.

"The studio."

"Meet you at my place in fifteen minutes," she says and ends the call.

My ballet studio is in the heart of downtown and only half a dozen blocks from Zahra's apartment building.

I put the marriage certificate back in its envelope and shove it in my bag with my laptop and phone, then pick up the mail to drop at Will's desk. I turn off all the lights, lock up again as I leave the studio, and start the trek to Zahra's place.

The walk does little to settle the festering rage within me or the thousands of questions. How did this happen? *When?* And most importantly, *why?*

I approach Zahra's newly-built apartment building, the doorman greeting me by my first name since I'm here all the time and use the key fob Zahra gave me to access the elevator. I exit on the twentieth floor and walk to the end, using my key to let myself in.

As usual, I take off my shoes by the door, switching them for my house slippers, and walk through the spacious, open-plan kitchen and dining toward the living area at the back of the space.

My whole one-bedroom condo fits in this space alone, but Zahra's apartment has two bedrooms, two bathrooms, a powder room, plus an office as well.

This place has meticulously chosen furniture in cool-tone muted colors, minimalist monochromatic art on the walls, and layered textures of wood, stone and softer furnishings. It's calming and clean, but still inviting.

My house also has minimal furniture, but my sofa is in terracotta velvet, I have a collection of framed photos of friends and family on my hallway wall, and my bed has way too many pillows.

Zahra's family walks the line between upper-middle class and wealthy; her dad's an architect and her mom's in corporate marketing, so her parents had a sizeable deposit aside for her to purchase whatever property she wanted when she turned twenty-five.

She played it smart and got in early on a project her dad was working on, swindled the developers into giving her a "friends and family" discount, and got her ex-boyfriend who was a broker to negotiate the best possible loan terms to get this fabulous place for an absolute steal.

I, however, come from the completely opposite background to my best friend. My parents are lower-middle-class parents; my dad does maintenance for the school district and my mom is a teacher at a public elementary school.

I grew up in the small two-bedroom apartment my parents have been renting since they got married, and the only indulgence we ever spent money on was my ballet.

My parents took me to a free class when I was four, and according to my dad, I was like "a duck to water". I absolutely fell head over heels in love with the art form the moment I stepped foot into the studio.

I met Zahra there when I was six. It was the only place we would see each other regularly since we went to different schools and lived in completely different areas.

My parents could afford regular classes until I moved up levels. They were about to pull me from the program until Zahra demanded her parents keep her friend in classes with her, so they did. They sponsored me from then on, even after Zahra decided she wanted nothing else to do with dancing.

By that point, Zahra and I were inseparable, and our parents were all close friends, considering Zahra and me as *their* children collectively.

Where Zahra's parents paid for me to do ballet, my parents would take us camping or my mom would tutor us. Zahra's dad took us fishing, and mine taught us basic car care and how to change a tire.

Both our moms talked to us together about periods and boys. That was the best-worst sleepover ever.

When we were in our senior year, I was auditioning for ballet companies and Zahra was applying for colleges. We both ended up in Boston. The company *might* not have known Zahra was my permanent roommate in the company accommodation they provided for me after she finished freshman year.

Those are some of the best memories I have with Zah. It was like the world's longest sleepover as we shared the bed in the studio apartment and spent way too many nights drinking cheap wine and talking and laughing so hard we would piss off our neighbors. We were content, but naturally, there were challenges.

I loved the cozy space, whereas Zahra was itching for more. I didn't care that the building's elevator was out of service more than it was functional, or that our intercom was busted the entire time we were there, but Zahra was missing doormen that knew her first name and swipe-access *working* elevators.

Even so, when it was time for me to move to New York and Zahra was staying in Boston for grad school, we both sobbed.

The time apart was hard, but let us solidify our own eccentricities. Comfortable practicality Phaedra, and quiet luxury Zahra.

So, even though Zah's asked me countless times to sell my little condo and move in with her here in this beautiful apartment, and despite me being here almost more than my own place, it still feels like I'd be living in *Zahra's* space, not like the little refuge that I curated just for me.

The door opening pulls me out of my reverie, and I turn to watch Zahra shrug off her coat, letting it fall to the floor in a heap, and kick off her heels, switching to her house slippers, then cross to the island counter and dump her handbag on the end.

"Show it to me," Zah says as she crosses and drops onto the sofa next to me.

I pull the envelope out of my bag and hand it to her. She pulls the certificate out, reads it, brings it closer and squints at it, then holds it up to the light. After her thorough inspection, she drops it to her lap and she mutters a curse.

"It's real, isn't it?" I ask quietly.

She looks at me, so many emotions flashing through her eyes. She shakes her head in disbelief and pulls her phone from her slacks pocket. "Not until the government confirms it."

She types furiously, her eyes darting over the screen, her brows furrowing the more she reads. Eventually she blows out a breath, and my phone vibrates in my lap.

"You can only confirm it in person at the clerk's office," Zahra informs me. "They aren't open on the weekend, so I made you an appointment on Monday. I have to be in New York for an interview, so I'll drop you off and, if it is legit, then we can talk about the annulment over lunch."

I nod along, my eyes returning to the offensive paper on the glass coffee table. "I don't know how the fuck this happened."

"Neither do I," Zahra adds. "It didn't happen at the club, so it must have happened at the penthouse." I watch her mind work as she stares out the window behind me. "You would have had to sign the marriage license, so it didn't happen when you were jamming to the piano man, or when we were drinking in the kitchen. And then..."

I jerk up as her eyes whip to me.

"Poker," Zahra says at the same time I say, "The *office*."

"What office?" Zahra asks, her focus solely on me now.

I sigh. "That's the thing. I *still* don't remember most of it." I tell her what I do remember: the books, the desk, my legs wrapped around Shaw—*Atticus.*

"That sneaky little fuck," Zahra spits out.

I nod, then frown. "But *why?*"

"That is a good question," Zahra says, reaching for the marriage certificate and lifts her phone up. "Let's see who this asshole is."

I take out my phone as well, opening an internet search page and typing in 'Atticus Oliver Shaw New York'.

Pages of results come up, but the first link grabs my attention. I click it, the logo of an 'S' with a slightly smaller 'I' layered over it.

It kind of looks like a dollar sign.

"Shaw Incorporated," I read out loud. "Looks like an investment firm or stock brokerage?"

"Mhmm," Zahra hums absentmindedly; the only other sound from her is vigorous tapping on her phone screen as I continue to read.

Atticus is the CEO of Shaw Incorporated, and their business is basically everything. Investments, property, start-ups, hospitality. They have their money in a lot of places, both domestic and global.

I click into the leadership portfolios and scan the team. Of course, my traitorous eyes linger on Atticus' stupidly beautiful face for longer than necessary before I drag my eyes to the information about him.

The only thing it really tells me is that he's been CEO for four years and lists the huge amount of business that's been handled under his reign, so I look up from my phone. My eye catches on the certificate in Zahra's lap, and I pluck it from her.

His date of birth is on this document. He's thirty-six. And a Leo.

I roll my eyes. Confident, charismatic, egotistical. *Of course,* he's a Leo.

I search the address he provided as his residence on my phone and find a real estate listing that's very familiar. That's the penthouse where all of this went down. Sky Building. Naturally, Shaw Incorporated owns the building.

"Holy shit," Zahra gasps, drawing my attention back to her. She's staring at her phone, mouth agape in shock. "Holy shit. Holy *shit!*"

"Zah?" I ask softly.

She looks up slowly, her mouth still open. She eventually snaps it shut and swallows hard.

I steel my spine. "Tell me."

"He's a Shaw," she starts.

I nod. "Got that."

"No, he's a *Shaw*. Like *the* Shaws of New York high society. The sister we met that night was Constance Shaw, the fucking supermodel." She turns her screen, showing a photo of Atticus, Constance, and the other guy we met that night. Looks like it's a photo from a black-tie event. "That's his best friend, Sloane Yorke, of the fucking Yorke jewels dynasty."

I grimaced. "Don't hurt me, but I don't have any idea what you're talking about."

"Do you ever listen to my work stories?" she asks, unfazed, as she readjusts on the sofa, tucking her legs underneath her. "Constance Shaw is the hottest model in the business right now. She has designers offering to lick her toes to wear their shit."

"That's disgusting," I comment.

"And Sloane?" Zahra continues. "The Yorkes are *old* money. They're the jewelers to fucking royalty. The dude probably wipes his ass with hundred-dollar bills."

"Jesus, Zah. What's with the grotesque imagery today?" I ask with a smile. "Let me guess. Atticus and Sloane are some of the most sought-after bachelors in New York?"

Zahra snorts. "Understatement."

I frown. "This information just makes it *more* confusing why Atticus married a drunk stranger."

Zahra tilts her chin considering that, but then shakes her head.

"Doesn't matter. New plan: you confirm the authenticity of the certificate, and we hope Atticus was dumb enough not to have you drunkenly sign a prenuptial agreement, then we find the hungriest divorce attorney on the East Coast and bankroll the rest of your life."

6

PHAEDRA

I SLEPT LIKE ABSOLUTE shit.

After having dinner with Zah and listening to her list out the plethora of lawyers that could take a man like Atticus for all his worth, I walked back to my studio with a pounding head and more confusion.

Usually, when life is a tangled mess, I dance to clear my head, but I knew this type of distraction could end up with me injuring myself for being careless, so I got into my car and went home. The whole weekend I was plagued with questions, making time slow to a crawl until I could find out if this was real.

And now I'm back in New York, and I have one of my answers.

> Clerk's office confirmed its authenticity.

ZAH

> Fuck.

> They fucking CONGRATULATED me.

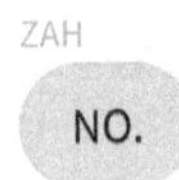

Zahra doesn't answer my text straight away. She should be just starting her interview, and knowing her ability to get people to talk, she probably won't be free for a while.

I sigh, sinking down to sit on the clerk's office's steps.

It's real.

I'm *married*. To a god damn stranger.

Sure, I had sex with the guy, but that's a social norm in this day and age. What's *not* fucking normal is making an inebriated woman sign a marriage license. And for what? It's sure as shit not for status.

Atticus has a net worth that makes hordes of grown men weep, *and* he's apparently one of the prince assholes of New York City.

Before I think about it, I'm looking up the address to Shaw Incorporated. Fuck waiting for a lawyer. I want answers *now*.

The building is in the Financial District, so I input the details into a rideshare car service and stand to wait by the curb. Thankfully, they don't take long to pick me up, but the eight-minute drive lasts for twenty because of the traffic. I thank the driver and get out across the road from the supposed Shaw Inc. building.

I turn around and my neck instantly cranes up. The building is all windows, reflecting the world around it in exacting detail. I drop my chin and cross the road. I recognize the huge metal 'SI' logo mounted on the marble wall in the spacious foyer from their website.

The foyer is warmer than the cool October weather outside, and the whole space is white marble with gray metal surfaces and large, brown leather seating in clusters throughout. There are multiple glass gates, which require the swipe of a keycard, that lead to banks of elevators, and two large desks with men and women in simple black suits sitting or standing behind them.

I approach an older man at the nearest desk who's looking at a computer. Maybe in his fifties, he's really fit for his age, his short hair is more gray than brown but he still has a full-head of thick locks, and he has kind blue eyes.

He smiles brightly at me. "Good morning, Miss."

"Hi," I say, returning his smile. "I'm sorry, I'm not sure who I need to speak to, but I have...an appointment with someone in this building."

"I can help with that," he informs, looking back at his computer. "Who are you here to see?"

"Mr. Shaw."

His eyes flick to me. "Which one?"

There's more than one?

"Felix or Atticus?" he supplies, obviously seeing my confusion.

"Are they brothers?" I can't help but ask.

"Cousins," he says with a conspiratorial grin. "Mr. Felix rarely gets visitors, and Mr. Atticus is constantly in meetings, so I'm going to take a guess and say you're here for Mr. Atticus?"

I look down at his name badge. Wade, security services. "I like you, Wade. Yes, I'm here for Atticus Shaw."

Pride blooms over his face as he types on his computer and then picks up the receiver of the desk phone in front of him and starts dialing.

"What's your name, Miss?" Wade asks.

"Phae Mills."

When someone answers the call, Wade introduces me, listens for a moment, then covers the microphone, looking up at me regrettably. "I'm sorry Miss, the secretary on the executive floor said you aren't on Mr. Shaw's schedule."

I know that, but...fuck. A ridiculous idea pops into my head, and I grit my teeth. "Tell them it's Phaedra *Shaw*."

Wade relays the new information, nodding along to whatever's being said to him, then he ends the call. He stands from his seat and buttons his suit jacket, stepping to the swipe gate and pressing his pass to the scanner, the glass gates opening immediately. "I'll escort you up personally, Mrs. Shaw."

My blood boils with fury as I force myself to follow Wade toward the elevators.

Mrs. Shaw.

Mrs. *Fucking*. Shaw.

We step into an elevator and it climbs with smooth grace as I fight the urge to punch something. I'll save the outburst for my *husband*.

Husband. I have a husband. This is fucking ludicrous.

The elevator door slides open on one of the top floors. The space is filled with sunlight, which is further amplified by almost every wall being glass and the abundance of white marble on the floors.

A woman behind a reception desk directly opposite the elevator greets us warmly as she stands.

"Can I take your coat?" she asks me, and I nod, pulling off the trench coat I borrowed from Zahra and thanking my former self for wearing a decent outfit today—high-rise black jeans and a cream knit sweater. I am, however, regretting the fuchsia sneakers that are glaringly obvious on the white floors.

Once I hand over the coat, the receptionist holds out a pass to me.

"This is for you, Mrs. Shaw," she says, urging me to take the black card on a retractable badge holder.

I pluck it from her hand with a tight smile.

"That will get you past the gates downstairs and through all the doors in the office," she informs with a smile.

I frown. "I don't think I—"

"Mr. Shaw insisted," the receptionist interrupts. "Now, to reach his office, you go through this door here, walk all the way to the end until the hall splits off east and west. Turn left and you'll find Hans, Mr. Shaw's assistant, at his desk."

I nod and turn to Wade, suddenly nervous. I don't want to walk through this glass maze by myself.

"This is where I leave you, Mrs. Shaw," he says, confirming my suspicions.

"Thanks, Wade. See you around."

He nods, backing away toward the elevator. "I'll be at the desk whenever you need assistance."

I nod my thanks to the receptionist and, using my all-access pass into Atticus' domain, I tap the card on the reader and push through the glass door into the hall. Staring straight ahead, I don't dare to peer into any of the offices I pass as I come to the end of the hall and turn left as instructed.

The doors off this hall are further apart and predominantly on my right; they're probably the big fancy offices of important people for the company. The hall opens up at the end to another reception area. It's much smaller and darker than the one at the elevators, as there are more solid walls than the rest of the floor.

To the right there are a couple of plush armchairs, and a glass door showing a conference room. Directly across from me there are closed wooden double doors with windows on either side that show another large seating area with a sofa and armchairs, and a stunning view of Lower Manhattan through the floor-to-ceiling outer windows. That's probably Atticus' office.

"Hello," a male voice says from my left, jerking my attention to him.

A man sitting at a black desk, maybe mid-twenties, looks up from his seat with a practiced smile. "I'm Hans."

I return his smile and walk over with my hand out to shake. "Phae."

His eyes widen and he scrambles to stand and grabs my hand with both of his. "Mrs. Shaw, I apologize sincerely. I, uh..." He lets out a nervous laugh. "I didn't know what you looked like."

Every time someone refers to me as 'Mrs. Shaw', my palms itch to throw something.

I force a smile across my face as I gently tug my hand out of his grip. "It's fine, and please, call me Phae."

Hans nods and clears his throat, tucking his hands behind his back. "How can I be of assistance today, M-*Phae.*"

"Is he available?" I say, angling my head to the office door.

"For you, of course," Hans says as he steps out from behind his desk. "Do you want me to bring you a drink? Water? Coffee? Wine?"

Wine? Really?

"No, I'm fine, thank you," I say as he leads me to the double doors.

Hans knocks twice, then opens the left door a fraction, angling his body into the small opening. "Your wife, Mr. Shaw."

I don't hear the words Atticus says, but the rumbling timbre of his tone sends a shiver down my spine.

Hans opens the door further and gestures for me to enter. I suck in a deep breath, nod my thanks, then step into the space.

The sofa and armchairs are pristine dark brown leather, the minimal furniture is metal and glass, and the white marble floor matches the rest of the building—the entire vibe of this space is exactly what I'd imagine for a high-powered CEO.

My eyes finally land on Atticus, and *fuck*, I forgot the man is *huge*. Even sitting behind a large glass desk, dressed in an expertly tailored dark gray suit, a tie, and white shirt, his presence alone commands all the attention in the room.

The color of his tie catches my gaze again.

Lilac.

He looks up, those sinful dark eyes meeting mine, pulling me immediately into their vortex. Seeing him completely sober, in the daylight, I'm struck by how absolutely, devastatingly handsome this man is. The inky black, tousled curls and short, neat black beard, the warm brown skin, perfect lips, and those damn eyes.

A smile curving across those delicious lips draws my attention, and damn it, I lose the ability to breathe.

"My beloved."

7

PHAEDRA

MY BODY HAS A visceral reaction to his voice, the low tone almost vibrating through me, but what he just said finally registers.

I turn to make sure the door is closed and Hans is gone, before whipping my head back to Atticus, putting every ounce of my desire to murder him in my glare. *"Beloved?"*

He's absolutely unfazed as he stands and readjusts his cufflinks. Another flash of metal snags my attention.

Left hand.

Ring finger.

A simple, thick gold band.

A fucking *wedding band.*

"What do I owe the pleasure of my wife visiting me at work today?" he says, pulling my attention away from his hand.

"I'm *not* your wife," I seethe.

He grins wider, his hand stroking down his tie. "Are you sure?"

I scoff, pulling out the certificate from my bag and holding it up.

"You mean this?"

He tilts his head, his eyes softening in amusement. "You carry yours around? How adorable."

I let out a light laugh and then tear the certificate in half.

"Did that make you feel better?" he says condescendingly.

"It did," I spit.

"Our marriage still stands, despite your little outburst." He's talking to me like I'm a petulant child.

I'm vibrating with rage. I take a few steps toward him and lower my voice.

"I didn't agree to this *marriage*," I spit the last word.

He raises a brow. "You signed the paperwork."

"I have no memory of doing so."

"There were witnesses," he points out.

"Yeah?" I volley back. "Who?"

"My best friend, Sloane," he supplies.

"Oh good," I chirp sarcastically. "Another conspirator to this *crime* that I get to kick in the balls."

"And *your* best friend," Atticus continues pointedly. "What was her name again? Oh, yes, Zahra."

I stumble back in shock. "She would *never*."

A devious grin twists his mouth as he tucks his hands in his pants pocket. "True... But she *does* sign non-disclosure agreements. However, she doesn't read them very well."

My jaw would be on the floor if I wasn't clenching my teeth so hard.

"This is a crime," I say slowly and clearly, so he can comprehend what I'm saying.

He shrugs. Fucking *shrugs*. "It could be?"

"It *is*."

"Okay?"

"You could go to jail."

"I doubt it."

"Not only will this marriage be annulled, but I will *sue* you," I threaten.

"I can afford it." He does that head tilting thing again. "Can you?"

"*Excuse* me?"

"Lawyers are expensive," Atticus reasons. "And trials are lengthy. Do you really want to go through all the trouble over a torn-up piece of paper and a name change?"

I blink in disbelief at the direction of this conversation.

"Why are you doing this?" I whisper.

Atticus has been standing in the same place this entire time, but now he finally moves.

"Because," he says as he takes slow, measured steps around his desk, his eyes never leaving mine. "I always get what I want."

I frown in confusion. What does that even mean?

As Atticus gets closer, I back away. Except I've somehow angled myself away from the exit and am now backing up toward the windows. Shit.

"What does that mean?" I voice out loud, never taking my eyes off him as I continue to keep a distance between us.

"It means exactly what I said," he says simply, not stopping his pursuit.

I shake my head. "You don't know me."

"I know a lot more than you think, Lilac."

Before I can ask what that means, my back bumps into something cold and I yelp, my bag sliding from my shoulder to the floor. The damned windows. Atticus uses the opening and takes three long strides forward, eating up the distance between us with his long legs. My heart hammers in my ears as he places his hands on either side of my head on the glass, caging me in.

My chest heaves in short bursts of air, the movement making my breasts brush his jacket. I tilt my head up, glaring up into his beautiful, deceptive face.

"Phaedra Darcy *Shaw*," Atticus says in a low tone, emphasizing my new supposed last name. "Twenty-seven. Born October first. Lives in Stamford, Connecticut." He reaches down and tucks the hair that's come loose from my plait behind my ear. "Happy belated birthday for last week, love."

"Atticus Oliver Shaw," I parrot in the same tone, swatting his hand away from me. "Thirty-six. Born July twenty-sixth. Manhattan, New York City." I roll my eyes. "That's all on the damned paperwork."

He smirks down at me, and my brain decides to notice at this inappropriate moment that his eyes aren't black, but a dark chestnut brown when they're in daylight. They're deceptively warm for a man that manipulated a woman into a marriage for no apparent reason.

"You graduated well in your senior year, but never applied for college," Atticus continues. "You auditioned for a few ballet companies until you landed in the corps for the Boston Ballet."

"That's public record," I reason, my voice warbling. My body is too hot. Did he do a background check on me before or *after* he married me?

"The art director was *very* impressed with you," he comments. "So much that he was going to shape you into his new principal, but then...you left." He leans in closer, his scent washing over me. I now know it's sandalwood and bergamot.

In a moment of weak curiosity, I might have sniffed a few fancy colognes until I found one that was close.

But none of those compare to a lungful straight from the source.

"He wanted to own you, didn't he, Lilac?" he asks softly. "Wanted to keep your sweet little cunt all to himself?"

The base of my skull tingles in warning, alarms blaring in my head.

"How... How do you know that?" I whisper.

"He told me," he says simply.

"He... What?" After I kneed that art director in the balls for groping me and threatening to file charges, he told me if I ever told anyone that he'd ruin my career in ballet. That still counts now, as reputation is everything as a teacher, so I've never said a word to this day.

Those chestnut irises darken to black pools of cold menace. "He chirped about a lot of fucked-up shit when I broke his second kneecap."

"You did *what?*" I balk.

"I would have taken his hands, but that would have been a *touch* overboard."

Sweat beads on my forehead. "You're insane."

A smile stretches over his face that I can only describe as *unhinged*. "Only for you, Mrs. Shaw."

The use of my new 'title' sends a burst of renewed fury in my veins. I raise my hands and shove at Atticus' chest hard—he barely fucking moves. Warm hands wrap around my wrists as I go to shove him again, and he pins them above my head. Maneuvering to hold my wrists with one hand, he trails the other down the side of my body. I try to jerk away from the sensations his touch causes.

His hand lands on my left hip, his thumb caressing the exposed flesh above the waistline of my jeans from my sweater riding up because of the position of my arms.

"After Boston, you came to New York." Atticus continues his report as his thumb rubs back and forth over my skin. "You entered the corps for the East Ballet Company and became an even faster favorite."

"Who did you injure for that information?" I grit out, feebly attempting to break his hold and ignoring that the goosebumps and some of the trembling in my body are for *completely* different reasons.

He chuckles, this time the sound *actually* vibrating through every contact point on my body. "*That,* I got from public record."

I wait. I'm assuming he knows the other things that happened to me at EBC.

"This time the art director didn't want to fuck you," he continues. "She *did* want to make you a soloist, though. So, she started training you as an understudy, which the rest of the company didn't take too kindly to." He sighs, the sound dripping in disappointment. "Ballerinas don't really grow out of their immature 'mean girl' behavior after high school, do they?"

I drop my head back against the window and let out a resigned sigh. The catty bullshit I experienced at EBC still replays in my mind frequently. Atticus bringing them up is a dick move.

"There was hope, though," he says with a small smile. "You were in talks of moving to New York City Ballet when the season was done."

I close my eyes, my mouth trembling. I never made it to NYCB.

"Enough," I say, barely above a whisper. "Please."

Atticus is quiet, his hands still on me, trapping me and caressing me at the same time. The hand on my hip flexes slightly, making me open my eyes and look up at him.

"How's your hip today, Mrs. Shaw?" he asks, eyes and tone sincere.

An involuntary tear slips out from the corner of my eye. Atticus tracks it, then leans in and kisses it away.

"My arms are starting to burn," I say, voice shaky.

One second I'm pinned against the window and the next Atticus drops my arms and scoops me up, bridal-style. He carries me to one of the armchairs and places me in it gently, then takes a seat on the sofa opposite me, leaning back and stretching his arms along the top of the cushions, lifting an ankle to rest on his knee.

My eyes flick to the door, and I notice the glass on either side is now frosted.

"Frosted means not to disturb," Atticus informs me.

"Can I leave?" I ask, turning back to him.

"Did you get everything you came for?" his tone casual.

"I came for answers, and all I got was more questions," I confess.

"What questions can I answer for you, Mrs. Shaw?"

"Why?" I ask again.

"I told you; I always get what I want."

"Why *me*, then?"

He doesn't answer, just continues to watch me.

I sigh, then change tactics. "I want an annulment."

"No," he says with finality.

"Then I'll continue with divorce proceedings."

"No," he says again.

I scoff. "You can't stop me."

His hand comes up to his chin, and he strokes it languidly as he regards me in contemplation. I'm transfixed by his long fingers caressing the dark hair along his strong jaw, imagining what it would feel like if *I* did that.

Snap out of it, Phae. You didn't come here to pet your husband.

His hand drops into his lap and I'm almost disappointed that the show is over.

"Is this what you really want?" he asks.

"Not to be married? Yes," I declare.

"Fine," he breathes. "I will consider it."

"*Consider it?*" I repeat incredulously. "There's no *considering*, there's only *accepting*."

"One month," he says suddenly.

I frown. "What?"

"Be my wife for the next month, and then I'll consider divorce," he offers.

I frown. "You want to fake a marriage?"

"It's not fake, you are *legally* mine."

I shake my head, scooting forward on the armchair. "I'm not going to lie for you."

He does that head tilt again. "Why not?"

"I don't know what twisted game you're playing, but I don't want to be a part of it."

A grin spreads across his face, his eyes sparkling deviously. "Don't think you'll win?"

"There's nothing *to* win," I counter.

"According to you, there's annulment, or divorce, to gain."

I opened myself up for that one.

"What if there were terms to this *arrangement?*" he offers.

"What kind of terms?" I ask cautiously.

He shrugs, his fingers playing across the top of the sofa's cushion. "Any terms you want to put in place."

I take a breath to comprehend what he's offering. "A month of marriage, *with terms*, in exchange for you agreeing to dissolve our marriage."

He drops his foot to the ground and leans forward, resting his elbows on his knees, his eyes searching my face.

"Lie for me, Lilac," he practically purrs. "Then we'll talk about it."

That's not a guarantee that I'd be free of this man at the end of the month, but it's a hell of a lot closer than I was at the start of this conversation.

"I'm assuming *you* have terms for this arrangement, as well?" I ask.

A satisfied grin blooms across his face. "I might."

I narrow my eyes at him. "I want to hear them first before I make my decision."

Atticus regards me with silent amusement for a long moment,

and then his expression shifts to all business as he straightens on the sofa.

"You will live with me," he starts.

"No."

He frowns. "Why?"

"I don't need to live with you for this charade."

"Yes, you do," he says. "We need it to be believable."

"How is it 'believable' when a wife randomly pops up on your arm?"

"Most people in my life know you exist," he announces.

My mouth drops open and all I can do is stare at him for a moment. "Excuse me?"

"My family and close friends all know who you are." He says it so casually, like he's not telling me a bunch of people know of my existence as his *wife*.

"Where do they think I've been?" I ask disbelievingly.

"Abroad."

"Doing what?"

"I'm a private man, Mrs. Shaw," he says in a serious tone. "That extends to my wife's privacy as well."

"What's this got to do with me moving in?" I ask.

"Now that you've come to the office and met a few people, they will know that you've returned and will expect my wife to be living with me."

Fucking hell.

"I have a life, job, and apartment, all in Stamford," I try to reason.

"I can arrange for someone to maintain your home while you're here," he answers immediately. "And I can have someone take you to and from your studio whenever you need."

"I have a car." My attempt to get out of this stipulation is waning rapidly, and he knows it. I sigh. *"Fine."*

He nods with a satisfied grin. "That wasn't so hard, was it?"

I roll my eyes. "Is there anything else?"

"Yes. You will need to attend a variety of events over the next month with me." Atticus holds his hand up as I open my mouth to speak. "Nonnegotiable."

"I was going to *ask*," I force out, exasperated, "what type of events, so I know what clothing to bring."

"I will provide everything you need," he says.

"I don't want you dictating what I wear."

"We can shop for what you need together then," he reasons.

"*Or* you can give me a credit card and I can go myself?" I retort.

He sits there in silence with an arch of a brow.

"I get to keep everything you buy," I declare with a saccharine grin.

"Naturally," he agrees.

"Next?" I breathe.

"You'll wear rings."

My eyes flick to his left hand. "Figured."

"We'll buy them tomorrow," he announces, reaching into the inner pocket of his jacket and taking out his phone.

"This is starting *tomorrow?*" I didn't expect my thirty days of incarceration to start on a Tuesday.

"I was going to say tonight," he says, his eyes flicking between me and his phone as he types. "But I understand you may need the night to pack."

He's giving me a *single* night to process everything that's happening. How fucking generous.

"I haven't agreed to this arrangement yet," I point out.

"But you will," he states with confidence, still typing away on his phone.

"You haven't even heard *my* terms."

That makes him pause his typing and look up at me expectantly.

So many things pass through my head, but I can't retrieve any of them to formulate demands. What do I want from this? What do I *not* want?

I say the first thing I can articulate. "Stop calling me Mrs. Shaw."

"No," he says immediately.

"My name is Phaedra Mills. I prefer Phae."

His eyes narrow at me. "Your surname changed when you signed the marriage certificate."

"Which I have no knowledge of doing, I remind you."

"You're mine, Mrs. Shaw. I won't stop claiming that." His possessive tone sends goosebumps across my skin. I fight the urge to squirm.

"At least call me by my first name," I say, my throat dry.

"Phaedra."

It's the first time he's said it. And *fuck*. Hearing my name on his tongue, with that deep, vibrating tone, makes my body *pulse*.

"You have to patron a ballet dancer for the next season," I blurt out, needing to move on before I ask him to say my name again, this time in my ear.

"Any particular ballet company?" Atticus asks. "Or dancer?"

I shake my head.

"Done," he says without hesitation.

That was *too* easy.

"You'll give Will a paid internship at your company," I demand.

Atticus raises a brow. "Who's Will?"

I cross my arms over my chest. "You've done a background check. I'm sure you know."

He lowers his phone to his lap. "I want to hear it from you. Who's. Will?"

Will being a potential sore spot for Atticus is absolutely laughable.

"Will does my paperwork at the studio," I say evenly. "And is an ex-student of mine. He's twenty, currently studying business. He also has a *boyfriend*."

Atticus stares at me with a hard expression for a few more seconds, and then looks back at his phone, breaking the tension. "Done."

"You can't fuck around with other people," I exclaim.

"I'm many things, Mrs. Shaw," he says, still looking at his phone. "But one thing I am not is a cheater."

"Good."

"I expect the same from you."

"Obviously," I mutter.

"Anything else, my beloved?" Atticus says, his tone rich with mock pleasantry.

"Yes," I chirp. "You can't touch me."

His head whips up so fast. "No."

"This is a *nonnegotiable*." I throw his own words back at him. "You're my wife—"

"*Fake* wife," I correct.

"*Wife*," he insists gruffly. "It's expected that I touch you, that *we* touch."

"When we have to put on the facade, I'll allow hand-holding, your arm around me, hands no lower than my hip, and light kisses, minimal on the lips." He opens his mouth to say something, but I hold my hand out to stop him. "In the privacy of your apartment, you don't lay a hand on me."

His mouth shuts with an audible snap. Satisfaction blooms in my chest—he's *seething*—but the fact he expected free rein to do whatever he wants with me really pisses me off.

We continue our stare-off for a long, tense moment until Atticus' face softens into something neutral. I'm immediately suspicious.

"I'll agree to only touching you when necessary in public," he starts, voice even. "And I'll agree to not touching you when we're alone."

I know there's a "but" coming.

"But the rule becomes obsolete if you touch me first."

Laughter bursts out of me. "That will *never* happen."

A sly grin lifts his lips. "Never say never, my pretty Lilac."

"So, you agree?" I reiterate.

"With my amendment, yes." He types something into his phone again, and then a second later, my phone chimes in my bag across the room.

"I'm assuming that's you?" I ask, deadpan.

He dips his chin in answer, then sweeps his hand to the bag. I stand and cross to it, pick up the whole thing, and bring it back to the armchair. I don't sit back down, instead putting my bag on the chair and digging out my phone.

There's an email from Atticus.

"Please review the terms discussed for a successful marriage?" I read out loud.

"What's the saying?" he asks contemplatively. "'Happy wife, happy life?'"

I scoff. "How does that even work when the wife in question will be happier *not* being a wife?"

I don't wait for an answer and continue reading the list he compiled with both of our terms and the details of the length of our arrangement. I shake my head at his noted outcome being "conversation about annulment".

I'm about to ask how he wants me to respond to agree to this farce when I read the last line.

"Agreement to be sealed with a kiss?" I ask, looking up at Atticus and startling.

He moved while I was reading, now standing a step from me and peering down with those wickedly dark eyes burning with intention.

"There's a no-touching rule in place," I say, thanking the universe my voice doesn't falter. "Kissing is touching."

"Rules don't take into effect until we've *sealed the deal.*" That goddamn rumbling tone does too many things to my traitorous body.

"I'm not kissing you," I declare petulantly.

Atticus leans in, his sandalwood and bergamot scent flooding me. "Because you'll enjoy it?"

"I can just send back a confirmation or sign something," I continue, ignoring him.

"I thought you'd be hesitant to sign anything since, the last time you did, you became my wife."

"Asshole." But he's right.

"Are you scared of me, Lilac?"

"No," I breathe.

"I think you are," he taunts. "I think—"

I pull him down by the neck and slam my lips to his, cutting off his words.

And then I fucking *melt*.

He tastes as good as I remember.

Feels even better.

Atticus' arm wraps around me, his hand grabbing an ass cheek possessively as he crushes me into his warm, hard body. My fingers crawl up his neck and sink into his hair.

When I close my fingers into a tight grip on his soft locks, he *groans*.

The sound spears pleasure directly to my clit, and it throbs, begging for his touch. Or tongue. Preferably both.

I inhale Atticus' woods and citrus scent like it sustains my existence as my tongue plays with his, savoring the taste of what is mine.

Mine.

That sentiment shoots through my whole body like a bolt of electricity, making me stumble out of Atticus' hold. Desire sits heavy in my body, pulsing between my legs, but I ignore it as I wipe at my kiss-swollen lips.

"Are we good here?" I pant, barely glancing up at Atticus, not wanting to fall into his lure again.

He's breathing heavily, but he doesn't move or say anything.

I turn sharply and pick up my bag from the armchair, not waiting for his response, and scramble for the door. Thank the universe Hans isn't at his desk to watch my escape.

Atticus' laughter chases me as I leave the office with his taste on my tongue. "See you tomorrow, Mrs. Shaw."

8
ATTICUS

THOSE ABSURD HOT-PINK SNEAKERS are almost a blur across the white floors as she runs from me.

Adrenaline pours through my veins, making my skin prickle, as watching her flee triggers an innate need in me to chase and capture. It's such a fucking rush to play this game with my wife.

Wife.

That sends a shiver down my spine. I've been waiting a long time to officially, *legally*, refer to Phaedra as mine. From that first glance, she was everything I've ever wanted, and now that she's tied to me, all I've worked for is finally coming to fruition.

I've been patient, biding my time and making meticulous plans for years, preparing for this day to come, and I can't help but bask in the heady weight of elation settling over me from my accomplishments.

I give myself another moment to revel, then turn sharply, cross to my desk and pick up the desk phone receiver.

"Mr. Shaw," Wade answers on the second ring.

"Mrs. Shaw should be down in a moment," I tell him. "Have someone ensure she gets to her destination safely."

"Yes, sir," he says without hesitation and ends the call.

Wade is part of the Shaw family's personal security team. Having been with our family for over two decades, he was the only security personnel who my father trusted with Constance until her line of work called for much more brute muscle. Now he works with me.

When I'm at the office, he prefers to work at the reception downstairs, wanting to be on the front lines preventing unauthorized people accessing the building.

That's when he's not watching over Phaedra.

I pull my phone out of my pocket, a message already in my notifications from Wade with details on who's watching my wife, and call Sloane.

He doesn't answer. I call him again.

"Jesus, Shaw, it's too early," he groans into the phone when he finally answers the third time.

"I would have expected you to be at the office by at least ten on a Monday," I chastise.

"I didn't get back from Monaco until three this morning," he mumbles, his voice muffled by his pillow.

I roll my eyes. "You left for Monaco Friday for *one* event *that* night."

"Yeah, and it finished Sunday afternoon," he counters.

I shake my head. He's been erratic since his last girlfriend dumped him three months ago. He falls for a woman every other day, but the ones that give him attention for more than a random hook-up he declares as the 'future Mrs. Yorke' until his overbearingness and quick jealousy force them away.

His remedy for his so-called 'broken heart' is to go on party binges or, when he travels, to declare he's never returning home.

I should probably put another tracker on him again.

"I need you at my house tomorrow evening after work," I instruct.

"What for?" he groans.

"Business. Bring your jewels."

Sloane chuckles deeply. "So, your runaway bride has finally returned?"

"My *wife*," I correct. "'Bride' infers we didn't marry."

He snorts. "If you call that haphazard ceremony by a minister you blackmailed into authorizing while the bride was clearly incoherent a legal ceremony. Then, sure."

"She's *mine*," I grit out, anger burning through my chest.

"Relax, Atticus. No one's trying to take her from you. You made sure of that when you trapped her in matrimony." I hear rustling like he's getting out of bed. "Why *did* you marry a random woman from the club, anyway?"

"Phaedra isn't some *random woman*," I growl.

"What do you mean?" Sloane asks. "I assumed she was some business rival's daughter you were using to make a power play, or you were doing it to piss off your dad, but from what I found online, she's just a random ballet teacher."

My fury turns molten. "You *researched* my wife?"

"Down, boy," Sloane says placatingly. "I was just curious why 'will never marry' Atticus was suddenly pulling tied-up ministers from a restroom and marrying a random chick with purple hair."

I pull my phone from my ear and fill my lungs with air slowly, calming myself down before I drive over to my best friend's apartment and smother him with a pillow.

Sloane is usually privy to the overly *theatrical* moves I make in my life. Hell, most of the time he's eager to take part.

But Phaedra was too important to share. I wanted nothing to go wrong. Everything had to be exactly right without tarnish. I only used other people in my plans when it was absolutely necessary.

I let out the breath slowly and then put the phone back to my ear. "Tomorrow evening, Yorke."

He audibly sighs in annoyance. "Fine, don't tell me, then."

"Tomorrow," I reiterate.

"Yeah, yeah," he huffs dismissively.

"Don't be late."

9

PHAEDRA

AS SOON AS I walked out of the Shaw Inc building, I called Zahra. The adrenaline seeped out of my body when I heard her voice, replaced with anxiety that wrapped around my chest almost immediately knowing she's going to have *many* things to say about this arrangement.

Which she did the moment I told her at lunch, and she's still on her tangent.

"We should give this to a lawyer," Zahra says again, reading the email on my phone. She shakes her head and passes me the device. "Actually, no, you didn't sign it, so it's not valid. We should find you an attorney for the divorce proceedings."

"Did you hear the rest of the story?" I ask, exhausted from this never-ending circle about what to do next.

"Yeah, yeah, thirty days, the kiss," she says, waving me off. "Do you really want to live with that man for a month?"

I shrug. "Not particularly—"

"And do you think he's even going to give you what you want?"

She gestures at my phone. "That 'contract' says a *conversation* about separation. It's not a guarantee."

I blow out a breath, sagging back in my chair. "Yeah. I know."

"Then why—"

"Because I can't *afford* it," I blurt out. "The only thing I have in this life is my studio and my reputation. He's a powerful man with money *and* influence on his side. A dent to my finances, but most importantly, *any* blows to my reputation will cause irreversible damage."

Zahra reaches across the table, taking my hand, her dark eyes soft with empathy. "You know my parents will—"

I shake my head vigorously, pulling away from her touch. "They *cannot* know. My parents either. They're already going to be disappointed that I was reckless enough to black out at a stranger's home, let alone sign fucking legal documentation."

"They're going to be upset at *both* of us," Zahra agrees. "I wasn't vigilant enough, and it was my idea in the first place."

"Don't blame yourself. It was a work thing," I dismiss.

"I should've kept it at the bar and not let us follow stupidly hot guys to a penthouse in the sky," she urges.

I sigh. "Why are we completely incapable of making decisions that won't potentially cause our extinction?"

We both laugh. We've been like this since the beginning. I'm surprised one of us hasn't ended up in prison.

I guess you could consider this arrangement with Atticus prison. A really luxurious, ostentatious, confusing prison that has breathtaking views of Central Park instead of bars, and a jailer that looks superb in a suit.

And probably out of it.

I shake that thought immediately. No matter what happens in the next month, there won't be any conjugal visits with my husband.

My role is to smile and look pretty on his arm. As a previous professional ballet dancer, I've done that many times with ballet patrons and company officials. It's a piece of cake. I smile. This time, I can even *eat* the cake.

"I know that look," Zahra comments, bringing me back to the present. "You're either thinking about setting his entire building on fire, or food."

I laugh. "Cake's on my mind. But fire sounds like a fabulous idea."

Zahra pulls the napkin from her lap and tosses it on top of her finished lunch as she stands, her hand out to me. "Let's go get cake, then we can discuss arson."

—— S ——

After a stop at two different bakeries, and convincing Zahra we didn't need to go to a hardware store for lighter fluid, we went back to my place with our treats.

Zahra lounged on my bed for a couple of hours as I packed my suitcase and then left me with the decree that she will drive me to the Sky Building tomorrow.

It's almost midnight as I crawl under the covers, my body exhausted, but my mind still spinning. I close my eyes once I'm comfortable, taking settling breaths and willing myself to sleep.

I try for a while, but my brain won't stop throwing questions at me. Why is Atticus really doing this? What does he mean, "I get what I want?" Why me? Why now? What events will we be going to? Is there a limit to the things he'll bankroll? How does he spend his evenings? What are his favorite foods? Does he sleep naked?

I open my eyes and blow out a breath. That's something I should *not* be thinking about.

My phone vibrates on my nightstand in a pattern that tells me it's a message. It's probably Zahra. We've had this spooky sense about each other when we're in turmoil since we were kids, so she's probably picking up on my wayward brainwaves and checking up on me.

I reach over and pick up my phone, about to swipe into the message, but my thumb freezes over the notification.

I jolt upright, my heart pounding wildly. What the actual fuck? I read the message again and note the sender. "Husband" could only be one person.

Atticus.

Instead of opening the message, which will show that I've read it, I unlock my phone and go into my contacts list. The only people I really talk to regularly are Zahra and my mom, so I rarely go into my contacts, but sure enough, there's one named 'Husband' with a New York City area code.

How did he put this on my phone? And *when*? And how in the fuck does he know I'm awake?

He can see you.

I immediately pull the sheets up to cover the flimsy camisole I'm wearing and look around. The room is dark, so I can't see shit, but from what I can make out, there don't seem to be any Atticus-shaped shadows or obvious blinking lights from a camera. But there is no way in hell I'm getting out of this bed to look around properly.

The only way to get any answers is to talk to him.

With a heavy sigh, I pick up my phone and finally open the message thread.

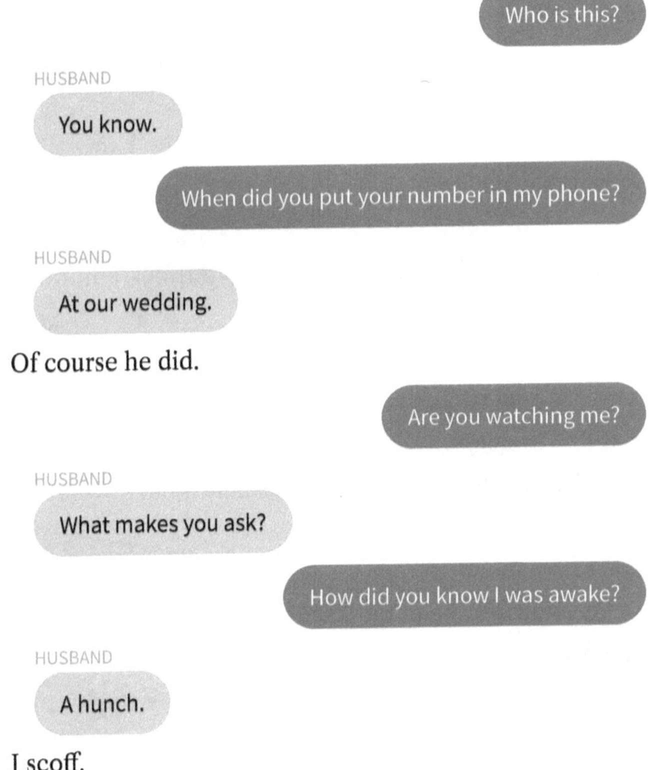

Of course he did.

I scoff.

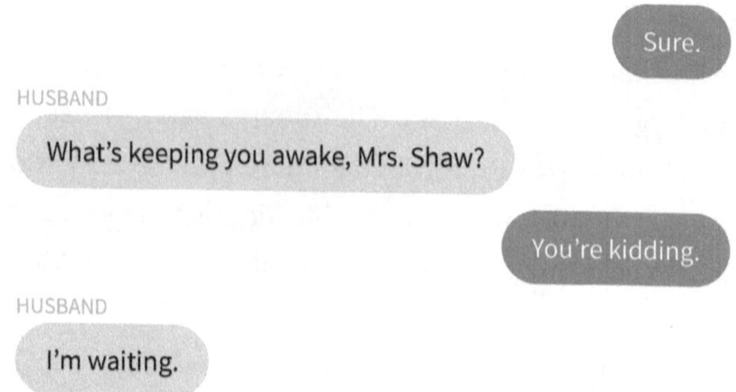

I roll my eyes and put my phone back on the nightstand. He can keep on waiting.

Just as I close my eyes, my phone starts vibrating again. Long vibrations. The audacity of this man to *call*. I ignore it, but just as it stops buzzing, it immediately starts again.

With an annoyed huff, I reach out and grab my phone, answering the damn thing.

"Do you mind?" I bark.

"I don't appreciate you ignoring me," Atticus admonishes through the phone.

I ignore the goosebumps over my skin at the tone of his voice.

"Answer my question," he demands.

"I'm trying to sleep."

"But you can't," he points out. "So tell me what's keeping you awake."

"I don't have to talk to you."

"But here you are," he purrs. "Still on the phone."

I roll my eyes. "You'll just call me again."

He chuckles, the rumbling sound making my thighs clench together. Fucking hell.

"You'd be correct, Mrs. Shaw."

"I told you to call me Phae," I huff.

"Is that what keeps you awake?" Atticus whispers. "Thinking about me saying your name into your ear?"

My heart beats faster at the thought. I close my eyes and shake my head. "I don't think about you at all."

"Liar," he growls.

"Isn't that what I'm supposed to do in this arrangement?" I ask. "Lie."

"Not to yourself, Lilac," he purrs. "You're thinking about that kiss, aren't you?"

I swallow. "No."

"I can't get it out of my head," he says, his voice hoarse. "The way you taste, the way you feel, even the way you smell."

I screw my eyes shut as my body hums at the reminder. I don't want to hear this, but my body is already attuned to his voice, his words.

"I want to know what your tight little pussy tastes like, *Phaedra*."

Heat sizzles under my skin as I choke on a whimper. "Atticus—"

"Say it again," he grunts.

I pause.

"Say it again, Phaedra," he pants. "Say my name."

I realize my hand is halfway down my body, traveling toward my throbbing clit. Fuck. I ball my fist and roll to my side.

"Come on, Lilac," he breathes. "Say it again for me."

"Atticus, *please*." My mind is hazy with lust, my body begging for release. I don't even know what I'm begging for. For him to stop?

To never stop?

He groans, his breathing heavier. "Yes, *just* like that. That's how you're going to sound when you're riding my face, begging me to let you come."

This time I openly whimper at that scenario playing out in my head. I can almost feel the graze of his beard on my thighs, the flick of his strong tongue, the vibrations of his approving sounds.

"Atticus," I say on a hitched breath.

"Fuuuck," he groans, long and hard into the phone, and I almost come just from the sound.

Then it dawns on me that I just talked this man to his *own* completion, and it's like cold water to my lust-heated body.

"Asshole," I hiss.

He hums lazily, the sound of shuffling heard across the line. "Sweet dreams, my beloved."

10

PHAEDRA

ZAHRA PULLS IN FRONT of Sky Building, where a man dressed in a black overcoat stands at the curb expectantly. He opens my door the moment Zahra parks.

"Good evening, Mrs. Shaw, my name is Harris, Sky Building's property manager," he introduces as I climb out of the car. He's a handsome man, maybe in his forties, with a polite smile.

Two other men in navy blue suits with gold buttons and gold trim with matching peaked caps exit the building and approach the car, pulling my bags out of the trunk.

"Do you have more bags being delivered, Mrs. Shaw?" Harris asks.

I shake my head. "Just the ones I have with me today. And please, call me Phae."

Harris looks offended at the suggestion, and I fight the urge to scream. This is going to be a long month.

"Remember to call me every day," Zahra announces from my side, grabbing our attention.

I nod and pull her into a tight hug. "I will."

"You should bang the manager," she whispers into my ear, making me laugh as I pull back. She grins cheekily and hands me my backpack, which one of the building staff immediately takes with a smile. "There's mace in there too, just in case."

"Jesus, Zah," I say between fits of giggles.

She turns to Harris. "If anything happens to her, I will hold *you* personally responsible."

Harris dips his chin. "I am at Mrs. Shaw's disposal."

Zah narrows her eyes and points a single finger at Harris. "Just make sure you don't end up at *my* disposal, got it?"

"I understand, Miss Mathers," he says earnestly. I'm impressed he knows Zah's last name, too.

Zah switches from menacing to sweet in a blink and then skips around to the driver's side. "Love you, talk to you later!"

"Love you too," I call as she slips into her car and pulls away.

I turn back to Harris, and he gestures toward the doors. "Shall we?"

I spend around half an hour with Harris in his office filling out paperwork, getting a set of keys and a security fob, and then he takes me on a tour of the building's amenities. When we return to the foyer from the most beautiful gym I've ever seen, Harris takes me around the main elevator bank to a wall of glass.

"Please scan here, Mrs. Shaw," he instructs as he gestures to the far right.

I press my fob to the scanner I didn't notice before, and it chirps once before the wall of glass slides open to a small private lobby with a single elevator.

"This is yours and Mr. Shaw's private elevator. It goes to all the amenity floors and also down to the garage in the basement as well. Though, if you require your car, you may also call reception at any time and there will be staff available to bring it to street level."

I nod along. His mention of cars reminds me I need to bring mine back here from home so I can go to and from the studio. Luckily, I only run classes four days a week, but I'm already exhausted thinking about all the travel I'll be doing in the next month.

"The only way to access the elevator is the scanner to the left," Harris continues, pulling me from my thoughts. "The top button on the panel is to your home."

I look at Harris with what I'm hoping is a smile, not a grimace. "Thank you, Harris."

He dips his chin. "My pleasure, Mrs. Shaw. If you need anything, please don't hesitate to contact reception."

I nod and force myself to walk up to the elevator scanner and touch my fob to it; the steel doors slide open immediately. Sucking in a breath, I step in and press the 'P' button, trying not to hyperventilate as the elevator rises rapidly, the pressure in my ears slightly uncomfortable. They clear as soon as the elevator stops on the penthouse floor.

I step out into another elevator lobby, mirroring the one downstairs. I walk over to another wall of glass, find the scanner, and touch my fob to it.

Light streams in, temporarily blinding me. When my eyes adjust, I walk into a stunning foyer. The floors are some sort of light wood in a herringbone pattern, and the walls are white, which contrasts the huge, colorful abstract paintings on either wall above the low, tan bench seats on each side.

The place has a surprising warmth to it that I wasn't expecting. I also wasn't expecting a welcoming party.

Two older women stand by the open door at the end of the foyer space. The gray-haired woman with glasses is wearing a black chef's uniform, and the other woman with crimson-red hair is in dress pants and a simple black sweater.

"Good morning, Mrs. Shaw," the red-headed woman starts. "I'm Rosemary, and this is my wife, Marta."

"Hello," I say with a small wave.

"Marta looks after the kitchen and meals, and I assist with everything else," Rosemary supplies.

Marta rushes forward with her arms out. "Welcome home," she beams and wraps me in a tight hug.

Rose winces from where she stands. "I apologize profusely for my wife, Mrs. Shaw. She's usually *much* more professional."

"I'm a hugger, so this is perfect." I chuckle and pull back. "And please, both of you call me Phae."

"After Rose shows you the house, Phae, come see me in the kitchen for lunch." With that, Marta disappears further into the apartment.

"She'll hold me to that instruction, won't she?" I ask Rose.

She gives me the barest of smiles. "She's very serious about feeding people."

My returning smile is wide. "And I'm serious about eating, so we're going to get along swimmingly."

Rosemary takes me on a full tour of the gigantic penthouse. It spans the entire floor of this level—a third of it is just the Grand Salon.

The vast open space has spectacular views overlooking Central Park and Manhattan through the floor-to-ceiling windows, enough lush seating for at least twenty—the furniture in rich earth tones—but its centerpiece is the sleek, black grand piano in the center of the room.

The piano is one of the few memories I have of this place from the first time I was here.

Rosemary stands by until I've had my fill of the views and have stepped out to inspect the loggia—a covered exterior space partially open to the elements—then directs me to continue towards the right side of the building. We walk through the formal dining room, and then into another open space with the kitchen, a breakfast table and cozy-looking family area.

We continue through to Rosemary and Marta's living quarters, which has a separate living area, small kitchenette and bedroom, then Rosemary leads me through the service corridor and back to the main foyer.

We start on the left side. Rosemary shows me Atticus' huge office. I barely glance at the wall of books and the large desk before scurrying out of there with heated cheeks, ignoring the vague memories of trying to fuck Atticus on that desk that shutter through my mind.

Rosemary leads me through a set of open double doors into a long, wide hallway that doubles as an art gallery. Several art pieces line the walls on the left, with soft lights shining above each one, and on the right there are quite a few doors.

"Each door leads to a bedroom with its own bathroom," Rosemary says as we stroll down the hall.

We stop intermittently to peek into a room or look at a painting. Similar to the rest of the penthouse, the furniture and tapestry in the rooms are in earth tones, complemented by the white marble bathrooms with brass fixings.

I also notice throughout the entire penthouse, vases big and small are filled with all varieties of lilacs. The purple and white bouquets give off their soft, sweet scent everywhere we turn.

We come to the end of the gallery where the hall veers to the left. There's only one door off this section, and another at the end.

"That goes back through to the laundry room, and to mine and Marta's rooms," Rosemary says, gesturing to the door at the end of the hall. She turns to the one we're standing in front of. "And this is to your primary suite."

Dread sours my gut. Clearly, Rosemary nor Marta have been clued in on the little scheme their boss is running. So *technically*, this would be "my" suite if my marriage to Atticus wasn't a sham.

I choose not to correct her and grit my teeth, nodding for her to open the door.

The first thing we walk into is a decent-sized seating area, with a television mounted on one wall and a wall of windows looking out to another covered balcony and the city beyond.

"Access to this loggia is only from this room and the other bedroom next door," Rosemary informs, gesturing at the door next to the sofa.

I nod and force myself to walk past the seating area, opening a sliding door into a large, open dressing room. Rows of suits in many colors line the hanging space along the wall to my left, behind glass doors.

To my right, the space is a large square room lined with more hanging space. The back wall is dedicated to shoes and bags on either side of the entrance to the marble bathroom, and a large island of drawers in the center of the room.

So much for taking me to go get clothes. The clothes, shoes and bags in this room aren't just Atticus' things; a vast amount of it is women's clothes. It looks like Atticus bought an entire fucking boutique.

I notice my suitcase, backpack and duffel bag sitting by the drawers in the center of the room.

"I wasn't sure of your preference to me unpacking your belongings," Rosemary says when she notices what has my attention.

"No need," I say quickly.

"I'm more than happy—"

"No, I promise I can do it," I reassure her.

Concern still creases her brow. "Is there something unsatisfactory I have done, Mrs. Shaw?"

"What? No. You're perfect. This place is perfect." I rush out, and then take a breath. "I'm just..."

Her light blue eyes search my face, her concern softening to understanding. "Overwhelmed?"

I sigh. "Very."

"You're new to this," she surmises.

"To being married?" I ask, confused.

"To this...lifestyle," she explains.

"I'm new to both," I admit.

Rosemary steps forward and places a gentle touch on my arm. "My role is to make yours and Mr. Shaw's life as seamless as possible. Give the word and it shall be done."

I place my hand over hers on my arm. "I'm a fairly self-sufficient person. I hope that doesn't offend you."

She shakes her head with one of those barely there smiles. "Of course not, Mrs. Shaw. But if there is *anything* I can do for you, you know where I live."

I chuckle softly and nod. She gestures for me to continue further into the suite. I really shouldn't—this is Atticus' most private space in this entire place—but curiosity wins, and I continue forward.

I step through the entrance on the other side of the dressing room, and it's not what I expected. I actually don't know *what* I expected.

This entire penthouse has a warmth to it, mainly from the thoughtfully picked furnishings, but it feels very "clean". Like a statement of a house. But this space, Atticus' space, feels lived-in.

It's a corner room with floor-to-ceiling windows showing more spectacular views, a glass desk with a large desktop computer and a comfortable-looking chair against one wall of windows. The other side has a chaise lounge in front of it, angled to enjoy the view, with a small stack of books on the end and a floor lamp hanging over the other side.

The only other furniture is a huge California king bed. The linens are the same rich earth tones as the other bedrooms, but unlike the other perfectly presented beds, this one isn't made—the blankets are haphazardly pulled up and the pillows are askew.

"Mr. Shaw told me that if you want any decor changed, that it will be done with urgency," Rosemary says, pulling my attention. "We can add anything to this room or change the others. He wants you to add your unique touch to your new home."

I try not to grind my teeth as I force a smile and nod.

Trying to make his prisoner more comfortable in their cell—what a benevolent warden.

Once Rosemary released me from the tour of the penthouse, I had a wonderful lunch with Marta.

As I devoured the best crumbed chicken and salad sub I've ever had, along with homemade fries and sweet tea, Marta and I had an in-depth conversation about my food preferences and the general structure of my day and week so she can work out timings for meals.

After lunch, I snuck back into the primary suite and moved all my bags to the other room connected by the loggia, so Rosemary or Marta don't get suspicious.

Once I put my suitcase at the bottom of the closet, I was too afraid to sit on the bed, knowing it'd probably feel like clouds and I'd fall asleep, so instead I changed into bike shorts, a matching crop top, and sneakers, found a small towel, and headed for the gym.

It's on the sixtieth floor with all the equipment you can think of, plus a large, empty group fitness studio I might test out another day. There isn't anyone here as I walk straight over to the matted area while tying my lilac hair into a tight, high bun and then stretch out my whole body.

I put my headphones on and blast metal music as I put myself through a rigorous strength routine, then do something I despise: a run on the treadmill. I don't last long, but I'm hot and covered in sweat by the time I'm doing my last stretches, and I've exhausted myself enough that my brain is *finally* quiet.

I wipe my face and turn off my music, pulling my headphones down so they're hanging around my neck as I leave the gym and try to remember where the right elevator is to the penthouse. I eventually find it and travel back upstairs, in desperate need of water and a snack, so I head for the dining room.

I stall in the entrance. An array of velvet-lined boxes, filled with a *fuckload* of glittering jewels, covers half the sixteen-seater table. I'm absolutely stunned at the millions of dollars of rocks that I don't notice there are people in the room until a voice rumbles through the space.

His voice.

"There she is."

11
PHAEDRA

IT'S RIDICULOUS HOW EASILY Atticus' stupidly perfect face and sinful, dark chestnut-brown eyes can disarm me.

I only saw him yesterday, but his whole demeanor feels different. This isn't the business tycoon Atticus Shaw that's negotiating marriage with a stranger. This feels like the guy who I crashed into with a glass of water and had a crazy bathroom romp with two months ago.

He's a manipulative bastard, Phae. The person you met was a lie.

I shake the sudden disappointment and pull my gaze from his face. Then I notice he isn't wearing a tie; the top buttons of his light blue shirt are undone, showing more of his flawless brown skin. And he's rolling up his damn sleeves, revealing deliciously corded forearm muscles and prominent veins.

Jesus Christ, why are men's forearms such a turn-on?

I force my eyes away from ogling my husband and move my attention to the other person in the room. A man about an inch or two shorter than Atticus, with short black hair, light brown complexion, pale eyes and an easy smile, dressed in a tailored gray suit and white shirt.

Tequila shots in the kitchen that fateful night.

Yeah, I remember Sloane Yorke.

Now the plethora of jewels makes sense.

"Mrs. Shaw," Sloane croons as he glides over with an easy grace toward me. "It's fantastic to have you back."

The moment he's a couple of steps away, leaning forward to kiss my cheek, I strike out, slapping him across the face. He jerks up straight, looking down at me with stunned blue-gray eyes.

"You know what that's for," I sneer, and then step around him, ignore Atticus, and head for the kitchen.

Loud chuckling follows me as I pull open the fridge and take out a bottle of water and a small container of chopped fruit Marta pointed out to me earlier today.

"I see why you like her, Shaw," I hear Sloane comment as I'm looking for a fork.

I feel his blazing heat against my back before I see his arm reach out to my right and pull open a drawer to reveal cutlery. His other hand rests on the counter next to me, caging me in.

"You're ignoring me," Atticus states in his signature low tone, his breath fanning over the back of my neck.

"I don't know what you mean," I say as I reach for a fork, but the drawer snaps shut.

"Don't play coy," he bites. "You need to answer when I call."

I turn slowly, glaring up into Atticus' eyes. "Being at your beck and call wasn't part of our arrangement."

Atticus leans down, bringing his lips dangerously closer. His proximity forces me to inhale his sandalwood and bergamot scent. It sticks to the back of my throat, and I hate that I want *more*.

Atticus' hand slides off the counter and somehow manages to pull my phone from the pocket in my shorts without touching me.

He holds it between us. "Did you block me?"

"No," I grit out.

"Show me," he demands.

This fucking guy.

I rip the phone from him and enter my passcode, open the settings, then angle the screen to him. "See this little button? That's called 'Do Not Disturb'. When you activate it, you don't get any messages or notifications. And when you turn it off..." I tap the button on the screen and my phone starts incessantly buzzing. "Would you look at that? Some asshole called me four times and texted me just as much."

Atticus doesn't move, but continues to glare at me, those dark eyes impossibly darker. I hope that look is him reconsidering this whole thing and that he'll release me from this farce, but my instincts tell me that won't happen. He seems to enjoy torturing me for whatever reason.

For another long moment of glaring at each other, Atticus rips open the cutlery drawer and walks off toward the dining room.

I notice Sloane standing in the entry—he was watching us.

"I thought you two were going to fuck," he comments with a shit-eating grin.

"Shut the fuck up, Sloane," I snap, pulling out a fork.

He presses a hand over his chest. "You know my name. I'm

honored."

I ignore him, pick up the fruit container and water, then walk past him into the dining room. I really want to sit on the opposite side of the table, far away from Atticus, but I don't have the energy to deal with anymore of his shit today, so I take the seat that's already pulled out next to him.

I crack open the bottle of water, taking a long gulp of the crisp liquid as Atticus pulls over the container of fruit. He removes the lid, takes my fork and spears a piece of pineapple, then pops it into his mouth. I'm too distracted by his jaw moving as he chews, his throat bobbing as he swallows, to see that he's stabbed a piece of watermelon this time and is holding out the fork for me to take.

I hesitate for a moment before taking the fork and sticking the fruit in my mouth. I'm expecting Atticus to take the utensil back and use it as some power play, but he just nudges the container closer to me, and moves his attention to Sloane, who's now standing on the other side of the table.

"I've been summoned here today because you're in need of rings of matrimony," Sloane says, addressing the both of us.

"Rings of matrimony?" I repeat.

Sloane nods. "Wedding band, engagement ring. The usual."

I side-glance at Atticus. "For a proposal that *didn't* happen."

He smiles at me. "I can propose to you right now if that would satisfy you, Mrs. Shaw."

I roll my eyes and concentrate on my fruit, choosing a piece of apple this time, and bite off half. Atticus pinches the stem of the fork with two fingers, angles it toward himself and pulls the remaining piece of apple off with his teeth.

"There's more in the fridge," I point out after swallowing the apple.

He grins, swallowing his stolen piece. "Tastes better because it's yours."

"Ah, young love," Sloane comments.

My head whips in his direction and I point the fork at him. "I will use this on you."

"You shouldn't flirt with me in front of your husband," Sloane tuts. "He's a very jealous man."

My glare drips with menace as I blindly stab another piece of fruit without looking away from Sloane. He just chuckles and starts a presentation on the jewels in front of us, talking about carats, cut, and clarity. I listen in silence while I eat my fruit, with Atticus occasionally stealing the fork for himself.

I'm finished with the food and water by the time Sloane wants me to try out sizing rings and then he asks about my metal preferences.

"I don't have a preference," I tell Sloane, as I'm deciding which size is more comfortable.

"May I suggest yellow gold?" Sloane supplies. "It will suit your complexion."

"That'll do," I say absently, pulling off the test ring and holding it up. "Let's go with this size."

"Perfect," Sloane murmurs, writing the size on his tablet. "Diamond for the engagement ring?"

I sit back and shrug. "I guess."

"Cut and carat? Setting?"

I've honestly never thought about this before. The three

boyfriends I've had in my life never remotely triggered the potential for marriage, and it was never a priority for me, so I don't even have a dream ring. I also thought I'd have Zahra or my mom with me doing these kinds of things, but Atticus forcibly bypassed all of them.

"Phae?" Sloane says softly, pulling me from my melancholy.

I pull out my phone from where it was tucked under my thigh. "Hold on."

I video-call Zahra, and she answers on the second ring.

"How much blood is there?" she says as a greeting.

Seeing her beautiful face and hearing her voice instantly relaxes me. I smirk and angle around, so Atticus is in the background. "He's not dead yet."

Zahra flips him the bird on the screen. "You're a prick."

"Lovely to see you again, Zahra," Atticus says in a bored tone.

"Phae might have stalled my plans to sue your ass for forging my signature, but don't think there won't be compensation involved."

Atticus rolls his eyes. "Send me the bill."

She laughs evilly. "You'll regret saying that."

Atticus grunts like he's unconvinced and moves his attention to his phone.

I move to sit straight again, switching the phone to the rear camera and pan over the jewels in front of me.

"Holy shit," Zahra breathes.

"What should I get?" I ask.

"You mean what should *we* get?" she corrects.

I smirk, my eyes flicking to Atticus—he doesn't move to protest. I flip back to the front camera and prop up the phone, then spend the next hour with Sloane and Zahra, going through jewels and ring design options.

We collectively decide on a yellow gold wedding band with eight tiny diamonds set intermittently around the whole band, and a moderate two-carat oval diamond on a simple gold band to match.

Zahra then proceeds to get both of us diamond tennis bracelets, or "friendship bracelets", as she calls them, as well as a pair of ruby studs for herself and emerald drop earrings for me. It's all charged to Atticus' account, hundreds of thousands of dollars worth of jewelry, and he still says nothing. After I chose the wedding rings, it seemed like he checked out of the whole experience, escaping into his phone.

After Sloane advises me and Zahra that our jewelry will be ready in five or six days, I end the call and Sloane swiftly packs up his jewels. Just as the table is cleared, Marta and Rosemary appear with dinner for the three of us.

Sloane's idle chatter keeps the silence at bay, with Atticus occasionally answering one of his questions, but I'm not actually listening to the exchange. This entire day has completely drained me of everything, and all I want to do is curl up and hide.

That notion suddenly overwhelms my system, so the moment I finish the delicious spaghetti carbonara, I'm out of my chair with my plate and excusing myself without a backward glance.

12

ATTICUS

"TROUBLE IN PARADISE?" SLOANE asks, pulling me from staring at the door Phaedra retreated through.

"None of your concern," I say, finishing my food.

I look up at Sloane's blue-gray eyes regarding me hesitantly. "Don't kill me for what I'm about to ask, but is she here against her will?"

I know he's only showing concern for Phaedra, which in theory I should appreciate from my best friend, but Sloane having *any* thoughts about my wife triggers an irrational impulse to draw blood.

"We made an agreement," I say simply, as I shove down the urge to stick a fork in his eye.

"A *mutual* arrangement?" Sloane presses.

"Yes," I hiss.

"Was she sober this time?"

"Sloane," I warn.

He throws his hands up defensively. "You know why I asked."

Yeah, and I don't like it. I take a calming breath, something I'm doing more and more of these days, before I continue.

"*Yes*, she was sober. *Yes*, it was a mutual arrangement. It even has terms and conditions. And *yes*, she can leave when she wants."

Sloane's eyes narrow. "But she won't or she doesn't get what she wants from this arrangement."

I can't help the sly grin that creeps over my face. He knows me so well.

Sloane chuckles as he shakes his head incredulously. "You're a bastard."

"I'm just trying to start my life with my wife," I reason. "She's the one who wants the marriage annulled."

"That's justifiable since she was *coerced*," Sloane points out.

"She'll come around," I say dismissively.

One way or another, Phaedra *will* accept this marriage. She'll even learn to be happy here in this life. And happy with me.

"What kind of arrangement is it?" Sloane asks, curiosity lighting up his face.

I stack my cutlery on my plate and pick it up as I stand. "You don't need to know the details."

"Oh, come on," Sloane whines as he jerks up and collects his plate and cutlery too, following me as I move toward the kitchen. "Give me a hint, at least."

I ignore him as I walk over and place my dishes in the sink, then cross to the cabinet door next to the wine rack and slide it open to reveal the small built-in bar. I pull out a bottle of gin and two crystal tumblers, then bring them back to the island counter.

"Is she coming to your parents' thing?" Sloane asks, placing his dishes on top of mine. He's referring to my parents' fortieth wedding anniversary dinner in two weeks.

"Yes," I respond, pouring both of us a drink.

"It'll be interesting to see how she fairs with the entire Shaw clan," Sloane comments, scooping up a glass. "Your dad will probably ask to see your prenup."

"Naturally," I grumble, then take a mouthful of gin.

Frederic Shaw at the first meet immediately questions someone's intentions, and thinks every interaction should involve an ironclad contract. It makes him a brilliant lawyer, but a shit husband and father.

Sloane raises a brow. "*Do* you have a prenup?"

"No."

Sloane sputters out a loud laugh. "Jesus, Shaw. And you say *I* make risky decisions."

It's already been too long since Phaedra has disappeared, and I'm tired of Sloane's commentary and attention on my wife, so I down the rest of my drink and place both of our glasses in the sink.

"Rush the rings," I say, sweeping my hand toward the dining room.

Sloane rolls his eyes, knowing I'm dismissing him, and pushes off the counter. "I'll send for Wade to collect them once they're done."

After waiting with Sloane in the penthouse's lift foyer until his security team arrives, I head directly to my room, eager to spend this first night with my wife. There might be a no-touching rule in place, but finally having her in my bed settles some of the hollowness that's plagued me for years.

This is how it's meant to be.

Except, when I enter our bedroom, she's not curled up in my bed. I turn and walk back to the dressing room—no bags. Nothing in our bathroom. What the fuck?

I take out my phone and pull up the security feeds from the penthouse lift lobby, scrolling through the last fifteen minutes. The only people I see are Sloane, his men, and myself. She didn't leave, so where the hell did she go?

As I'm about to exit the primary suite, the loggia snags my attention and I chuckle. My clever little lilac. I pivot to the glass door and slip out into the cool October night. I grin—the door to the other bedroom connected to this space is ajar.

Keeping to the shadows, I cross over to the door and peer in. Soft, warm light glows through the space from a lamp on the nightstand, and I can just hear a shower running. I spy a suitcase at the bottom of the closet on the opposite side of the room, and a laptop set up on the desk.

I'm making a note on my phone to purchase a larger desk for our main bedroom when the shower turns off and a hushed "shit" echoes from the bathroom. Phae darts out wrapped in a towel, hair wet down her back, and rummages through her suitcase, pulling out a pack of sanitary pads, then disappears back to the bathroom.

I pull up the calendar on my phone, marking today's date. It's a couple of days later compared to her last cycle. She must be stressed, or maybe not eating well. I send Marta a message with the list of foods my wife prefers during her cycle.

I also notice the reminder for next week, so I pull out the second phone synced to Phaedra's device, book in her contraceptive injection renewal appointment with her doctor on the clinic's website, and set up a reminder on her calendar. These things will be a lot easier when we sync our schedules.

Phaedra reemerges from the bathroom, so I pocket both phones. She's now dressed in black sleep shorts and a white camisole, with her hair now wrapped in a towel.

Christ, she's beautiful.

Her smooth pale skin would be the perfect canvas for my handprints and bite marks. She should be wearing a ring of pretty lilac bruises to match her hair from my tight grip around her neck, while I watch her gasp for air as I fuck her until her eyes roll back.

Lust pumps through my veins at the thought as I press my hand into my hard cock, trying to relieve some pressure as I watch her move about the room, adjusting the lighting, testing the variety of pillows on the bed and tossing aside the ones she doesn't like, then padding over to sit in front of her laptop.

Like many nights before, I consider slipping into the room, sneaking up and picking her up from behind, delighting in the struggle she'd give before pressing her into the mattress and filling my lungs with her fear-spiked vanilla and lilac scent until I'm strung out, then claiming her as mine over and over until she begs me to never stop.

A thrill rolls down my spine as I wrangle those dark desires back into their chains. I don't want Phaedra terrified of me—not that much, anyway. She needs to think about me every waking moment, to the point of insanity. Every moment away from me should eat at her soul like it has for me all these years.

I take a slow inhale while the sudden onset of fury flashes over me. I force myself to back away to our bedroom. I will grant Phaedra the next four or five days of peace, but then my wife has *many* transgressions to answer for.

13

PHAEDRA

AFTER MY NOT-SO-SUBTLE ESCAPE yesterday from dinner, I locked myself in the room I've claimed and showered, which was the exact time my body reminded me I was due for my cycle to start.

The light ache in my lower body as I went to bed turned into full-on nightmare cramps this morning, and they're a reminder that sometimes I really despise owning a uterus.

Thank the scheduling gods, I don't have any classes until the day after tomorrow, so I spend most of the morning in bed being miserable. I don't have my usual comforts like my heat pack or my tea, so the next four or five days are going to suck.

By late morning, my hunger wins out over the comfort of the luxurious bed, so I pull myself out and have another shower, which soothes some of the ache in my back, and once I'm dressed in loose sweats and a large crewneck, I venture to the kitchen.

I'm expecting Marta and maybe Rosemary to be milling about, but I didn't expect Atticus to be home. Dressed in a crisp, white button-up shirt, no tie, and black suit pants, he sits at ease at the kitchen counter typing away on a laptop.

"Good morning, Phae," Marta chirps happily, as she dries a frying pan with a hand towel. "Are you hungry? I can put something together."

My eyes flick to Atticus—his focus is still on his laptop.

"Uh...yes, that would be amazing," I say to Marta. The muscles in my abdomen ripple in a painful roll, and I fight to keep my composure. I gesture toward the sofa in the family area on the other side of the large room. "I need to sit. Please, nothing too heavy. A yogurt would be plenty."

Marta nods, and I shuffle over to the plush gold L-shaped sofa. Relief washes over me as I sink into the corner, the cushions soft enough to relieve the uncomfortable pressure on my hips and back, but not too soft that I'll become one with the sofa and never move again.

I readjust my position, tucking my knees toward my chest and burrowing further into the comfort. I glance at the television mounted on the wall, longing to watch a random disaster film or animal documentary, but that would require me to move and find a remote.

Suddenly, the television turns on and I blink. What the—

"Sit forward," Atticus' deep voice instructs softly behind me, and I jerk my head toward it.

He looks like a dark, avenging angel looming over me with...a heat pack?

Stunned into compliance, I shift forward, and he fits the hot-pink heat pack between my lower back and the sofa. I audibly sigh at the relief from the warmth seeping into my muscles, and my eyes flutter closed involuntarily. A soft rattling sound makes me open them again. Atticus holds out a bottle of ibuprofen and a bottle of water. I take both from him and realize both bottles are still sealed.

"So you know I'm not trying to poison you," he says, noticing what has my attention.

I give him a sardonic smile. "Thanks."

One side of his lips quirks up as he produces a television remote and places it on top of the sofa cushion, then retreats to the kitchen. I frown at his retreating form. How did he know? He has a sister; I guess he's seen it all before.

My attention returns to the pill bottle as I open it, taking out two and chasing it with the water. Marta appears with a tray, and she places it on the sofa next to me.

"Here you go," she beams. "Yogurt with berries and dark chocolate pieces. Honey in the small bowl. And then there's cinnamon tea in the pot and a little carafe of milk in case you wanted it today."

I stare at the tray with a slack jaw.

"How did you know?" I ask, looking up at Marta.

She gives me a warm smile. "Mr. Shaw informed me."

My favorite tea, food, and preferred pain-relief methods. How in the actual fuck did he know about all of that?

"Thank you, Marta," I say. "I'm very grateful."

She reaches down and pats my knee, lowering her voice. "I remember how hellish cycles can be. I'm so glad they're over for me."

I nod my agreement, then she turns back toward the kitchen. My gaze shifts to where Atticus was at the counter, but he's no longer there. Maybe he's going to work now that he's seen his prisoner is still present.

I turn my attention back to the television and, after some trial and error, I finally find a disaster film to watch and dig into my breakfast. I'm feeling a hell of a lot better by the end of the movie and, before I start the next one, I decide on more tea.

I take the food tray from earlier back to the kitchen and load the dishwasher, then rinse out the teapot and refresh the infuser with more tea as I wait for the water to boil in the electric kettle.

Questions float back to me, and I pull out my phone and open up my message thread with Zahra.

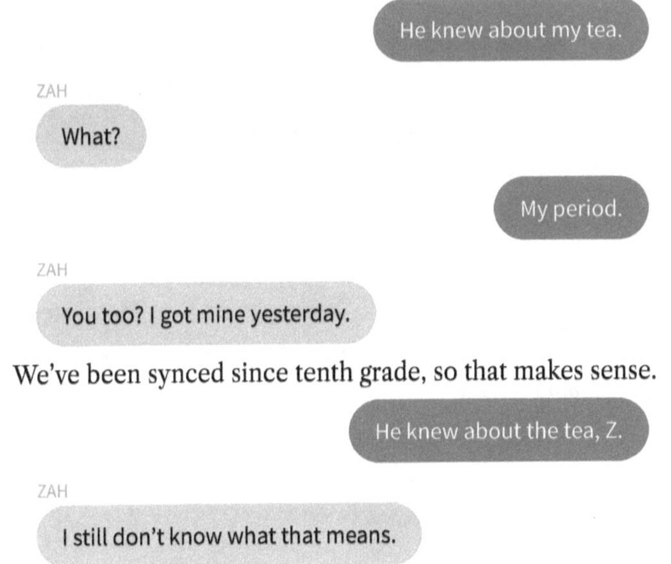

We've been synced since tenth grade, so that makes sense.

> The cinnamon tea. The one I use for bloating.

ZAH

> You mean the hot bark water you think helps?

I snort. Zahra is very anti-tea.

> Atticus told Marta. It's even the same brand.

ZAH

> Who's Marta?

> Atticus' live-in chef.

ZAH

> You have a live-in chef?!

> Focus, Z. We're talking about the fact that Atticus knew about the tea. He also knew about the heat pack, and my favorite food to eat.

ZAH

> He probably just looked up the best ways to help a woman on their period. And he has a sister.

I nod to myself—that's what I thought earlier. The water has finished boiling, so I put my phone down and cross over to the kettle, bringing it back to the pot to fill.

As I'm returning the kettle to its base, realization smacks me in the face. I cross back and snatch up my phone.

> How the hell did he know I had my period in the first place?! It's not like I announced it.

Zahra calls me as a reply, and I answer immediately.

"That *is* really weird," she says.

"*And* he was here like he knew it was coming," I say softly.

"Okay, now you're being paranoid," she chides. "He wouldn't stay home to play nurse. He runs a billion-dollar empire. That's definitely just a coincidence."

I sigh. "You're right. But how did he know all the other stuff?"

"Powers of deduction?" she supplies. "Are you wearing sweatpants and looking miserable?"

"Rude," I chuff.

"I'll take that as a yes."

"Still doesn't explain that he already knew my preferences and had the supplies beforehand."

Zahra hums in thought. "Maybe he just had a *really* good, or creepy, private investigator doing his background check?"

I frown. "That's another thing—"

"Phaedra, my dearest love. The bestest best friend in this universe. You're going to send yourself to a psych ward with all these questions. So he did a background check, and he knows you like dirty hot water during your monthly shed."

"Your visuals are always impeccable," I say dryly.

"At least he's courteous enough to give you your comfort things and leave you alone."

I huff out a burst of air. "I want to go home."

"Eyes on the prize, babe. There's only twenty-nine days left until you're free of that man, and then we can go on a really long holiday to the Mediterranean with his monetary compensation for your troubles."

That pulls a laugh from me, but I stop as it agitates the muscles in my abdomen. "So I do and say nothing?"

"Exactly," Zahra agrees. "Exist like a ghost haunting the penthouse. You're pale enough."

I shake my head with a grin on my face. "You're an asshole."

"I know," she beams.

"I'm going to watch a documentary series on sea animals and drink my dirt water," I tell her. "Talk to you later?"

"I'm going to make a martini and soak in the tub. Love you, babe."

"Love you too."

— $ —

I must have dozed off two or three episodes into my binge session because when I wake up, I'm curled up on my side under a super soft blanket I didn't have before, and there's a news broadcast at low volume on the television.

Blinking the sleep out of my eyes, I sit up slowly, my head pounding a little, probably from a lack of hydration. There's a fresh bottle of water next to the ibuprofen on the coffee table, so I lean forward and pick up both.

"Are you hungry?" Atticus' voice comes from next to me, startling me.

Dressed the same as before—the sleeves of his shirt rolled to his elbows this time—he's sitting at the end of the sofa working on his laptop, a couple of feet from where I had my head on some throw pillows. I'm surprised I didn't feel his presence the moment

I woke up.

There's something less frenetic about him right now. He usually oozes intensity even if he appears relaxed, but tonight he seems comfortable. Settled in some kind of way.

When I don't answer him, he stops typing and looks at me. The energy shift I felt yesterday still lingers in his dark gaze, still confuses me. Is he the fun, albeit a little intense, stranger I met at the bar, or is he the off-kilter rich guy that only makes decisions to appease himself?

My educated guess is that he's both. And now, I have to navigate the intricacies of those pieces of this man in the hope I'll last a month without potentially committing a felony, or doing something even worse, like caring about him.

"Lilac?" he prompts lightly, pulling me from my thoughts.

"Hmm?"

"You should eat with the pills," he says.

My stomach decides to respond audibly to his instruction. At that, Atticus puts his laptop on the coffee table and walks toward the kitchen, his long strides eating the distance quickly. I take two pills, then push back the blankets and stand, stretching out my legs and visiting the restroom.

When I return, Atticus is sitting in his spot on the sofa again, watching the news, eating from a huge bowl in his hands. I shuffle past him quickly and take my spot again, picking up the extra bowl of food from the coffee table. It's some sort of grain salad with a fresh, zesty dressing.

We eat in a surprisingly comfortable silence together. Atticus' attention is on the television and mine keeps drifting to him.

My questions from earlier in the day start zipping around in my head again. Zahra's words try to keep them at bay, but I want answers.

"How did you know about the tea?" I ask softly.

The question pulls Atticus' attention to me, chestnut-brown eyes tracking over my face like he's looking for something. I don't know what for, but I feel exposed and I can't quite understand why.

He eventually looks down at his food, loading up his fork. "I've said it before, I know a lot more than you think."

I frown. "What does that mean?"

"You're asking the wrong questions," he says cryptically before shoving the loaded-up fork into his mouth.

What does *that* fucking mean? I aimlessly push the delicious food in my bowl around as I watch him eat, trying to work out how to play this damn game with him.

"Did you do a background check on me?" I ask.

"Yes," he answers simply.

"Before or after our wedding?"

His eyes flick to mine. "Both."

That question surprises me. He knew who I was *before* the club? Realization once again slaps me in the face. He's the *owner* of *Deux*.

"Have we met before?" I ask, trying to sift through every single memory I can conjure. He had to know who me and Zahra were before sending that invitation to his club.

His eyes glow as his lips curve slightly, almost like he's proud that I'm putting pieces together. "Yes."

My heart pounds quicker. We've met before. When? Why don't I remember? I'd remember Atticus. His entire presence is something you *can't* forget.

"When?" I ask out loud, my breathing stilted.

Atticus abruptly stands and holds his hand out. "Finished with your food?"

I stand from the sofa, anger spiking as I step toward him. "You didn't answer my question."

A wicked grin spreads over Atticus' face as he shrugs. "I'm bored with your line of questioning."

I take another step toward him and stop inches away before I shove him in the chest, remembering our arrangement stipulations about touching.

Delight flashes in his eyes—he's just fucking with me.

Without touching him, I stack my bowl in his empty one that's in his hands and step back. I collect my water and ibuprofen, then walk around the other side of the coffee table and head to my room.

It was reckless letting Atticus lead me to almost breaking the no-touching rule. I won't put myself in that position again.

14
PHAEDRA

THE NEXT WEEK GOES by in a blur. I've taken Zahra's advice and have become a ghost, having minimal run-ins with Atticus and resuming my life like the only thing that's changed is my postal code.

Zahra picked me up from the penthouse on Thursday when I was due back in the studio, so I didn't need to ask Atticus for a ride, and after classes I picked up my car from my house and drove back. The exhaustion from the extensive travel has helped with the whole ghost strategy, as I've basically eaten and passed out every night.

By the weekend, I've gotten into a pretty good routine, and my cycle's finished, so it's looking like the rest of this month may be easier than I thought.

The sun has long set by the time I pull up in front of the Sky Building. My legs and core muscles protest a little from the dance routine I went through before I left the studio as I climb out of my car and pull my duffel bag from the back seat.

Harris appears from the building in his usual uniform with an easy smile. "Good evening, Mrs. Shaw."

"Hi, Harris," I say, handing him the keys and thanking him before heading toward the elevator.

I make my way straight to the kitchen, finding Marta in a fluffy robe stirring something on the stove.

"Marta," I announce in confusion. I glance at my phone; it's after ten. "You shouldn't be awake."

She ladles soup into a bowl. "Harris told me you just arrived. I figured you'd be hungry."

"I could have put together a sandwich," I say.

She waves me off as she crosses to the island counter and sets the bowl on a tray, which already has a plate of sliced crusty bread, a small bowl of grated parmesan cheese, and a glass of white wine.

"Just leave the tray when you're done and I'll handle the dishes in the morning," she says as she takes my bags and then disappears further into the penthouse.

Deciding on a new spot for dinner tonight, I take the tray to the Grand Salon and, not wanting to ruin any of the furniture, I find a spot on the floor near the grand piano and set the tray down.

I sit facing the window, looking out to the beautiful, glittering view of New York at night as I demolish the hearty chicken and vegetable soup, all the bread, and finish with the glass of wine. I pick up the tray and take it back to the kitchen, leaving it on the counter as instructed, then head toward the door that leads to the service corridor.

I turn the handle, but it snags. It's locked. I frown; it's never locked. Well, actually, I'm usually in bed by now, so I wouldn't know. Marta and Rosemary probably lock this section, so they aren't disturbed overnight.

I head toward the dining room but realize I left my phone in the Grand Salon. I stop at the entrance when I find Atticus standing in the spot where I was eating dinner.

Dressed only in a navy-blue button-up shirt, no tie, and dark gray suit pants, he's peering out the window, with his hands folded behind his back. Like a king observing his kingdom.

As if he senses my presence, he turns toward me and holds something up. My phone. I give him a watery smile and walk toward him.

As I move closer, I notice he seems tense. Or maybe I'm imagining it. I've avoided eye contact as much as I can in the last week, but as I get closer, I see the sharpness of his features, the hard glint in his eyes.

"You're in contact with him," Atticus states.

I pause by an armchair a few feet from him. "Who?"

The muscle in his jaw ticks. "You know who."

I shake my head in confusion.

"Dylan."

My mouth drops open. *What?*

Atticus takes a couple of slow steps toward me, turning my phone screen toward himself.

"*We should talk,*" he reads, then looks at me. "How long?"

My heart hammers as I instinctively step backward. "How long what?"

"How long have you two been in contact?" Atticus keeps advancing forward slowly as I move back, trying to work out what's happening right now.

I shake my head. "We haven't spoken since we broke up."

"Are you lying to me, Lilac?" he asks. His tone screams danger.

"What? No." I suddenly halt in my escape, my anger spiking. "What gives you the right to read my messages?"

Atticus continues prowling forward. "Is he why you're avoiding me?"

"Once again, attention wasn't part of our deal," I remind him, holding his intense glare as he stops inches from me.

"Is that where you were tonight?" he asks, pitching his menacing tone lower. "Are you fucking him?"

"No," I spit.

"Then where were you?" he demands.

I fold my arms across my chest. "Why don't you ask whoever spies on me on your behalf?"

A taunting grin spreads across his face. "Now, why would you think you're being watched, Lilac?"

"Because I'm not stupid, *Shaw*," I say mockingly, then snatch my phone from his hand. "I was at my studio. Where I always am when I'm not here. I haven't seen Dylan since we broke up, and this is the first time he's contacted me. And I *won't* be responding to him. Are we done?"

Atticus leans forward, bringing his face so close to me I get a lungful of his sandalwood and bergamot scent. "I never want to hear his name on your lips again."

I roll my eyes, step back and pivot sharply, entering the dining room. I cross to the other door, which leads to the foyer. As I'm passing through, I jump as Atticus appears at the Grand Salon's entrance from the foyer.

"I didn't say we were done, Mrs. Shaw," he says, moving toward me.

My heart kicks into a new speed as my instinct to run takes over my whole body. I shuffle a little faster toward the hallway gallery, but not too fast that he knows that he's affected me.

"Does he know you're married?" Atticus says, his voice seems to echo throughout the penthouse.

When I turn left down the hall, I peek in his direction. He's still following me, his long legs eating up the distance despite his languid, easy stride. It's like he knows he doesn't have to be quick to catch me.

With fear overpowering my system, and the need to have a door between me and Atticus, I cross to the first bedroom and turn the handle.

Snag. Locked. *Fuck*.

I turn to face the direction I just came from. Adrenaline blasts through me when I see Atticus waiting at the entrance of the hallway.

I stumble backward, my hand sliding across the wall as I blindly feel for the next door.

Atticus prowls toward me again. "You know that I'm a jealous man."

I reach the next door, and grab for the door handle—locked. My breathing becomes short as panic mixes into the adrenaline, and I continue down to the next door.

"You are *my* wife," he declares, still moving toward me. I grab the next handle—*locked*. I swallow a whimper and continue, moving faster. "And I don't take kindly to other men having *my* wife's attention."

I finally reach the room I've been using for the last week, the last door, and grab the handle. *Snag.* I look down at it and try again, rattling the handle. No, no, *no.* Why is it fucking *locked?*

When I look up, I realize Atticus has gotten *much* closer. I scramble back blindly, trying to work out how the fuck to get out of this situation. I don't even know what he wants or why he's chasing me. If it's to scare me, then he's doing a fantastic fucking job.

"Do I have to remind you of the terms of our arrangement?" Atticus asks, still advancing slowly.

My heart is going to burst through my chest at the ferocity it's beating. I shake my head vigorously as my back smacks into a wall.

No, not a wall, it's a door. I grab the handle and almost cry when it doesn't snag. When it opens, I almost fall onto my ass but catch myself on the arm of a sofa. I'm in the primary suite, which is connected to the other room via the loggia.

I scramble toward the glass door, and of course it's fucking locked.

I turn to the sound of the suite door clicking shut. Atticus leans against it with his arms folded behind his back, watching me.

"Remind me again," he says evenly.

"Of what?" My voice is hoarse.

"Of our arrangement."

My bottom lip trembles and my eyes sting from tears, but I refuse to let them fall.

"What do you want from me?" I plead softly.

He tips his head to the side, regarding me in that predatory way of his that makes my skin break out in goosebumps.

"I want so many things," he breathes.

"W-what if I can't give them to you?"

"You can," he croons softly. "You will."

We stand in silence for a few moments. I cling to the door handle like it'll magically unlock, and Atticus continues to watch me with unwavering focus.

"One month," I whisper, breaking the tense silence. "Our arrangement is for one month of marriage."

"And?" Atticus asks neutrally.

"Cohabitation, events, monogamy."

"Are you holding to that last one?" he asks, his eyes narrowing.

"Yes," I hiss. "Are *you?*"

Atticus' whole demeanor changes at my question. He *relaxes*.

"There is no one but you, Mrs. Shaw."

"You can't touch me," I blurt out, my clutch on the door handle still a death grip.

"As you like to remind me," he says as he pushes off the door. He sweeps out a hand toward the rest of the suite. "Shall we?"

His swift change in attitude has me completely off-kilter. "Shall we what?"

"Bed," he supplies.

I point to the door. "I need a key."

He tsks and shakes his head. "Sleeping separately is no longer an option."

"Why?"

"Too many questions."

Since my laundry is always fresh, and my bed made, I'm guessing

Rosemary has probably already questioned why her boss's new bride is sleeping separately.

I nod, dropping my gaze and motioning to the sofa. "I can sleep here."

"Not an option," Atticus declares, drawing my gaze back to him.

I shake my head. "I don't want—"

"*Bed*, Phaedra," he barks. "I won't hesitate to break a term of our arrangement and carry you there if I have to."

My body tingles at the mention, but I ignore it and sigh heavily as I walk further into the main suite, giving Atticus a wide berth. I walk into the bedroom area and around the huge bed to the far side that doesn't look slept on and sit on the edge.

I can hear Atticus' deep chuckle farther into the suite, probably still in the dressing room. I look down at my phone; the screen lights up with the damned message that got me in this room.

DYLAN

We should talk.

Why the fuck is he contacting me now? It's been two and a half months since he told me he was moving to New York for work, and he didn't want a girlfriend who refused to move with him "holding him down."

He honestly did me a favor because despite me trying to come around to the idea of moving back to New York, I don't think I would be ready any time soon.

I snort softly at the irony that I'm currently here, living in New York City. At least this is only temporary.

I look over at the nightstand and notice a blue charging cable. *My* blue charging cable. Of course, it's already here.

Footsteps approach as I reach over, plug my phone in to charge, and place it down on the nightstand.

"I'm going to assume all my stuff is in the bathroom," I say, staring out at the city lights.

Atticus' half-naked form suddenly appears in the window's reflection and my mouth goes dry. Holy *fuck*.

If I thought Atticus was intimidating in the suits he wears daily, it's nothing compared to the lethal predator of pure muscle they hide underneath. Dressed in nothing but low-slung black sweatpants, every defined ridge of muscle and an expanse of smooth dark brown skin is proudly on display.

With the sheer size of him and the grace with which he moves, the man is a walking warning sign to stay the fuck away. I wouldn't want to encounter Atticus in an alley alone, and yet here I am in his bed.

My eyes roam the light dusting of hair across his chest, down to the trail below his abs that escape into his pants. I drag my attention away from his crotch, remembering *exactly* what's hiding in those sweatpants.

"All of your things are on the right vanity," Atticus says as he crosses to his nightstand.

"Perfect," I breathe as I avert my gaze, ignoring the sudden batshit idea to lick Atticus' abs and escape the room.

15
ATTICUS

S ATISFACTION WARMS MY CHEST as I watch my wife skitter past me to the bathroom, eyes never leaving the floor. Her sweet and floral scent floats past me, settling deep in my chest. I look forward to this whole room smelling of her.

I cross to my side of the bed, pull the linens back, and sit on the mattress. Propping myself against the padded headboard and pillows, I check a few emails as I listen to the quiet hush of the shower running. I reply to a few of them, but the moment the shower turns off, my focus immediately switches to my wife.

She comes back into the room dressed in a loose, white T-shirt and silky purple shorts that hug her perfect ass. Long, wild lilac curls lay down her back, her eyes still avoiding my direction as she circles the large bed and quickly pulls back the blankets, tucking herself inside right on the edge.

Her nervous energy gratifies the darkness that's ever present in my mind, but it also frustrates me because, despite "attention" not being in our arrangement as Phaedra has pointed out, that's what

I want—her undivided attention.

"Comfortable?" I ask Phaedra, who's curled up facing away from me.

"Yes," she says softly, despite being visibly rigid.

"You didn't even test the pillows," I point out, peering at the three stacked against the headboard. She's essentially using her arm as a pillow.

My comment makes her roll slightly so she can look at me over her shoulder in confusion.

I grin. "Don't want you getting a sore neck, my beloved."

She turns back and sighs, then pulls herself to her knees, facing the pillows. I watched with rapt attention as she picks up each pillow and bashes it around, then tosses the two she doesn't like off the bed. She picked the softest one, like I knew she would.

Placing her preferred pillow down calmly, Phaedra smoothes the fabric before curling back on her side, facing away from me.

"Goodnight," she murmurs, then reaches out and turns off the lamp on the nightstand.

I turn off my own so the room is dark, but I don't move from my seated position. "Sweet dreams, Lilac."

I close my eyes and listen to Phaedra's breathing, my mind drifting to earlier tonight. I watched Phaedra eat in peace on the floor of the Grand Salon for a while, enjoying seeing her content in her own little bubble within my dominion.

I had already locked all the doors in the apartment and was waiting for the perfect opportunity to speak to my wife, who had been ignoring me for the entire week. Leaving her phone behind was that perfect opening until I saw that message from that fucker,

Dylan.

The audacity of the man to think he was worthy of her attention after he broke it off. He didn't deserve her attention in the *first* place.

Dylan needs to be dealt with.

Pulling myself from thoughts of reprisal, I realize Phaedra's breathing is slow and deep. Opening my eyes, I test if she's truly asleep by finally sliding down the bed and rustling the blankets a little. She doesn't move. I reach out and trace the curve of her shoulder. Still nothing. I grin. My wife sleeps like the dead.

Laying on my side, facing Phaedra, I continue to trace my fingertips along the back of her arm, across her shoulder blades, and then through her hair fanned out over the pillow. So soft and long and thick. I resist the urge to wrap the tresses around my fist, instead detangling myself from her hair and returning to the task at hand.

I grip her bicep and tug softly, rolling her until she's on her back. Reaching across her body, I hook my arm around her waist and slide her closer to me smoothly.

Once our bodies are against each other, I slide my arm under Phaedra's head and pillow, then pull her body over mine as I roll onto my back, settling her over my side, tucking her head into the crook of my neck.

My still-sleeping wife sighs softly, her breath tickling over my clavicle as she unconsciously wraps around me further, tucking a leg between mine, now using me as her own personal pillow.

I swallow the groan of absolute ecstasy pulsing through my blackened heart from the feel of Phaedra finally touching me after all this time. Burying my nose in her hair, I suck in her scent like a man possessed. Because I am—possessed by the voraciousness of this beautiful creature at my side.

When she wakes in the morning sprawled out on top of me, the tedious 'no-touching' rule will be obsolete and I'll be able to touch her as I please.

And then her atonement for stealing pieces of my soul begins.

I hum pleasantly at the thought, settling further into the comfort of my bed, tucking my hand through the leg of Phaedra's shorts and gripping her hip, and finally, *truly*, relaxing.

As I drift off to sleep, I eagerly await my dreams, knowing they'll be of my exquisite wife.

16
PHAEDRA

I STIR FROM SLEEP and open my eyes, only to shut them again from the glare of the sun. I didn't consider being on the other side of the building nor the extra windows when I went to bed last night.

I snuggle further into the expensive sheets, fully intending to get another hour or two of sleep before facing the day. It's going to suck going back to my secondhand mattress after sleeping on luxury ones for a month.

I smile—I'm definitely going to sneak in an order for new bedroom furniture on Atticus' dime before the end of our agreement.

As I'm dozing off with daydreams of new mattresses, the current one I'm lying on shifts under me.

I frown. What the—

There's shifting again, and the hand that's gripping my thigh under my shorts now slides further up to cup my bare ass cheek.

My eyes fly open, ignoring the stinging from the sudden

brightness, and I jerk my head up. Smooth brown skin over corded neck muscles, short beard over a sharp jawline.

Hooded, warm chestnut-brown eyes regarding me heatedly.

"Good morning," Atticus drawls, his voice rumbling through his chest under me.

I simply blink at him, my brain desperately trying to work out what's happening. I was sleeping. *On* Atticus.

I'm touching him.

"No," I breathe.

Before I can scramble away, the world tilts as Atticus heaves to the side, trapping me under his huge body and crushing his lips to mine. My brain screams at me that this is wrong, but my treacherous body goes languid, disintegrating into pliable mush.

His tongue thrusts into my mouth, marking its territory with a possessive sweep as our lips and teeth war with each other. Dizzy from his scent in my nose and his taste on my tongue, I paw at his tense, hard body, clutching at smooth, warm skin. I don't know if I'm trying to get him off me or pull him closer.

Atticus' vice grip on my ass cheek disappears as his hand slides out, then he forces his leg between mine, adding delicious pressure to my core. His now-free hand slides up under my T-shirt, trapping my left nipple between two fingers and pinches hard.

I rip my mouth away from his on a gasp as pain lances through me, shooting directly to my core and making my legs clench around his wide thigh.

"Are you a little pain slut, Lilac?" he croons as he rolls my nipple between his fingers. My legs tremble uncontrollably with each stroke of his thumb over the stiff, aching peak.

"No," I grit out immediately, forcibly loosening my body, not wanting to give him the satisfaction of a reaction to his touch.

I'm lying to him, and to myself. As a ballet dancer, you're used to pain, but it becomes background noise. However, when you give up your innate self-preservation during an intimate act and allow someone to purposely inflict pain, that focused intensity releases this numbing haze afterwards that I've unintentionally experienced only once before, but craved ever since.

I've never had that level of trust with a partner to ask again. And I'm not ready to admit to Atticus, of all people, that he's the only person I've considered asking.

Annoyance at my blatant lie flashes in his dark chestnut eyes as he pinches my nipple again, harder this time and twisting it slightly. It takes everything in me to temper down the rising tide of pleasure flooding my system, triggered by his painful ministrations.

The sharp pain disappears from my nipple and a light sting lances over my cheek. I freeze.

Did he just *slap me?* It was more of a love tap, but... This fucker really just *slapped* me.

"You want to try that again?" Atticus growls in my face as his hand grips my jaw, forcing me to look directly at him.

"Fuck you," I sneer, trying to pull my face out of his grip, but he just squeezes tighter.

"You will after you answer my question without the lies." His smirk is cruel. "Am I going to find your cunt dripping for pain, Mrs. Shaw?"

Use of that title pulls me out of the lust-trap as fury burns in my entire body. I shove at Atticus' chest hard and buck my hips. The move must surprise him because he tips to the side. I don't realize we're close to the edge of the mattress until Atticus' massive frame shifts off me and he continues off the bed.

Serves him fucking right.

But at the last second, Atticus scoops me up by the waist and I'm jerking forward at a frantic speed, falling with him. He crashes onto the floor with a heavy *thunk*, and I land face-first on top of him, my teeth knocking together as my chin slams into his hard pectoral.

Heart pounding and ignoring the dizziness from the impact with his chest, this time I don't wait to scramble off Atticus, not caring that my elbows and knees are landing in soft parts and making him wheeze out a breath.

I just manage to get clear of his body and onto my knees when a tight grip in my hair renders me immobile.

"Running from me just makes the punishment worse," he warns, twisting more of my hair around his fist and moving to stand.

"Punishment?" I grit out, wincing at the painful tugging on my hair as he steps around to face me. "For *what?*"

He sneers down at me, a looming threat ready to decimate. "For lying to me."

"What? I wasn't—" I hiss as Atticus pulls harder on my hair until my neck is straining and then eases the pressure. That glorious haze washes over me, and I fight to keep my eyes from rolling closed.

With his free hand, Atticus shoves his sweats down, freeing

his cock. *Fuck*. Hard and thick, smooth and slightly curved. A prominent vein running the length, a temptation for my tongue. Fucking perfection.

"Hands on my thighs," Atticus barks, pulling me out of my dick hypnosis.

I look up to stare directly into his face as I do as I'm told, sliding my hands up his clothed thighs until I'm sinking my short nails into warm flesh near his pelvis.

He tracks every movement, his eyes dark pools of lust searing every inch of me they touch. I'm drunk off his attention, desperate to keep it for as long as possible, no matter how we ended up here.

"Open your mouth," he orders, his voice lower and gravelly. *Desperate*. We both are. "Tongue out."

My jaw drops open, tongue out flat and waiting.

Atticus wraps his free hand around his cock, stroking it languidly and spreading the clear liquid weeping from the tip.

"No teeth," he sneers, the unspoken threat bearing down on me like a suffocating beast, making goosebumps break out across my whole body.

He watches me for a beat, and when I don't move an inch, he shifts forward as he tugs on my hair so that I rise taller on my knees. He watches intently as he feeds me his cock in one smooth thrust, bottoming out about halfway down, my throat seizing around the head, cutting off my oxygen.

Atticus groans, his lids drooping in bliss. "This fucking mouth."

My throat constricts more, making drool drip down my chin. My muscles tremble as I struggle to breathe, my vision going hazy with tears.

As I'm about to give in and tap his thigh, Atticus draws back slightly, dragging his cock along my tongue slowly as I rasp in a breath. Before he can thrust back in, I take control and surge forward, sucking him in until he's restricting my airway again. This time Atticus is the one trembling as his eyes roll closed, and he drops his head back with a strangled moan.

Jaw straining from his girth and with tears leaking down my face, I pull back, dragging my mouth over his length with hard suction, as I slide my hand from his thigh to wrap my fingers around the base of his cock.

I work him hard and deep, my throat relaxing to get more of him in my mouth as I work the rest of the length with a tight, rhythmic grip.

It's messy—saliva coats his cock, my chin, my hand—and I hate to admit that I fucking love it. But this isn't for my pleasure. This is for control.

Atticus is completely at my mercy, the only sounds coming from him are desperate pants and heady moans as he keeps a grip in my hair.

Once I can get most of his dick in my mouth, I change the position of my hand, sliding my saliva-slick finger to cradle his balls and apply slight pressure.

"Oh...*fuck*," Atticus groans, his grip on my hair tightening. His hips start to buck frantically into my mouth, and I give in to the rhythm, applying a bit more pressure with my hands and digging my nails into his thigh with the other.

"I'm going...to come," Atticus pants, still thrusting.

I hum around his cock.

The vibration sets him off as he shoves in on a strangled cry and fills my mouth. His taste coats my tongue as I pull away from him. He untangles his hand from my hair, still trying to catch his breath with a bewildered expression, watching me stand from the floor.

I hook my hand around his neck and pull him down as if to kiss him, but as soon as he angles closer, I spit his come on his face.

"You're pathetic," I whisper, then shove away from him and stalk towards the bathroom, heart hammering in my chest and adrenaline buzzing through my veins.

17

PHAEDRA

I'M ON EDGE AS I'm washing my mouth out, waiting for Atticus to appear behind me and dole out some wicked punishment, but by the time I'm done, there's no sight of him.

I take a second to steel myself, then walk back into the dressing room and change into gym shorts, a sports bra, cropped T-shirt, and running shoes before going back to the bedroom for my phone.

I snatch the device from the nightstand and walk out, seeing a familiar shirtless figure on the loggia. Before Atticus can see me, I slip out of the room and head for the kitchen.

Marta is in her black chef's uniform, humming as she stirs a large pot on the burner. Rosemary sits at the island counter in her usual shirt and slacks combination in front of a laptop, reading glasses propped on the end of her nose, her eyes tracking across the screen as she types.

"Good morning," I greet as I walk to the fridge and open it, pulling out one of the fresh green juices Marta makes each day.

"Good morning, Phae," Marta sings. "What can I get you for breakfast?"

I cross to the fruit bowl on the back counter and pull a banana from the bunch, then lean up against the marble. "I'm hitting the gym first."

Marta nods in understanding and resumes her humming.

"Any other plans for today, Mrs. Shaw?" Rosemary asks from her spot.

"Not at the moment," I say, as my phone vibrates in my hand.

ZAH

> I'm in the city for the next two days. Your husband better not get in between us.

I grin at the screen. It's like the universe knows I'm in desperate need of bestie time.

"Actually, I might have plans later," I say absently as I'm asking Zahra to send me an itinerary for her trip.

"And your plans today, Mr. Shaw?" Rosemary asks, and my whole body freezes.

I keep my eyes fixed on my phone, my heart pounding in my ears as I wait for Atticus to respond. He's probably about to say some out-of-pocket comment about this morning, and then I'm probably going to punch him.

Suddenly, his warm body presses into my front, my nose bumping into a pink shirt-covered chest as his arm locks around me. I angle my head up so I'm not sucking in more of his citrus and woods scent, ready to berate him for invading my space, but before I can say a word, Atticus leans down and lands a sweet kiss on my lips.

"Good morning, my beloved," Atticus says in that delicious rumbling voice with a lazy smile.

"Uh, hi?" I say dumbly, because...*what?*

"I'm in back-to-back meetings today," he answers Rosemary, as he plucks the banana from my hand and peels it while he still has me pinned to the counter with his body.

"Will you be home for dinner?" Marta asks Atticus as I watch him take a bite of the fruit, then hold it out to me.

"To be determined," he says, waiting for me to take the banana.

"It's yours now," I say, refusing to play this game.

I reach to the bowl again behind me, pull another banana from the bunch and start peeling it without taking my eyes from him. As I raise the banana to my lips, Atticus leans down and bites the tip off.

"What is your obsession with eating my fruit?" I ask.

He shrugs and downs half the banana in his hand, still pinning me to the kitchen counter.

"It's rude," I comment before taking a bite of my new banana.

This time when Atticus leans down toward my fruit, I shoot my arm out so it's not in biting range, but he continues forward and presses a firm kiss to my lips, his tongue teasing the closed seam.

He hums an approving sound that makes my body clench.

"Delicious," he purrs, before finally stepping back. I hate to admit I miss his body heat the moment it leaves me.

Cheeks warm at that realization, I clear my throat and force my attention back to my phone, reading through Zahra's plans for the next two days. It takes me two passes to actually understand what I'm reading.

She's currently working on an article about an up-and-coming artist, so she's got interviews today, the art collection's debut at a gallery tonight, followed by an after party. Tomorrow, she has more interviews and a studio tour, but then her night is free.

> Tomorrow night, you're mine.

ZAH
> Your assertiveness turns me on.

ZAH
> I also put your name on the guest list for the gallery and the after party tonight.

I shake my head and grin.

> I'll think about it.

She sends me a string of hearts, and then I pocket the phone and finish eating my banana. Atticus returns to the room carrying a black leather briefcase, now sporting a medium-gray suit jacket that matches his pants, and a navy tie.

My eyes catch on the way those pants fit around his thick thighs, because, *damn.*

I snap my mouth shut and avert my attention before I'm caught staring, but by Atticus' smug expression, it's too late.

He has his briefcase open on the counter and pulls something out, then crosses to me.

"I didn't get a chance to give these to you last night," he says, picking up my left hand. The object in his other hand is a black velvet ring box, and when he opens it, my mouth goes dry.

"Jesus," I whisper, as I watch him first take out the first ring; it's not the gold band with sporadic little diamonds that we settled for. Instead, it's a whole row of small round diamonds set in gold that wink at me as he slides it onto my ring finger.

Then he pulls out the largest diamond ring I've ever seen.

Atticus hums a contented sound and lifts my hand to admire the rings on my finger before pressing his lips over them. "Much better."

"This looks way too big for two carats," I say, eyes glued to the massive fucking rock.

"That's because it's just over four, and about two carats in the wedding band," Atticus informs me. "Now people can *really* see it."

"I...can't take these out in public," I reason, eyes moving from the ring to Atticus' amused expression.

"You can." The *"you will"* echoes in his pause as he tucks a stray curl behind my ear.

"There's insurance on this, right?"

Atticus chuckles. "Yes."

For a split second, I'm caught by how his laughter dampens his intensity, the warmth returning to his chestnut-brown eyes. An unusually soft expression that stokes the flames of my curiosity. I want to know *this* Atticus.

Remember what happened just this morning, Phae.

"Good," I say with a nod, sidestepping out from between Atticus and the counter.

Before I can run away and sort through my confusion, I'm jerked back and spun around. Then Atticus' lips are crushing to mine as he bends me at the waist in an elaborate flourish. I cling to the lapels of his jacket, keeping myself steady, as his tongue slides against mine, scrambling my brain further.

His teeth sink into my bottom lip, enough to sting but not break skin. The small hurt sends a rush of endorphins through my system, making my breath catch and my fists tighten further, inadvertently pulling him closer.

Then he angles us upright, dragging his teeth off my lip before letting it go with a rumbling sigh that resonates in my core as my body *aches*.

My eyes flutter open to his hooded gaze.

"Will you miss me?" he whispers.

Reality comes crashing in like a cold, slapping wave, and I push out of his touch, clearing my throat.

"Bye," I throw over my shoulder as I rush out of the room, heart pounding and eyes fixed on the floor.

Trap, that man is a trap.

A beautiful, delicious, nice-smelling trap I keep stumbling into and only narrowly missing its jaws when they try to clamp down on my common fucking sense.

If I'm going to survive the rest of my term with Atticus, I need to be smarter about this game of cat and mouse.

18

PHAEDRA

I HIDE IN THE bedroom for a while, scrolling aimlessly on my phone until I'm sure Atticus has gone to work, and that Marta and Rosemary are preoccupied with other things, before I venture out and go to the gym.

Muting my phone notifications and blasting heavy rock music, I go through a hard strengthening routine and another dreaded run on the treadmill, pushing myself to the limit until I'm pouring with sweat and my thoughts are incomprehensible.

A low vibration of tranquility warms my whole body as I'm returning to the penthouse, not realizing I'm limping slightly until I'm entering the bedroom—maybe I went a little *too* hard.

I head straight for the shower, taking my time under the scorching spray, applying color-boosting conditioner to my hair and leaving it to sit while I dive into the abundance of products that have clearly been added recently to buff and scrub my body until my skin is smooth and glowing.

After rinsing out the purple concoction from my hair, I turn off the shower and secure the damp strands in a towel that's unfortunately white—I hope Rosemary won't be too mad about the staining—then take a large fluffy towel from the heated racks and wrap it around my body.

The thought of clothes on my warm skin feels like the worst idea right now, so I make my way into the bedroom where I left my phone and sprawl out on the haphazardly made bed.

My notifications turned back on while I was in the shower, so there's a slew of them waiting for me. I frown. Most of them are missed calls from Atticus.

I don't want to return his call purely out of spite, but he wouldn't call *five* times unless it's important, right?

I tap his name, bringing the phone to my ear as I roll to my side, my nose almost buried in Atticus' pillow.

"Phaedra," he answers, his deep tone reverberating through the speaker.

My stomach flips. "Atticus."

He's silent. I use his name so little out loud that apparently it still seems to confound him when I do. That kind of sway over him makes a grin tug on my lips.

"You rang?" I prompt.

He clears his throat. "Yes. Several times."

"I was at the gym."

"I know."

I'm confused for a moment, but then I sigh. "You have access to the building cameras."

"I do," he confesses simply.

I roll my eyes. Figures.

"How's your hip?" he asks randomly.

I frown. "Fine. Why?"

"Because your workout seemed quite strenuous. And you've been in the bedroom for some time."

I jerk up. "There are cameras in *here*?"

His low, wicked chuckle rolls through my whole body, settling me instantly.

"Not in any of the bedrooms," he informs me.

"But throughout the penthouse?" I ask, laying back down.

"Yes."

"Do you watch them frequently?"

"When you're there, all the time," he confesses.

I open my mouth to say something, but nothing comes out. I should find that outrageous, but...I don't. I seriously need to see a shrink.

"Was there a reason you called so many times?" I ask, refocusing our conversation.

There's shuffling on the line, like Atticus is moving. "What are you doing tonight?"

I stare at the ceiling, absently playing with the edge of the towel around my body. "Not sure yet."

"But you have *potential* plans." I can hear the faint hum of ambient office sounds and doors shutting in the background.

"I do."

"With who?" he asks, an echo of demand in his otherwise neutral tone.

"Does it matter?" I breathe.

"It matters a *great* deal, Mrs. Shaw."

The danger warnings in the back of my head are pitifully dull as my body buzzes—like a shot of adrenaline directly into my bloodstream. The hand that was toying with the towel now moves further down my body.

"Is it *him?*" Atticus seethes, the rumble in his voice making my thighs spread open.

"Who?" The towel parts and my fingers glide over short, soft curls before sliding through my arousal.

"You know who."

His words from just last night filter back to me.

You should know that I'm a jealous man. And I don't take kindly to other men having my wife's attention.

"Is this...*jealousy* I hear?" I purr.

Atticus sighs, exasperated.

I close my eyes, my fingers finding my clit, circling over it with firm pressure. I swallow the moan in the back of my throat as pleasure shimmers through my core.

"Admit it," I say, my fingers working faster.

"What exactly do you want me to say?"

"The truth," I breathe. My mind is hazy with pleasure as I work myself with more pressure.

"That's a complicated question," he says neutrally.

"That wasn't your answer last night when you saw that message from—"

"Do *not* say his name," he growls, and *fuck*, my cunt spasms.

"Then admit it," I pant. "Admit you're jealous."

"I'll admit I will do unspeakable things if someone gets between us, *wife.*"

I swallow a whimper and my thighs tremble.

"That's quite a promise to live up to, *husband*," I tease. "And you say you aren't jealous."

"I said it last night," he counters.

"But you won't admit it now?"

"Why are you so desperate for a reminder, Lilac?"

"Because pressing your buttons gets me wet." My impending orgasm peaks, making my hips roll as I work my clit faster. "Do you enjoy being nothing but a toy to me, Atticus?"

"Phaedra." It's a warning.

"Say it again," I demand, my voice desperate. "Say my name."

I hear the sound of a door opening and several low voices overlapping. "I'm about to start a meeting."

"Are you wishing it was me spread out over that boardroom table right now, Mr. Shaw?" I pant.

Atticus clears his throat, mumbling about needing a minute to someone, then the voices fade further into the background.

"What are you doing?" he demands softly, his tone clipped.

"Are you hard right now?"

He makes an angry sound at the back of his throat. "Yes."

"Aw, poor baby's going to be all worked up for his important meeting."

"Fuck," he whispers.

"Too bad you don't have cameras in here," I sigh. "You'd be getting *quite* the show."

"*Fuck*," he repeats, this time strangled.

"*Please*, Atticus," I plead. "Say my name again. For me."

"Phaedra," he croaks low, his voice tenuous.

"Oh, *yes*, again," I pant. "I'm so close."

I hear the strained soft groan; I imagine that he's here, doing it directly into my ear. "You're fucking killing me, *Phaedra*."

An intense orgasm rushes through me, and I let out an ungodly sound as I continue working over my clit, prolonging the blissful torture. When my brain comes back online a few moments later, all I can hear is Atticus' heavy breathing on the line and the faint continuous murmur of people talking in the background.

"Have a good day at work, Mr. Shaw," I purr into the receiver, then end the call.

19
ATTICUS

PHAEDRA'S HEAVY BREATHING, GASPING moans, and desperate shout of pleasure almost sent me to my fucking knees in front of the executives of my company, and that *really* pisses me off.

That tricky little sorceress throws me off-kilter so easily, and that's simply unacceptable. Even now, her keening sounds reverberate through my head, eating away at my sanity, her words whispering in my ear.

Say my name again. For me.

Using the words I said during our first phone conversation was tactical, and it hit its mark tenfold. Well played, Mrs. Shaw.

I shift in my seat. Sitting here listening to my team drone on about profit margins while my cock is painfully hard is the worst kind of torture.

My fingers drum on the table as I try to act engaged in whatever the fuck is going on in this meeting right now, even though I'm desperate to leave.

Thankfully, Felix picked up my distraction and has been taking point, while I imagine all the ways I can punish my wife for this little stunt.

Her body confessed she's a little pain slut this morning when she got all worked up from our rough play, so draping her over my knee and spanking her ass red probably won't teach her a lesson.

But images of Phaedra's perfect ass at my mercy sends a rush of lust through my system. I could tie her hands behind her back, hook my leg over the back of her knees, and wrap her hair around my wrist tight, leaving her completely trapped.

God, her struggle would be *electric*. The hatred glowing in those beautiful topaz eyes would fuel the twisted part of my soul that thirsts for her.

And if she cried?

A shudder runs down my spine as I take calming breaths through my nose, my cock pulsing, begging for attention, *her* attention.

I pull my phone from the table, unlock the device, and immediately open the surveillance system feeds. I flick through the ones from the penthouse, not finding Phaedra anywhere, annoyance burning again in my chest that I don't have cameras in our bedroom.

That's going to change, since Phaedra will probably hide out now that she knows.

Wait... No, there she is. And—

Fuck.

In my office, dressed in nothing but one of my white shirts and matching socks, Phaedra sits in my chair with her feet propped up on the edge of my wooden desk with her knees spread and her hand between her legs. Her eyes are closed, head tipped back slightly as her body writhes, the hand playing with her pussy working at a quick pace.

I'm transfixed, watching her free hand cup her breast, pinching the nipple through the shirt as her breathing comes out in shorter bursts, her sock-covered toes curling into the desk.

A wave of lust courses through my body, mixed with a healthy shot of agitation. Phaedra's putting on a show just for me, *knowing* I'd bring up the feeds at some point, adding more fuel to the fire she started with that damn phone call.

Phaedra should enjoy these victories in our little game, because my wife is going to learn very quickly that I *never* lose.

I know the moment she comes when she almost jerks out of the chair and her knees tremble as they clamp around her hand. I wish I was alone so I could watch with the audio.

The snapping of laptops being shut pulls me back to the present. I stand abruptly, pocket my phone as I turn from the table and thank everyone over my shoulder as I storm out of the boardroom.

Hans stands immediately at his desk as I breeze past in a hurry.

"Clear my schedule," I instruct when I exit my office with my briefcase.

I only just hear Hans acknowledge me as I continue out of the office.

Wade barely pulls up in front of the Sky Building before I'm exiting the car. Usually, I'd come in through the basement, so the woman covering the desk jumps up, surprised at my appearance. She splutters something as she steps out from behind the desk, but my focus is getting to the penthouse.

As I swipe my fob to open the sliding door to the private foyer, the elevator doors across from me part. The vision walking out roots me in place.

Strappy silver sky-high heels, smooth, toned legs, and a sinfully short light gray skirt hugging ample hips. The white satin shirt tucked in at the waist is unbuttoned to the bottom of her sternum, showcasing the curves of my wife's perfect breasts but not flashing anything important.

My gaze follows the exposed olive skin to her bare, slender neck, then glossy, bitable, plump lips, before finally connecting with sparkling golden-topaz eyes. The darker make-up accentuates the color, and the elongated shape gives her a feline gaze.

Her lilac hair is up in some sort of low style, with a few loose curls framing her face.

"You're home early," Phaedra says, as she fishes out her phone from the pocket of a tan coat draped over her arm.

I cross to her and take the coat, holding it open for her. "Trying to sneak off without me knowing where you're going?"

She shrugs nonchalantly as she slides her arms into the coat sleeves.

Her aloofness triggers the jealous beast roiling inside me. I lean forward, my lips brushing the shell of her ear. "Who are you meeting up with, Lilac?"

"My other husband," she deadpans, attention still on her phone. I can see she's messaging Zahra.

Hands trailing down her arms, I snake one arm around her waist, pulling her flush against me. Her lilac and vanilla scent wraps around me like a sensual embrace. She doesn't resist, willingly melting against me, but her thumbs are still moving over the screen of her phone.

I slide my hand under the coat, my fingers stroking the exposed skin along her sternum. "I enjoyed your little show in my office."

That finally gets her attention.

"You were watching," she states rather than questions.

I hum a confirmation anyway as my fingers slip into her shirt, grazing a hardened nipple. No bra, no covering. Daring little Lilac.

She twists her head to look at me. "While you were in your meeting?"

"Yes."

A sly, victorious smile tips those tempting lips.

"Teasing me won't end well for you," I warn.

"Not used to things not going your way, Mr. Shaw?" she taunts. Her breathing is shorter as she presses further into me while I continue to play with her nipple.

"I *always* get my way, Mrs. Shaw."

She scoffs, then turns to face me. With her heels, she's

considerably taller, but she still needs to tilt her face up to me. "What do you want?"

"What you promised." I pull my hand from her breast and slide it down the center of her body, pausing at the waistband of her skirt.

"Promised?" she breathes, her fingers playing with the curls at my nape. "What exactly did I promise?"

"You. Spread out over my desk. My face buried in your cunt."

Her pupils dilate, her breathing a little tighter as she raises an arched brow. "I promised none of that."

I step forward, moving Phaedra back until she's pressed in the elevator doors. "But you want it."

"Do I?" she asks. One of her hands slides out of my hair and grips my wrist, dragging my hand from the waistband of her skirt to the hem of the short length.

Holding Phaedra's burning gaze, I move my hand under the soft fabric, fingers traveling up her thigh until I'm cupping her naked core.

My fingers slide through her arousal, and I groan my approval.

"All of this for me?" I croon, playing over her clit, delighting in the way her breathing hitches and her thighs closes around my hand.

"Maybe this is for someone else," she taunts.

I thrust two fingers into her dripping heat. "Liar."

"That's...what I do," Phaedra pants. "Lie."

"You only lie *for* me, Lilac," I remind her, my fingers working faster into her. "Not to me."

Her head falls back on the door, her lids heavy with pleasure as

I continue to pump in and out of her body, adding my thumb to press firm circles over her clit.

"Give it to me," I grunt into her ear.

"No," she whines, even as her body flutters around my fingers, her grip on my hair and wrist tightening.

I dip down and bite into the side of Phaedra's throat hard.

Phaedra lets out a desperate shout as she comes, her body squeezing my fingers tight, more arousal sliding over my hands and down her thighs. I release her throat from my teeth and run my tongue over the marks as I continue my ministrations until she's pushing my hand away.

I brush my wet finger along her bottom lip before crushing my mouth to hers. She tastes of vanilla and sex as our tongues dance and teeth clash.

Hunger, sharp and infinite, claws at my chest; my thoughts are on nothing but wholly possessing Phaedra. She occupies every moment of my existence, and yet it's not enough.

An exaggerated throat clearing behind me makes Phaedra pull away. I almost turn and growl at the intruder like a beast.

"Am I interrupting something?" Zahra asks, the tone feigning innocence.

"You're just in time," Phaedra chirps, her voice still breathy, as she slides to the side, and shuffles away.

I turn to see Zahra standing with Harris. Her eyes dart between me and her best friend, smirking openly. Harris has the decency to be looking at the floor.

"Phaedra," I call, just before she disappears around the corner. She pauses and turns back to me.

"You're a stunning liar."

20

PHAEDRA

"**N**OT A WORD," I warn Zahra as we cross the foyer.

"I wasn't going—"

"Shut your beautiful mouth," I snip.

She laughs openly as we exit the building and slide into the black town car waiting at the curb, the driver standing by the back door with a smile. He closes us in and swiftly moves around the car, getting into the driver's seat and pulling away.

"Phae," Zahra starts.

"Please, don't, Zah," I breathe, closing my eyes, not wanting a Zahra lecture while my body is still buzzing from that foyer escapade.

"Phae—"

"I know I'm playing with fire, okay?" I cut her off. "And I know this won't end well, but the man already has his hooks in me, and I need to reclaim my power back. And if that means using sex as a weapon, then so be it."

The car is silent. I glance up at the driver through the rearview mirror. We make eye contact before he quickly looks away.

"What I was going to say," Zahra exclaims, ignoring my outburst. "Is that you have a hickey."

Housed in a multi-story, red-brick building in an industrial area of Chelsea, the gallery, *Sabbia*, is a large open space with an expansive mezzanine, white walls displaying huge colorful canvases, light timber floors and meticulous lighting.

We've been here for an hour and the gallery is now teeming with people, from flamboyant artist types to clean-cut business executives, huddling in clusters around different art pieces, with hospitality staff floating around serving canapés and champagne. There's a light hum of conversation through the space and a vibrant energy about the art on display.

Playing with the end of my hair that's now out of its clip, I admire the work in front of me. It's an abstract interpretation of the naked female body, a monochromatic piece in shades of black and gray, using extravagant strokes and paint splatter. The whole piece somehow catches the light in a way that makes it feel alive. I squint at the piece and lean forward; I'm pretty sure there's also—

"Tiny shards of glass," a smooth male voice says next to me.

"Mixed into the paint?" I ask, straightening and turning to the man.

He's a little taller than I am in heels, dressed in a loose-fitting black T-shirt and equally loose-fitting black pants with red velvet flat shoes peeking out of the wide hems. Mixed metal chains of varying sizes and lengths adorn his neck and wrists, contrasting his dark outfit and pale skin.

His hair falls in dark brown waves to his shoulders, and he sports short facial hair and a relaxed smile. My eyes flick up to his pale blue eyes that are on the art in front of us.

"Getting the pieces small enough to mix well but large enough to refract light was a pain in the ass," he says, his eyes moving to mine.

"You're the artist?" I ask.

He dips his chin in confirmation, but his eyes never leave mine. "And you, my dear, are a work of art made flesh."

I smirk, but I feel the blush heat my cheeks. "Do you say that to all the girls?"

His smile is downright sinful as he opens his mouth to say something, but his attention shifts to my right.

My skin tingles, and I know exactly who has his attention before Atticus' warm arm wraps around my waist.

"Good evening," he says in his low, rumbling tone as he pulls me to his side.

"Mr. Shaw," the artist says in a rush as he *literally* bows. "It's an honor."

"You seem to have met my wife." The biting, possessive edge in the way he said "wife" makes me look up and frown at him.

God, I shouldn't have looked. Dressed in a deep burgundy suit, with a black shirt and no tie, not one of his dark curls out of place, his beard trimmed, dark eyes burning with intensity and his scent wrapping around me, Atticus is *devastating*.

Possessive jealousy slithers through me like an angry snake at the thought that he's out in public looking *this* good, but I smother that sucker before it takes root.

"My beloved," he almost purrs.

"What are you doing here?" I ask, low enough only he can hear while keeping a smile on my face.

Instead of answering me, Atticus turns his attention back to the artist. "I'd be interested in hearing more about the exhibition."

The artist beams as he nods, then sweeps his hand out to the art piece in front of us and starts explaining its origin and method of production. I peek up at Atticus, surprised to see that he's actually interested in what the artist is saying as we move around the space.

Over the next thirty minutes, Atticus doesn't let me leave his side as the artist presents, but he makes sure he replaces my glass of champagne every time the staff approaches us. Which means I'm already four or maybe five glasses deep, and being such a lightweight, I'm fairly buzzed.

Someone comes up to the artist's side and talks softly into his ear, then he makes his excuses to us before leaving.

"Do any of these interest you?" Atticus asks casually, admiring the work in front of us.

I step out from his hold, elbowing him in the ribs as I go, and face him with my arms folded across my chest.

"So, what, you're stalking me now?" I ask.

A smirk lifts his lips, but when he turns to me, there's anger in his gaze. "He wants to fuck you."

"Who? The artist?"

He nods curtly.

"Is that all you ever think about?" I snipe softly.

"Yes," he says simply.

I scoff. "What a waste of time for the great Atticus Shaw."

His smile deepens, but that anger burning in his eyes remains. "You think I'm great?"

"I think you're an asshole."

"But a *great* one."

"Yes, the great Prince Asshole of New York," I snap angrily and then turn my face away. Infuriating fucking man.

Warm fingers suddenly trace the edge of my shirt, then tug on a curl, but I refuse to look back at him.

"You're mad at me," Atticus starts. "That's okay, because I'm *furious* with you."

Affronted, I turn back to him. *"Excuse me?"*

His eyes remain on the tendril of hair he's playing with. "You think of this, us, as a game."

"It *is.*"

He nods. "Yes, Lilac, it is. But you're a fucking novice dueling with someone leagues above you." His fingers release the lock and skate up my chest to trace the hickey on my neck that's obscured by hair. "I've been in this game for a lot longer, with more pieces on the board."

"How long?" I ask curiously.

His depthless, dark eyes flick to mine, and I stop breathing. "Years, Phaedra."

My heart hammers in my chest. *Years.* He's known about me for years. Our conversation on the sofa from last week filters back to me. He insinuated we'd met before that fateful night at his club.

Apparently, *years* ago.

I ask the question I've been asking since this whole "game" started. "What do you want from me?"

"I want you to stop putting yourself in danger by trying to best me. I don't take kindly to my wife being in peril."

I shake my head. "That will never happen."

He sighs. "You won't win, Lilac. I know what moves you're going to make before you—"

My laugh cuts him off. "*Now* who's the liar, Atticus?"

His head tilts slightly as he regards me with confusion.

I step closer to him, stroking my left hand down the center of his chest, the rings sparkling in the lights. "You have *no idea* what my next move is, and that is pissing you off, isn't it?"

The anger sparking in those dark depths is answer enough.

This time I sigh, patting his chest sympathetically. "Don't try too hard, honey. You don't want to strain something."

I take several steps back out of his reach as fury incinerates whatever was keeping him docile. He takes a step toward me, retribution blazing in his eyes. Adrenaline zips through my veins, the promise of another round of this ridiculous game about to begin. So, with liquid courage, I turn my back to him and walk away.

My skin tingles, knowing he's following as I weave through the crowd, trying to work out my escape without Atticus snatching me up outside, when I see the perfect exit. I change direction and walk up to Zahra, who's standing with the gallery manager and the artist.

Zahra smiles as I slide up to her side, and then her eyes widen when she clocks Atticus behind me.

"Mr. & Mrs. Shaw," the manager says in a polite tone. "We thank you again for joining us tonight."

"It's been a pleasure," I say to her, then move my attention to the artist who's looking at me and avoiding Atticus. "Your work is incredible."

He inclines his head graciously. "You're very kind, Mrs. Shaw."

"My husband and I have been talking about refreshing the art in our apartment, and I think several pieces from this collection will be fantastic."

The manager and the artist both look between us in shock.

"Of course, Mrs. Shaw," the manager says in a rush, picking up the catalog for the show from the table behind her.

I pluck it from her hands and turn to Atticus. His face is perfectly neutral, but I can feel the wrath rolling off him.

"How many did we decide on?" I ask innocently.

He flashes a pantie-soaking smile laced with a hint of menace. "As many as your heart desires."

I swear I hear the gallery manager whimper. Grinning, I step across to the artist's side, standing close to him and open the program between us. I point out several of the most expensive pieces, asking his advice on where I should put them in the penthouse, making sure our arms brush as much as possible.

Once I've selected five pieces, I close the program, and pass it to the manager, return to Zahra and loop our arms together.

"Zahra and I have another engagement, so my husband will handle the final sales and delivery."

The manager nods eagerly, setting her attention on Atticus,

while I angle me and Zahra toward the exit.

"I fucking love you," she whispers as we move away.

"Oh, wait," I call, stopping and looking back. "I think we'll also take the glass woman, too. For the bedroom."

I blow Atticus a kiss and then walk away.

21

PHAEDRA

THICK SMOKE AND PULSING lights fill my vision as I move with the heavy beats of the music. Instead of going to the respectable bar that the after party was taking place, Zahra found a questionable basement club in the East Village for us to escape to.

The place is relatively small, and there's so much smoke from machines that it's hard to breathe or see. It also smells a little stagnant, the bar is perpetually sticky, and the bathroom has ambiguous hygiene standards.

I fucking love it here.

Zahra and I have drunk so much tequila that I really can't feel my body and, even if I could see through the smoke, the world would blend in a slurry of color.

Delicate fingers grip my wrists, pulling my attention.

"Bathroom!" Zahra yells over the music, then pulls me through the crowd.

As usual, there's a line, so we plant ourselves at the end and lean up against the wall of the hallway.

"I can see your nipples through your shirt," Zahra slurs as she touches the warm skin of my torso.

I bat her hands away with a giggle and look down. Sure enough, my shirt is damp with sweat and clinging to me, with the shape of my peaked nipples clearly visible.

I shrug. "If someone touches, I throw hands."

Zahra takes my hands and kisses over my knuckles. "I got your back, champ."

I push her off again with a giggle as I move with the line, keeping my back on the wall so I don't fall over.

"Do you have my phone?" I ask Zahra. We left our coats in the town car, and I don't have pockets, so I gave my phone to her to hold, and I haven't seen it in a while.

"Yeah, hold on," she grumbles as she fishes through her small, cute crossbody bag. She pulls out two devices, checking the protective cases to distinguish between the two, then passes me the one with pink bows on the back.

The brightness of the screen makes my eyes sting as I try to read the time through my spinning vision. It's almost one in the morning. There are also quite a few missed calls from Atticus.

I snort-laugh. "Oh man, Atticus is going to be pissed."

"Who fucking cares?" Zahra barks loudly. "He's incon...inconse..."

"Inconsequential?" I offer.

"Yeah, that."

I let out a breath, moving with the line and handing back my phone. "Yeah, I know, but—"

"No buts, Phae," Zahra cuts me off, shoving our phones back in her bag. "He's a little worm and you're the bird."

I snort. "You're making no sense."

She grabs either side of my face, squishing it as she kisses me hard on the lips, then pulls back just enough that she can look at me in the eye. "Boo, Atticus."

I nod, bumping our noses together. "Boo, Atticus."

Satisfied, she releases my face, turns me toward the now-empty hall, and smacks my ass. We both laugh as we stumble forward into the bathroom, waiting behind one woman for a short time before two stalls become available—she takes one and Zahra and I take the other together.

After both using the facilities, washing our hands and fixing up what we can of our smudged makeup, we head for the bar. Surprisingly, we find an empty section and squeeze in between two groups to wait for the bartender, who's currently at the other end.

We eventually get our tequila shots and orange juice chasers, drink both, and then I pull Zahra back toward the dance floor. Near the edge of the dense crowd, I crash into a hard body.

Steady hands grab my biceps. "Easy there."

I whip my head up. Tall, slim frame, familiar light eyes and light brown hair. "Dylan?"

His eyes widen as he takes me in. *"Phae."*

I take a step back, shaking my head, but Dylan's grip on me tightens.

"We need to talk," he insists.

I'm absolutely not doing this tonight, or *ever*.

"No, we don't," I say, but he ignores me and pulls me through the crowd.

"Hey!" Zahra shouts, and shoves at Dylan, but one of his friends grabs her.

"Dylan, what the fuck!" I try to wrestle out of his hold, but it's tight. He's going to leave fucking bruises.

We end up in the bathroom hallway, where he traps me at the end against a "Staff Only" door. I check the handle behind my back, but it's locked. When Dylan finally releases my arm, I strike out and slap his face hard enough that his head jerks.

"I guess I deserved that," he says, rubbing his face as he looks back at me.

"I want to leave." I move to step to the side, but he slaps his hand on the doorjamb near my head.

"I need to talk to you," he asserts, his tone almost...desperate?

"I don't care."

"Are you really married?" he asks.

I frown. "Who told you that?"

His light blue eyes search mine, then drop to my left hand. "So it's true?"

"What's it to you? *You* broke up with *me*, remember?"

He rakes his fingers through his hair, clearly distressed. "Shit."

"I need to go—"

"Back to that *psycho*?" he spits. He takes a steadying breath. "Phae, please. You need to listen to me. Atticus is not who you think he is."

I scoff. "And who exactly am I supposed to *think* he is?"

"I don't know, some elite bachelor you managed to tie down."

A laugh bursts out of me, and I cup my hand over my mouth.

"Whatever farce he fed you," Dylan continues, ignoring my outburst. "None of it is true. That guy is seriously bad news."

I swallow the hysterical laughter, and wipe at the tears at the corner of my eyes.

"You really thought three months after you left me you could come swooping back into my life and save me from someone you think is the boogeyman?"

"I couldn't come any sooner," he reasons. "Technically, I shouldn't be here *at all*."

"What does that mean?"

He shakes his head and cups my face. "It doesn't matter. I'm here now, babe. Here's the plan: I'll talk to my uncle, the divorce lawyer, and we'll get you out of this."

I smack his hand away from me. "Don't *ever* touch me again."

"Phae—"

"Fuck off, Dylan. I don't want you *or* your help."

He shakes his head in disbelief and takes a step back. "But you want *him*?"

"It's none of your fucking business," I shout.

"Please, Phae, we can fix this," he tries again.

"There is no 'we'," I point out. "And did you ever consider I can look after myself?"

"Not against *him*," he argues. "He's literally insane."

"Stay out of my life, Dylan. If you contact me, or anyone in my life again, you won't like what happens next."

"He's already in your head," he says dejectedly, as he drops his head. "I'm so sorry."

"I don't know what you're babbling on about. I'm leaving now and if you stop me, I will hurt you."

Dylan stumbles back and leans up against the opposite wall, a hopelessly lost look on his face as he continues to stare at the floor. I don't wait around a second longer, scrambling away toward the bar.

I find Zahra near the entrance of the hallway, still trying to fight off the hold of Dylan's friend. I shove the guy from the side, surprising him, and he releases her. I take her hand and we head straight for the exit.

"What the fuck was that?" Zahra demands the moment we're in the frigid October air.

"Dylan being a fucking idiot," I say, rubbing my arms as my teeth chatter. I regret leaving my coat in the car now.

"I'm going to go back in there and fuck him up," Zahra announces, stumbling back toward the entrance. The bouncer catches her before I can, and I give him a grateful look.

"Don't worry about it, Zah. I got a good shot in. Let's just get the car here before I freeze my nipples off."

She huffs but digs her phone out of her bag and stabs at it before bringing it to her ear. I take my phone out of her bag as well and put in my passcode. The sudden urge to call Atticus washes over me, but I quickly shake it off. I don't need to put up with his jealous bullshit tonight. I'll stick with the original plan and stay with Zahra at her hotel, then deal with him in the morning.

The deep growl of an engine pulls my attention from my phone as a shiny red sports car pulls in front of the club. The driver gets out, and my plans change completely.

"Phaedra." Atticus' voice carries clearly in the space between us.

He circles his car and walks toward me. I close the distance with hurried steps, slamming myself into his warm body, burying my face in his chest and snaking my arms under his coat, wrapping them around his torso tightly.

I don't give a shit how he found us. He's here.

"Jesus, you're freezing," he comments as he pulls me closer, and wraps the coat around me, fully encasing me against him.

The warmth of his body sinks into my bones, slowly relaxing my taught muscles. I could stay like this forever.

"What happened?" Atticus asks, pulling me back to the present.

I lift my head from his chest and look up into dark, dark eyes. "Nothing. Let's go."

The frown he's sporting deepens. "Phaedra."

I shake my head. "Take me home, Atticus."

22
PHAEDRA

I STAY WRAPPED AROUND Atticus as we wait until Zahra's car arrives, even as he accepts my coat and bag from the driver and Zahra blows me kisses goodbye.

I eventually release my tight grip on him when he places me in his car. I sigh and close my eyes as my body sinks into the heated leather seats and I use my coat as a blanket, vaguely feeling Atticus securing my seatbelt.

"I'm surprised nobody stole this baby," I comment as he starts the car, the engine rumbling to life under me.

"They wouldn't dare," he says, pulling away from the curb.

I loll my head to the side and peek at him. "Does *everyone* know who you are in this city?"

He smirks as he changes the gear. "Pretty much."

I scoff. "You're so entitled."

He shrugs. "Maybe."

I watch him drive for a while. The way he moves so smoothly, how he's so relaxed. I realize he's no longer wearing his coat, dressed only in burgundy suit pants and a black shirt with the sleeves rolled up to his elbows. Such delicious forearm muscles.

"How did my art acquisitions go?"

I'm expecting him to tense up, but he remains languid, even tapping on the wheel to the tempo of the soft music I didn't realize was playing until right now. I think it's jazz, but my ears are ringing slightly from the club.

"It went smoothly," he informs.

"Can you buy me a mattress?"

He looks at me briefly with amused confusion. "Usually I'm asked for jewelry and clothes, and you want...a mattress?"

"I need that cloud magic in my life," I sigh wistfully. My daydream of mattresses cuts off when I register what he just said. "Wait, *usually*? How many random people have you married?"

"You're the only Mrs. Shaw," he says, his tone serious.

My heart flutters.

"When was the last time you had sex?" I ask curiously.

A cheeky smile plays on his lips. "Define sex."

"Penetrative," I supply.

"Our wedding night."

Flashes of our bathroom escapades invade my mind and I shake them off quickly. "I meant sex that wasn't with me."

"Two years ago."

My eyes widen. "You were celibate that *whole* time?"

He nods, slowing down for a light.

"I don't believe you."

He turns to me with an amused expression. "There were offers. I wasn't interested."

"So you're an intentional fucker," I surmise.

He shakes his head at me. "Such colorful language."

"What are you going to do about it?" I challenge.

Atticus chuckles, the sound so rumbly it blends with the car's purr. "I definitely have some ideas."

My skin tingles with anticipation, but before I can ask for explicit details or a demonstration, I rein in the tequila-induced deviant and ask something I've been curious about since he showed up at the club. "How did you find me?"

He reaches over and taps my phone that's lying in the center console.

"You tracked my phone?" I assume.

He nods once.

I sigh, not at all surprised. I probably should have made that conclusion sooner. "Since when?"

"I knew where you were the moment you left the gallery."

"I didn't mean just tonight." I *know* he's been doing this for longer than today.

He stops the car at a red light and looks over at me.

I raise a brow.

The muscle in his jaw works and then he looks back at the road as the light goes green. "From the beginning."

Years. He's been tracking me for years. Maybe it's the alcohol, but, once again, his answer doesn't surprise me. And it somehow doesn't bother me.

"When was the beginning?" I ask.

The car slows down again, then we turn right and go down a ramp that's lit by white lights that sting my eyes. I only register we're in Sky Building's parking garage when we drive past my car. Atticus maneuvers into a parking spot easily and turns the engine off.

He gets out without a word, walks around the car and opens my door. I detangle myself from my coat and take off my seatbelt, passing him the heavy fabric before scooping up my phone and bag and getting out.

Placing a warm hand at the curve of my back, Atticus leads us to the elevator doors, swipes his key fob, and the doors open immediately. It's a silent ride up to the penthouse and walk to the bedroom.

"Are you going to tell me what happened tonight?" Atticus asks behind me as I stumble toward the dressing room.

He steadies me by grabbing my hips and walks me to the island unit of drawers in the center of the space. He lifts me to sit on the top, his hand sliding down to my ankle.

"Nothing I couldn't handle," I answer, as I watch him unbuckle the straps of my heels and pull them off.

"I didn't ask if you could handle it," he points out, pulling the shirt out of my skirt and unbuttoning it. "I asked what happened."

I grab the ledge of the drawers and slide down until I'm standing between them and Atticus.

I crane my neck up. "You're ridiculously tall."

He continues looking at me with a stern expression.

Sighing, I reach for the zipper of the skirt, dropping my gaze to his chest and mumble, "Dylan was there."

Atticus grabs my chin and tilts it up. "Come again?"

"Dylan was there, and *no*, I didn't call him."

"What did he want?" he demands.

"Wanted to know if I was really married." I shimmy out of the skirt, letting it drop to the floor. "He also seemed to know *you*." I chuckle to myself. "Especially when he was calling you insane."

"Did he touch you?" Atticus asks, ignoring my commentary.

I hesitate.

"Where?" he demands, his voice dropping an octave.

I peel down the shirt to my elbow, revealing my bicep. As predicted, there's a developing grip mark.

I peek up and almost wince. Atticus' face is a sculpture of fury, his dark eyes glued to my arm.

"Where else?" he asks, tone *glacial*.

I pull the other arm down, but I don't have any bruising on that side, so I pull the shirt back up. "Nowhere else."

Atticus reaches out to the exposed arm, cupping it lightly, his thumb brushing over the mottled skin.

"Are you in pain?" he asks.

"No," I say quickly. I grab his wrist gently, drawing his attention away from my arm. "I'm fine."

He holds my gaze for a moment, his dark eyes focused intensely on me like he's looking for the lie. He must decide to believe me, because he nods once and takes a step back, sweeping his hand out to the bathroom. "I had Rose draw you a bath."

His demeanor is still icy, so I don't argue with his offer and walk over to the bathroom. The steam and soft scent of jasmine coming from the huge tub is like a siren call as I cross to the porcelain beauty, pull off my shirt, and climb in. Atticus scoops up my hair as I submerge into the heat and sit back against the side, my eyes automatically closing as I groan in bliss.

I feel Atticus twist my hair and secure it with a claw clip that materialized from somewhere, and then he kisses my temple.

I open my heavy eyelids and turn my head toward him. "Are you joining me?"

A soft but victorious smile tilts his biteable lips. "Not tonight, my beloved. I have a few things to take care of."

I turn in the water with a frown. "Right now?"

Atticus is on his haunches, resting his forearms on his knees. "Unfortunately."

I fold my arms on the edge of the tub and rest my chin on them. "You never answered my question."

"Which one?"

"When was the beginning? Of *this*."

His dark eyes search my face, and then he straightens, placing his hands in his pants pockets. My gaze travels languidly up his body. He's power personified, both in the sheer mass of muscles he possesses, but also in the energy that he exudes. He's definitely someone to fear, but I'm realizing that...I don't. Not anymore.

"Are you ever going to tell me?" I ask, dragging myself from that revelation.

He pulls one of his hands out of his pockets and cups my chin gently. "Yes."

"But not yet?"

He nods, releasing my face. "Not when you're intoxicated."

I snort. "You married me when I was at least six times more drunk than this."

He smirks, but it doesn't reach his eyes. "The opportunity was too perfect."

I splash water at him. He steps out of the way easily.

"Enjoy your bath, Mrs. Shaw," he says with a slight bow.

I turn in the tub. "Enjoy your work, Mr. Shaw."

23
ATTICUS

A PLEASANT HUM SITS comfortably in my chest as I travel in the elevator back down to the parking garage. Chasing Phaedra is an addictive thrill. I never wanted complacency, but I'm starting to look forward to how she's going to push every single button I possess, create more, and then press those as well.

She's a formidable opponent and, though she won't admit it, I know she likes our little games too.

I can feel the soft smile on my face as I exit the elevator, walk back to my red Maserati, and open the trunk.

My smile stretches wide at the scene before me. Dylan and his acquaintance struggle in their binds, their arms secured behind their back and legs with a healthy amount of duct tape. My nose crinkles at the smell of beer and sweat wafting up from my car—I make a mental note to get it professionally cleaned.

With their mouths also taped closed, their muffled shouts are useless as I haul Dylan and then his friend out, dumping them on the floor.

The friend is now unconscious as his head connected with the concrete, but Dylan continues to flop around like a fish out of water. Leaving him to his feeble escape attempt, I take a tight grip on his friend's ankle and drag him through the garage.

At the furthest end of this floor, I open the door that reads "Maintenance." The only furniture in the room is a simple desk, chair, and some random building supplies on shelving lining the back wall.

Wade sits at the desk, reading the newspaper. He looks up over the rim of his glasses as I drag my catch in. "Need me to get the other one?"

I shake my head, then spin on my heel and exit. I chuckle as I return to my car—Dylan has managed to roll maybe seven feet from where I dumped him.

Pathetic.

He wails behind his tape as I take hold of his ankle and haul him to the room, then shut the door behind us. I sink to my haunches in front of Dylan. The lighting is low, the only sources being one naked lightbulb hanging from the ceiling and the lamp on the desk Wade is using to read, so I'm not sure if he's sweating profusely or crying.

"How unpleasant to see you again, Wendell," I say, using his last name.

He tries to say something, but it's just garbled sounds.

I click my tongue disapprovingly. "No one said you could speak."

I straighten and walk over to Wade, who's now standing in front of Dylan's friend. He's already cut and ripped the tape off his mouth, but he's still unconscious.

I stomp him in the ribs, and he wakes with a yowl.

"What's your name, kid?" Wade asks.

He makes pained sounds in response.

Wade bends down and grabs a handful of his hair, shaking him. "*Name.*"

"N-Nick," he wheezes.

"Last name," Wade demands.

"Mc...McMahon."

Wade releases his hold on Nick and crosses to the shelving unit behind me, rummaging through the items.

"Well, Nick," I sigh, my hands returning to my pockets as I peer down at him. "Care to explain your actions?"

Panicked eyes bore into me as he shakes his head furiously. "I don't know what you're talking about."

I raise a brow. "No?"

"Please, man, I don't...please let me go."

I grimace. I despise begging. Unless it's Phaedra, preferably on her knees. I shake that delicious thought before I'm hard and focus on the task at hand.

"I can't let you go, Nick. You upset my wife and her best friend. That's simply unforgivable."

"I didn't!" he whimpers. "It was all Dylan. He told me to!"

I shake my head disapprovingly. "Selling your own friend out for your life. Not very loyal, are you, Nick?"

Nick's attention moves from me to Wade as he returns to my side; his eyes could not be any wider in horror.

Wade passes me a sledgehammer and Nick shrieks. "Fuck, no!"

"You think this is for you?" I ask. "Oh, no."

Relief washes over him.

"No, Nick, you aren't worth my attention."

The gunshot, even with a suppressor, reverberates through the room, and my ears ache at the sound. Wade whistles a low tune as he switches the safety back on his weapon and returns to his position at the desk.

Stepping around the blood and brain matter on the concrete, I cross to Dylan. He stares at Nick, his face ghostly white, his breathing labored.

Resting the head of the sledgehammer in Dylan's eyesight, I lower onto my haunches next to him again.

"Now, *you*," I start.

Dylan's head whips to me, a high-pitched stressed sound spilling out from behind the tape.

"We had an agreement, Wendell," I remind him. "Do you remember what I said if you broke our deal?"

I follow the tear sliding down his temple as he glances at the sledgehammer.

"The terms were simple. You were to leave Phaedra alone." I sigh, disappointed. "But you didn't, did you?"

More tears. And now his whole body is trembling. Satisfaction pulses through me, making my head spin.

"I gave you enough money to leave my city, to start a new life literally anywhere, yet you didn't." I cock my head to the side. "Why is that, hmm?" Anger flashes through me. "Did you think you could take my wife with you?"

I stand up abruptly at the thought. "Did you really think I would allow you to take what's mine?"

I lift the sledgehammer and swing. It connects with Dylan's left tibia with a spectacular crunch, and he *sings*.

"You think she'd even want you back?" A hit to his other leg: a glorious snap. "You aren't worth the ground she walks on." Both kneecaps cave in. "You shouldn't breathe the same air." I destroy his ribcage.

I'm panting as I drop the sledgehammer and pick up the knife Wade left for me on the desk. Blood seeps out from behind the duct tape, the gurgling and wheezing not enough to satisfy the rage still festering in my chest.

"I should have ended you the moment you laid eyes on her." I kneel on what's left of Dylan's concave torso, grab a handful of his sweat-slick hair and skewer his left eye, twisting and wrenching it from the socket. I carve out his right eye as well.

Terror vibrates Dylan's vocal cords, a harrowing, broken melody that settles some of his debt to the beast roiling within me, but compensation won't be complete without a soul, and all debts *must* be paid.

Tightening my grip in his hair, I lean down, bringing my face close enough so he can feel my breath. "You called me insane, and you're right. For Phaedra Shaw, I'm absolutely certifiable."

I slice through his vocal cords. Blood sprays across my front: the warm, slick liquid soaking into my shirt and coating my skin. The pleasant hum from earlier returns, and I take a cleansing breath, the iron scent filling my lungs.

"Feel better?" Wade asks from my side as I stand, dropping the knife onto the corpse at my feet and accepting the rag he holds out.

"Yes," I admit, as I wipe my face, neck, and hands. "Are the arrangements made?"

Wade snorts. "What do you think I am, an amateur?"

I chuckle softly, dumping the soiled rag on the floor even though I can still feel where I missed places. A soft knock draws our attention as it opens. Harris appears in his pristine uniform and gloved hands, with a soiled laundry bin behind him.

"Any laundry, Mr. Shaw?" he asks.

I pull off my shirt, step over the body, pass it to him, then gesture behind me. "Wade has the rest."

Harris bows his head as I step out and head toward the elevators. I roll my shoulders, trying to dispel more of the tension, but there's an itch deep in my bones.

An itch only my wife will be able to ease.

I grin—it's Phaedra's turn to repay her debt.

24
PHAEDRA

I'M WOKEN FROM MY dreamless sleep by a rough tug on my ankle. My heart hammers as I slide down the bed toward a large, dark figure. Disoriented, I kick out wildly, trying to get out of his hold. I was too drunk to find clothes before diving into bed, so I'm fighting my assailant buckass naked.

A deep, vibrating laugh fills the darkness as my legs are yanked up and spread wide before the man crushes me beneath his heavy frame. Bergamot and sandalwood fill my lungs, easing some of my panic, but the pungent reek of iron brings it all back.

"Are you bleeding?" I croak out before Atticus' mouth crushes to mine.

Everything stops, every atom of my existence tuned to Atticus. I taste only him, feel only his strength covering me, the warmth from his skin seeping into me. It's both overwhelming and confronting and maybe a little confusing but, somehow, it's also comforting and so simple.

Atticus is unapologetically himself, no matter how fucked up he is, and he seems to pull out parts of me I keep locked down for fear of retribution. Ballet demands perfection, and I strived for that image both on and off the stage. It's so inherently ingrained into me that I've forgotten what it was like to be myself.

I don't know how, but Atticus can bypass all that practiced precision and coax out the unpredictable hellion that I've denied for so long. He makes me see red, and react in ways that I never expect to, and I'm pretty sure he enjoys provoking me.

I might like it too.

There are so many reasons I shouldn't be here, but right now, I don't fucking care.

I sink my teeth into Atticus' bottom lip hard and he pulls back with a hiss. Illuminated only by the lights of the city, he's mostly shadows, a heaving beast staring at me with pitch-black eyes that promise *everything*.

I shove him, putting my weight into it, bucking and writhing, trying to get out from under him. He blocks my swings, then strikes out and grabs my throat with a firm grip.

"Stop," he growls.

I claw at his forearm. He squeezes tighter. My heart races, languid heat pulsing in my veins as I continue my struggle. I must break skin with my nails, because Atticus makes an annoyed sound in the back of his throat, then both of my wrists are trapped in one of his hands and wrenched above my head.

Atticus lowers himself, his naked chest flush against mine, his weight restricting my diaphragm movement. I can barely breathe, and I love it.

"Get off me," I wheeze out.

His laugh drips in menace. "I don't think I will."

My bottom lip trembles.

"I've wanted you like this for so long," he purrs. "Trapped under me. At my complete mercy." He sucks in a breath. "What to do? Where to start."

He sounds drunk on lunacy.

I try to buck him off me.

He moans, burying his face against my neck. "That's it, my beloved, struggle harder."

I thrash, trying to dislodge my wrists, but it's pointless. Frustrated tears escape down my temples.

"Atticus," I whimper. "Please, let me go."

"Is that what you really want, Lilac?" he asks softly, his face lifting from my neck.

Fuck no.

"Yes," I whisper.

His grip on my neck disappears, his fingers trailing down the side of my body. They slide between us and over my core. He chuckles when he sinks two fingers into me easily.

"Dirty little lies escape your mouth," he says into my ear. "But you always make such a mess."

Arousal drips out of me as my legs tremble; his fingers curl inside, hitting that spot that makes my vision dim.

"Atticus," I breathe. It sounds like a plea: to stop and to never stop a blurred line.

"Do you drip just for me, Phaedra?" he asks, as his fingers pump in and out of me, sending me further into delirium.

"No," I pant.

His grip on my wrists tightens, and he shoves a third finger into me, the stretch from the intrusion a painful burn.

"What did I tell you about lying to me?" he admonishes. "Admit that this perfect pussy only drips for me."

I shake my head, which he must see or feel because his fingers suddenly disappear from inside me, and he moves so I can see again. Still holding my wrists, he grips my hip and flips me onto my stomach roughly, his palm coming down hard on my ass cheek.

The unexpected pain causes me to yelp, and the heat radiates across my skin, making me dizzy with pleasure.

"Stop," I croak out, trying to roll away, but Atticus pins down my thighs by kneeling over them, making me immobile.

"Tell me this cunt is mine," he demands, then slaps the other cheek harder this time, and I choke on another yelp.

"Fuck...you." I grit out.

His laugh is terrifying. "You will, but not before you give me what I want."

"Wha—What is that?" I pant.

He caresses my heated flesh. "I want your screams."

He delivers two more blows, each harder than the last. I let out a keening sound through clenched teeth, and tears stream down my face.

"Come on, baby, scream for me."

I try to hold it together, but two more quick, hard slaps land over my tender flesh, and I cry out.

"There it is," he growls, caressing his work. "Now more."

Atticus completely covers my ass and upper thighs with harsh, punishing spanks. My screams get louder and my tears flow freely.

I beg him to stop and try to get away, but his grip on my wrists and his leg across my thighs keep me at his mercy.

Every strike causes more pain than the last, but every time Atticus' hand connects with my skin, my clit throbs with need and my body clenches, begging to be filled.

"Christ, you're stunning, Mrs. Shaw," Atticus pants, his fingers trailing over the hot, sore flesh of my ass cheek. "You wear my marks so well." He delivers another punishing slap and I cry out. He chuckles, the sound a deep rumble. "And you scream so sweetly."

Suddenly, his knee pinning me and his grip on my wrists disappear. Then I'm pulled down the bed again until my feet touch the floor with my torso still laying flat. Atticus grips my hair at the root tightly, shoving my face into the mattress.

It's wet under my cheek.

"Messy, messy wife," he admonishes as he kicks my legs open wider. "Let's see if we can ruin the floorboards."

Atticus enters me in one hard thrust, and I stop breathing. No, I *can't* breathe because he's just shoved all my organs out of the way to make room for his cock. And *fuck*, the burn, the stretch. I don't think any amount of foreplay can prepare me for his girth.

"*Fuck,*" Atticus moans and my whole body spasms around him at that single word.

Then he pulls out slightly and thrusts back in impossibly deeper. My eyes roll closed as unintelligible sounds fall out of my mouth.

Keeping his grip on my hair, his free hand grabs one of my sore ass cheeks, making me wince. And just like our first time together, he spreads me open as he starts fucking me with hard, measured strokes.

God, how is he *deeper?*

With every thrust I whimper, the sensations scrambling my brain as my body builds up to ecstasy.

"Perfect," he huffs through clenched teeth, his pace never wavering. "So fucking perfect."

This *is* perfect. The spectacular consolidation of pain and pleasure, of power plays and trust, of fear and relief. It's an inviting pool that promises splendor beyond compare, or it could mean a vicious demise in its murky depths.

"Is this what it felt like?" he asks roughly. "With *him?*"

There's only one person he would be talking about. "No, never."

"He never should have had you." His pace quickens, the thrusts deeper. "Never should have known who you were."

I make some sort of sound in response while he fucks me into a stupor.

"He was a *stranger,*" he stresses, his grip in my hair tightening. "Why did you speak to him?"

He's asking questions I literally can't fathom when his dick slides over so many nerves that I'm going into overdrive. "I—"

"He was just a random man who moved into your complex. You need to be more wary of strangers."

"I am," I rush out.

Atticus barks a laugh. "You followed me into a bathroom at the club."

He's not wrong, but I don't have the brain function to talk about this right now.

"Atticus," I whisper.

"It's okay now," he coos. "He won't bother you again. He's gone."

I think I should be concerned about that statement, but Atticus' hand on my ass has moved to my clit and is applying the perfect pressure and pattern over the sensitive flesh for me to see stars.

"You're mine," Atticus declares.

"Atticus," I moan, my tongue thick in my mouth.

"Say it," he growls, his hip bones bashing into my sore ass with every punishing thrust. "I want to hear that smart mouth say it."

I shake my head, my mind swirling, my body on the edge. A few more passes over my clit and—

His fingers stop moving, and I choke on a sob.

"Do you want to come?" he asks.

"Yes," I rasp. If I don't rid my body of this tension, I might actually die.

"Then say it."

"I'm yours," I rush out desperately. "Yours, all yours. *Please*, Atticus."

His only response is to pinch my clit hard, and I detonate. That rising tension is now a cascading crescendo of pure bliss. I'm in such a completely different dimension that I barely register Atticus fucking me to his own completion, then collapsing most of his weight onto me.

"All mine," he grumbles into my ear. "Completely."

We're like this for a while, trying to catch our breath. Atticus shifts off me at some point and pulls out, and I hear and feel our combined mess drip out of me.

"My perfect mess," Atticus muses wistfully again, and then scoops me into his arms.

As we enter the bathroom, I'm barely holding onto consciousness as we step into the shower, but I could swear when we pass the mirror, I see blood streaked over our skin.

25

PHAEDRA

I HAVEN'T EVEN OPENED my eyes, and my head is pounding. Tequila. It's always fucking tequila that gets me.

My body feels like it's made from concrete, and my stomach feels as if it's filled with burning kerosine. I groan in misery.

My pillow chuckles lazily under me.

"Why are you making so much noise?" I grumble, my cheek not moving from Atticus' chest.

He traces my bare thigh I have hooked around his waist. "How are you feeling?"

"I think I'm dying."

He chuckles again, the vibrations of the sound jostling me too much, making me groan once more. He laughs harder.

"If you keep shaking me, I will puke all over you," I warn.

"I didn't know I was married to such a lightweight."

"Divorce me," I mumble.

"Never."

I don't move, relishing Atticus' fingers tracing over my skin and listening to his strong heartbeat under my ear. I doze off for a bit, but then I remember it's Saturday.

"What time is it?" I ask.

Atticus' hand disappears from my skin, and I regret asking immediately. "It's seven-thirty."

I jerk up into a seated position, my eyes stinging at the sudden brightness. "Fuck."

Atticus squeezes my waist gently. "Everything okay?"

I look down at him and have to stop my jaw from falling open. The man is unbelievably hot. Wide, thick frame, sculpted muscles, beautiful dark brown skin, a light smattering of short chest hair, and a happy trail from his belly button that disappears under his boxer briefs.

"Damn," I whisper.

"Like what you see?" Atticus rumbles, flexing abdominal muscles people dream about.

I shake myself out of my stupor and clear my throat. "I have classes starting at nine. I have to go."

His grip loosens on me as he nods, and I scramble off the bed, finally noticing I'm dressed in nothing but Atticus' T-shirt. Last night's events are hazy, but those memories will pop up later when I'm not racing around. From the soreness in *particular* places, I can take a guess at what transpired.

I comb through my clothes, picking out workout tights and a cropped T-shirt, find fresh underwear and a sports bra, then bump the drawer closed with my butt. I yelp at the pain radiating at the contact.

"What the..." I trail off as I cross to the floor-length mirror, turn my back toward it and lift the shirt.

"Atticus!" I shout. "What the *fuck*?"

Both cheeks are mostly red with burgeoning purple blotches in the central areas. I also have circular marks that look suspiciously like fingerprints on my lower back and hips.

"What a glorious sight in the morning," Atticus sighs from the dressing room entrance.

I drop the shirt hem and turn sharply to him. He leans against the doorframe with his arms crossed over his chest and one ankle crossed over the other, totally relaxed in all his almost-naked glory.

"We'll talk about this when I get back tonight," I seethe, then pivot to the bathroom.

After wincing and griping through a quick shower, I get out and wrap myself in a towel, then cross to the vanity, and brush my teeth. When I come up from spitting a mouthful of toothpaste, I jump at the large form behind me in the misted mirror.

"Can you not sneak up on me?" I grumble, wiping my mouth with the end of the towel.

"Bend over," Atticus instructs.

I look over my shoulder. He's dressed in a white shirt and black slacks, and his hair looks wet. He must have showered in another bathroom.

"Your fist will have to suffice this morning," I snipe.

His grin is absolutely criminal. "As much as I'd like to fuck you all day, I'm here with this." He holds up a nondescript white tube. "Arnica cream for the bruising. Unfortunately, *not* lube."

I roll my eyes and reach toward the tube, but Atticus pulls it out of my reach. He swirls his finger. "Turn around."

I don't have time to argue with him, and he knows that, so I huff loudly as I turn back and lean over the vanity.

Atticus is quick and efficient, lifting the towel and gently applying the cream over my tender skin with no funny business, then covers me again and steps to the other sink to wash his hands.

I apply deodorant and then drop the towel to change, not caring if he watches me dress. Obviously, he saw me naked last night.

I feel his attention as I throw on my clothes and twist my wet hair it into a tight high bun and secure it with two hair ties.

"Rings," he instructs.

"I don't wear them when I teach. Can you put them away?"

He's picking up the jewelry as I turn and exit the bathroom in search of shoes. I halt in the dressing room—my usual work duffel bag is out on top of the island drawers, along with a fresh pair of socks and sneakers. Atticus' briefcase and a suit jacket sit beside my stuff.

"If we don't leave now, you'll be much more than ten minutes late," Atticus says as he breezes past, picking up his suit jacket.

"You're going to the office on a Saturday?" I ask as I rush to grab the socks and put them on.

"I'm working today from the studio," he says casually.

I frown as I tie my laces. "Studio?"

"That's where we're going, yes," he says, amused.

I straighten, blinking at him. "You're...coming. To my studio. In Connecticut?"

He smiles, picking up his briefcase and my duffel bag. "You're edging toward fifteen minutes now."

Despite being *twenty* minutes late because Atticus insisted we pick up coffee and food on the way—which he had preordered and also got me one of my favorite green juices to "detox"—all the classes ran smoothly, and shockingly none of the parents complained about the delays.

Will told me that's because the moms and dads were too busy whispering about the mystery businessman in my office. The businessman who spanked me red and purple then fucked me like he owned me last night.

Yeah, *all* those memories came flooding back on the drive here as I tried to choke down my granola and yogurt with heated cheeks and shallow breaths.

I'm walking out to the reception area with my last class of the day when a trio of moms approach me with sly little grins.

"We *must* know who that handsome man is in your office," one mom of my teen students' demands.

"New management?" the second one asks, eyes still on my office.

"Another teacher?" the third one asks.

The first one scoffs. "Please, he's too...*big*...to be a dancer."

They all giggle like their teen children.

"That is my husband," I say carefully.

All three heads turn to me so fast, I'm surprised none of them injured themselves. Their eyes drop to my bare left hand.

"You got *married?*" the first one says, frowning.

"When?" the second one asks.

"We celebrate three months in two weeks," a deep voice says from behind me.

All three of them gasp and take a startled step back. One of them looks a little pale.

Atticus lifts my hand, sliding on my wedding rings, then kisses them and wraps an arm around my waist. The moms *swoon* and I fight an eye roll.

"Same time next week?" I say, trying and failing to pull their attention.

"I'll ensure we get here on time," Atticus promises.

"Oh, no, it's fine," the first mom waves us off, her voice breathy. "We get it. The honeymoon period."

Atticus pulls me closer. "Indeed."

The moms finally leave at the urging of their kids, but not before bidding us goodbye *twice*.

"You can't come to the studio anymore," I declare as the place empties, "Doe-eyes for Atticus" Will included.

Atticus smirks as he crosses to the doors and locks them. "Why?"

"You're too...large."

He laughs, the sound deep and rich. *"Large?"*

I huff as I walk to my office. "You're distracting." I gesture at his work papers and laptop covering my desk. "And you take up too much space. *And* Will is scared of you."

Atticus leans on the doorframe, amused, and damn it, why does he look so good doing that?

"He isn't scared of me," he reassures. "Pretty sure he wants to lick me."

Now I roll my eyes, looking underneath all of Atticus' papers. "Apparently everyone wants to do that."

"Do *you* want to lick me?" Atticus purrs. I can hear him moving closer.

"I already have," I point out, shifting his laptop.

"You have?" he asks lightly, perching on the edge of the desk next to me. "I don't seem to remember."

"Old age really takes its toll on memory," I comment.

"What are you looking for?"

"A stack of bills." I frown. "They were here somewhere."

"They've been taken care of."

My head jerks up to Atticus. "What?"

"Will's got the checks," Atticus says simply.

"You paid my studio's rent," I exclaim. "The utilities for here and my apartment. My mortgage."

"I paid the utilities for the next year on both properties, settled your entire mortgage with the bank a week ago, and I have contracts for you to sign for the ownership of this building."

I blink. Then blink again. I don't think my heart is beating. I... "Think I'm going to pass out."

Atticus wraps an arm around my waist, pulling me to stand between his legs. I lean against his chest as he rubs my back rhythmically, my vision swimming as my brain reboots entirely.

"I also have a realtor on call for when you want to look at studio space in New York," he says after a while.

I lean back enough to look at him. "Why?"

"Coming back and forth to this studio will take a toll on you. We can hire someone to teach the classes at this location, and Will checked out so we can trust him to keep things running smoothly. "

"You did a background check on Will?"

He gives a quizzical look. "Of course I did."

"Why would I want studio space in New York?" I ask as I step out of Atticus' hold.

His expression hardens, and he crosses his arms. "You want to stay in Connecticut?"

Why is he questioning this? I live here, work here.

"This is my studio," is all I can say.

He regards me for a second and then nods once, pulling his phone from the inner pocket of his suit. "I'll have the realtor pull properties for sale. There are some sufficient apartments that are being developed, but I'll have him pull houses in Greenwich as well."

"Why...why would you need an apartment?" I ask.

"*We* need a home," he clarifies without looking up from his phone.

"But you..."

He's talking about the *future*. Plans for more than the month that we agreed to.

My heart pulses fast in my ears as I stumble back a few more steps. I need to think, to breathe, to *run*.

If I run, he'll catch me—he's proven that multiple times—but I need to *move*.

I walk over to my duffel bag and pick it up off the floor. "I'm going to dance."

26
PHAEDRA

S WEAT COVERS MY WHOLE body as I spin and travel and jump across the studio until nothing is left in my head. I might hate running, but I *love* dancing. I need to do it more because it's the only thing that makes the world make sense.

I execute the final moves of my routine as the classical music comes to a close. Dressed in pink tights, a black leotard, and a short black wrap skirt, I assess my *croisé devant* through the mirrored wall, the only sound my heavy breathing echoing in the studio.

"Perfection." Atticus' soft tone fills the silent space. I see him in the mirrors, watching from the back wall near the entrance.

I step out of the position and walk to the front, lifting and resting my ankle on the barre to stretch out my leg. I hear his shoes on the wood floors as I bend this way and that, switching legs, stretching out my whole body, then sinking to the floor and pressing my back against the mirrors, hugging my knees to my chest.

Atticus surprises me by sitting down next to me on the floor with his legs stretched out, one ankle crossed over the other.

"I love this," I say wistfully, resting my chin on my knees, looking around the studio space. "I love the beauty of the movement, the intensity and complexity, the need for iron control of your body and your mind. A single degree wrong in your form, and the visuals are off. You brace wrong, and a lift doesn't work. A distracted mind, and you're injured."

Tears, both of sorrow and frustration, sting my eyes, but I refuse to let them fall, distracting myself instead with pulling the ties out of my hair and finger-combing through the wild mass of purple waves. "I was distracted when it happened."

"Your injury?" Atticus asks softly.

I rest my head back against the mirrors and nod. "The corps found out about the Boston incident. Thought it was true, and I had slept my way to New York." I snort. "Surely, I would have slept my way into a soloist or principal position, not the bottom of the barrel, which everyone else concluded pretty quickly. But there was this one dancer, a soloist, who didn't like me from the start."

I look at Atticus, who's watching me impassively. "And I mean, from the *moment* I walked into EBC. I hadn't said a word to anyone, and I'd become enemy number one."

I start untying my pointe shoes. "I blocked it out mostly. It was high school 'mean girl' behavior, as you call it. But then the art director wanted me as an understudy for one of the principals that was rumored to be leaving, and that's when things got bad."

I pull one pointe shoe off and start undoing the other. "*She* was the instigator. The endless whispering and rumors always started with her. But when the NYCB chatter traveled around the company, it got worse because then it was *everyone.*" I pull off the other shoe and drop my legs into a crossed position, placing the shoes in my lap. "It finally got in my head, and I was distracted for our first performance. One of the last leaps I landed wrong, causing damage to my hip that ended my career."

"A labral tear," Atticus adds. He probably got that information in my background check. "Many dancers return after surgery and rehab."

I sigh heavily. "I was done after that. I didn't have the mental fortitude to go through the trials of company hierarchies again. I don't give a shit about an audience or the notoriety, just the dance. If that means those assholes won, then so be it. I truly don't care. I think I enjoy teaching more than performing."

"It gave you back control," Atticus comments.

I nod. "I'm teaching them about their conduct as dancers *and* the perfect pirouette."

"More puppet master than puppet," he posits, amused.

I smirk at him. "A leaf from your playbook."

Atticus tilts until our foreheads are almost touching. His liquid brown eyes dance with mischief, drawing me in like a snare designed just for me. "Feels good, doesn't it?"

"Is that why you do it?" I ask. "Because it feels good?"

His eyes drop to my lips. "It's immensely satisfying when things bend to my will."

"Really?" I muse, breathless, suddenly warm. "And you never bend?"

His tongue sweeping over his bottom lip snags my attention. "There is...one exception."

"You" hangs between us. I don't want him to admit it, but it's also the only thing I want to hear from his bitable mouth. I look away, body heated and breathing labored as we sit together with the tension, allowing it to settle into anticipation across our skin.

I could act on this pressure between us—the invitation vibrates from Atticus with his every breath—but with every physical connection, I lose more fragments of reality. This is only temporary, these yearnings a result of proximity. Nothing more.

"You want to move here," I say after a while.

"Not necessarily," he says, and I hate that his answer stings a little. "But you're here."

And just like that, the sting dissipates.

"Our agreement ends in two weeks," I point out.

I can see his objection, so I lift my hand to stop him before he can say anything.

"We agreed to talk about it at the end, so let's park this until then?"

The muscle in his jaw works, but he inclines his head.

I return his curt nod and push up from the floor. "I need to change, then we can go."

Atticus stands. With no shoes on, I have to crane my neck to look at him, reminding me how much bigger he is than me.

"In regard to our arrangement," he starts, and my stupid heart patters a little faster. "We have to attend a dinner next weekend."

"What kind of dinner?"

For the first time since I've known him, Atticus looks uncomfortable. "An anniversary dinner, for my parents."

My stomach drops. "An anniversary dinner with others means

it's a milestone."

"Forty years," he says, his answer clipped.

"I'm assuming the invitation was for more than just us?"

He nods. "Most of the Shaw clan, many friends. It's a small, intimate dinner."

I let out a breathy, panicked laugh as I start toward my bag by the door. "Oh, yeah, no problem. Just a bunch of the city's, hell, the *world's* most influential people in one room. *Super* casual."

"The prince politely declined, so pretty casual," Atticus comments as he follows me.I halt and spin. "*Prince?* Of where?" I throw my hands out and turn back. "You know what? I don't even want to know."

27
PHAEDRA

"**I** STILL DON'T KNOW what to wear," I fret to Zahra, my phone laying on the island next to me on speaker as I look at the wall of clothes in the dressing room.

Tonight is Atticus' parents' anniversary dinner and despite going through this entire wardrobe and having multiple conversations with Zahra over the last week, I still haven't decided. At this point, I'm going in the T-shirt and panties I'm standing in.

"What do I always say?" she asks, exasperated. She's mad because it's seven in the morning on a Saturday, and I woke her with this dilemma after fretting about it myself for an hour.

"If in doubt, slut it out," I deadpan. "This isn't the occasion for my ass hanging out, Zah."

"Your fine, peach-shaped ass should *always* be out," she stresses. "But, fine. Cross off white or ivory because that screams bridal. Avoid black, so there's no talk of funerals or mourning. Your hair is going to attract attention, so no super bright colors."

"So..."

"Wear green." Atticus' voice startles me as he appears at the entrance.

He's wearing black sweatpants and a sleeveless compression shirt, breathing heavily. I woke up to his message telling me he'd be at the gym, but since I haven't seen him in anything but boxer briefs or a suit, my brain didn't compute that he'd be in gym clothes. And I'm reminded once again how unfairly perfect this man is.

It's been an ordinary week, both of us working and existing together, then waking up curled around each other in bed each morning. But nothing more, so it's been a dry, barren week for my libido, and apparently, she's suddenly *parched*.

"Ooo, yes," Zahra coos on the phone, snapping me out of my ogling. "That emerald-green satin shift dress. The calf-length one with all the straps down the back. That one would be perfect."

I frown at the phone. "I can't wear underwear with that one."

Zahra's laugh is diabolical. "Thank me later, love you, bye!"

She ends the call before I have the chance to berate her.

"Why green?" I ask Atticus curiously as I watch him cross the room while peeling his shirt off. I hold in a groan.

He stops next to me, heat radiating off his bare chest, his eyes a dark pool of addiction I'm struggling to avoid.

I tear my gaze away, my eyes dropping to his torso. The skin on the left side of his rib cage—just under his beautifully sculpted pectoral—piques my attention. There's a series of symbols tattooed in black ink, rows of dashes and dots running down the side of his body, each line a different sequence. They aren't noticeable since they're quite thin and maybe six inches long, which is surprising since there are a lot of rows.

I reach out and graze my fingertips over them, trying to decipher their meaning. Then I realize I'm touching Atticus.

"Sorry," I rush out, pulling my hand away, but Atticus grabs my wrist and brings my fingers back to his skin.

"Every inch of my skin is available for you to touch at any time, Lilac."

"What do they mean?" I ask, stroking over the lines.

"My everything," he answers.

I'm too distracted by the feel of his smooth skin to dispute his cryptic answer. I absently step closer, and his body heat travels through my fingertips as they glide up over his chest and clavicle, then to the base of his neck.

"You have two here, too," I whisper, tracing the lines of dashes and dots on the left side of his throat. You'd never see them when he's wearing a collared shirt.

Arms suddenly wrap around me and Atticus' mouth crashes into mine. Lips, teeth and tongues dance as I'm lifted onto the island top. My legs immediately go around Atticus' waist, pulling him flush against me, his already hard cock applying delicious pressure between my legs.

One of his hands sinks into my hair at the nape and the other on my hip, as my hands dive between us and slide into his pants, my fingers wrapping around his girth.

He moans into my mouth, his hand on my hip flexing as I pump him lazily, reveling in every pulse and twitch.

I pull away from his kiss, panting. "I want..."

"Tell me," he urges, his hips rolling. "Say it."

I look into obsidian. "I want you inside me, Atticus."

He wastes no time, using his grip on my hip to pull me closer as I shove his pants down. He slides his hand over my damp panties, pushes them aside and lines his cock with my entrance. We both moan in a perfect symphony as he thrusts into me to the hilt, the stretch a welcome pain as my brain goes offline.

I tighten my legs around his waist as he starts to move, his thrusts hard and deep, pleasure mixed with a little pain ricocheting through my whole body. But I want more, *need* more.

I grab the wrist of his hand still tangled in my hair, and tug until his fingers wrap around my throat.

"Squeeze," I pant. "Squeeze, *please*."

Atticus doesn't hesitate, squeezing tight, pressing into the muscles and restricting airflow. My eyes roll back as he pushes me down, pinning me by his throat hold and fucking me harder.

"You're fucking perfect," he growls as my vision goes black at the edges. "My perfect little wife."

"Yes," I choke, my grip on his forearm firm.

"Is that what you want? To be mine?"

I say nothing, but I squeeze his forearm harder.

"You look so fucking good under me," he grunts. "So breakable. Like I can just—" His grip tightens around my throat and my whole body spasms, pleasure bursting through my veins.

Atticus' laugh is maniacal, his thrusts never wavering from their brutal pace. "You want to be broken, don't you, my beloved?"

"Y-yes," I wheeze out.

"Let's see how many pieces we can make," he muses, as my vision and hearing fades, my grip on his arm loosening.

Survival instincts kick in then, and I start clumsily pawing at Atticus' arm, trying to dislodge his hold, but the pressure in my head is already heavy.

"Yes," Atticus huffs, but he's muffled by my heartbeat in my ears. "Fight me, love."

I try, I do, but I'm absolutely going to pass out.

And then his grip disappears.

The tsunami of euphoria slams into me along with oxygen and it ignites a blinding orgasm that turns my world white. I feel nothing and everything, every nerve ending firing and misfiring. For a second, I think I did pass out and ended up in another dimension, but I soon return to my warm body.

More like overheated because Atticus is draped over me panting, his head nuzzled between my breasts, his cock still buried in me. My fingers sink into his hair, playing with the thick curls while our breathing returns to normal, and then for longer.

Eventually, he lifts his head and kisses me sweetly while he pulls out. A rush of our combined arousal leaks out of me, making me shiver.

Atticus stands and looks down with a satisfied grin. "What a beautiful mess."

My cheeks heat as I give him a coy smile, even though my heart has started hammering again.

He's right, this is a mess.

—— § ——

"Wake up, Lilac," Atticus' voice rumbles in my ear.

I frown, burying my face further into the pillow. Waking up seems like the worst idea.

Atticus' laugh vibrates through my back, all the way to my fingertips. "Come on, you have an appointment."

My frown deepens. After our rendezvous in the dressing room, Atticus and I showered together, then went to bed to take a nap. The only plan for today is this anniversary dinner.

"Appointment?" I say, my voice muffled.

"It starts in fifteen minutes." Atticus' fingers trail down my naked back. "I also have bagels and coffee."

I open my eyes and roll onto my back, peering up into Atticus' amused face. "What kind of bagels?"

"Plain with blueberry cream cheese and fresh strawberries."

"My favorite," I sigh. "Your private investigator did a very thorough job on that background check."

His grin widens. "He sure did."

I reach and stretch my arms up, making the sheets slip down and revealing a nipple. Atticus bends to suck it into his mouth, grazing his teeth over the sensitive peak, and then slides off with a pop and sits up, reaching for the goods on his nightstand.

I sit up, tucking the sheets under my arms, and accept the iced coffee from Atticus. I realize he's wearing a dark blue henley with the sleeves pushed up to his elbows and black jeans.

"It's weird seeing you in anything but a suit," I comment as he places a paper bag in my lap.

"A rare occurrence, but it happens," he says, pulling out some sort of seeded bagel that's overloaded with salmon and cream cheese.

We eat in comfortable silence for a few moments, Atticus smashing through his whole bagel and getting into his second as I'm finishing my first half.

"What time is it?" I ask after swallowing my last bite.

"Almost one," Atticus supplies, collecting our trash. "Plenty of time for Diego to work."

"Diego?" I frown. "My...hairdresser?"

"Yes."

"You made Diego come *here?* He doesn't do house calls."

Atticus scoffs before taking a sip from his takeout coffee cup. "He does for me."

"Do you *know* my hairdresser?" I mean, he would from his super thorough background checks, but this feels different.

Atticus plucks my empty coffee cup from me and stands from the bed. "For years."

Realization dawns. "What's your favorite color?"

He arches a brow. "Lilac purple."

"Did you, by chance, tell that to your dear *friend* Diego a year ago?"

His sly grin says it all.

28
PHAEDRA

I 'M CLINGING ONTO ATTICUS' arm with a death grip as we walk into the Oak Room of the Plaza hotel. I stall at the entrance, distracted by the intricate dark oak paneling throughout the space, and the beautiful chandelier that's the center focus of the ridiculously high ceilings. Then I register that the place is teeming with people.

I did research on the way here and I recognize government officials and socialites in the crowd, but I wasn't expecting actors and Hollywood darlings in the mix.

"*This* is small and intimate?" I ask Atticus softly as he pulls us further into the room.

"For my parents, it is," he says, nodding in greeting at multiple people as we walk past. We enter another area to the right that's smaller, with an ornate bar, low-level seating and more people.

"Atticus!" We both turn toward the female voice. I've seen Atticus' sister in magazines and in videos on social media—and apparently on my supposed wedding night—but Constance Shaw is stunning in person.

Plump cheeks, defined jaw and chin, full lips, gorgeous light brown skin that contrasts her striking light green eyes that made her famous, and long dark lashes that match her shoulder-length, glossy, bouncy, tight black curls. She emits sunshine from every pore.

Her tall, lean body has all the right curves, accentuated by the form-fitting strapless dress that's black at the top and blends into ruby red at the bottom with a high split up the right side. Men and women alike stare after her as she glides over on towering heels and wraps Atticus in a brief hug.

"I thought you were in Prague," he says as she pulls back.

"I'm going back tomorrow." She turns to me, those captivating eyes sparkling. "I didn't want to miss *finally* meeting my sister-in-law."

Before I can introduce myself, Constance pulls me from Atticus' side into a firm hug. "I'm Constance."

"Oh, I know," I say with a nervous laugh as she releases me and steps back. "Phaedra, but please, call me Phae."

She sweeps a stray strand of my freshly dyed lilac hair behind my ear. "I'm obsessed with this color."

"Thank you." I used to dance on a stage in front of thousands of people and I'm here absolutely starstruck by my husband's sister. If I can't handle this introduction, I'm not going to survive the night without making more of a fool out of myself.

Constance steps to my side and hooks her arm through mine. "Let me give you the lay of the land."

"Am I that obvious?" I breathe, trying to dispel some of my

nerves.

"You're fine," she reassures, then cuts a look at Atticus on my other side. "*Somebody* shouldn't have thrown you into the deep end."

Atticus' fingers lace with mine. "Phaedra is capable of more than you think."

Constance rolls her eyes, then casts her gaze over the crowd in front of us. "There's really no one important in here."

"The mayor isn't important," I say, eyeing him at the bar.

"You did your research," Constance comments, impressed. "The mayor is Atticus-level important, which means boring. Let me introduce you to Constance-and-Phae-level important people."

"Please don't drag my wife to any of your degenerate celebrity parties," Atticus says to Constance as he brings my hand to his lips and kisses the back of it before detangling our fingers.

I smirk at him. "I'll call you for a pickup?"

Constance laughs. "Oh, I like her already."

She pulls me to the bar, orders us each a cinnamon whiskey shot with an apple juice chaser. We clink our shot glasses together before tossing them back, then we snag a full champagne flute from a tray at the end of the bar before continuing out to the main room again from another door.

Constance proceeds to approach actors, people in the fashion industry, and a host of other celebrities with me at her side, introducing me to each person like we've known each other for longer than three minutes.

When we are halfway around the room, we finally run into a

familiar face.

"Ah, Mrs. Shaw," Sloane drawls over his tumbler of clear liquid and ice. "Lovely to see you again."

Constance steps up and gives Sloane a brief hug before returning to my side. "You've met?"

"We've had the pleasure," I deadpan.

Constance laughs. "Oh, so you already know he's an asshole? That's excellent."

"Has Conny tried to sneak you off to an orgy yet?" Sloane volleys.

She grimaces. "Ew, do not call me 'Conny'. You're just jealous I never invited you." She crosses her arms over her chest. "Besides, I don't do those anymore."

"That's good to know," Atticus says dryly, appearing at my side.

He hands me the drink he's holding, then wraps his arm around my waist. It's a tumbler of gold liquid with a foamy top and a bright red cherry resting on the ice. I take a sip—Amaretto Sour, one of my favorites.

"Those rings are such beautiful wedding rings," Sloane comments obviously, his eyes flicking from my left hand around the glass to my ears. "And those earrings. I wonder who the designer was?"

"You know it's rude to get a hard-on from your best friend's wife wearing your jewelry," Constance admonishes.

Sloane grins, reaching out and caressing the pear-shaped diamond drop earrings she's wearing. "I'm also hard from *you* wearing my jewelry, little Shaw."

"You're disgusting," Constance says, but there's no weight in those words.

I lean into Atticus. "Are they dating?"

Constance and Sloane's faces screw up in disgust at my question.

"She's like my brother," Sloane says, taking a sip of his drink.

"We kissed once, and I almost puked," Constance adds, stealing Sloane's drink and finishing it. I smirk; liberating other people's drinks must be a Shaw trait.

"They're more siblings than I am with Constance," Atticus comments.

"That's because Atticus was too busying parenting all of us," a new male voice says.

Constance darts across our group and jumps into the arms of the newcomer. "Phin!"

When she pulls away from the man, my eyes widen.

Still holding his forearms, Constance looks at me. "Phae, this is—"

"Séraphin Baptiste," I finish.

He's way taller than he appears in his films—rivaling Atticus' height—and his wide and built frame cuts a fine figure in his black-on-black suit. The man is beguiling, with short, neat facial hair, full lips, sharp cheekbones and short black twists atop his head with the sides freshly faded, but what stalls my brain are those crystal-blue eyes against beautiful bronze skin that are literally hypnotic.

And... "You're wearing glasses," I blurt out before I can stop myself.

Séraphin chuckles, pushing the gold wire-frame glasses further up his nose. "Contact lenses are the worst. If I'm not on set, I have these on."

That Cajun drawl, sweet *lord*. If I didn't have some liquid courage in my system and Atticus wrapped around me, I definitely would have fainted.

"Phin, this is Phaedra Shaw, my wife," Atticus introduces. "Phae, I'm assuming you know of the blockbuster movie star Séraphin Baptiste?"

Séraphin rolls his eyes at Atticus' jovial jab as he grasps my free hand with both of his and shakes it gently, those baby blues regarding me fondly. "The Shaws are like family, and family calls me Phin. It's a pleasure to meet you, Phaedra."

"Call me Phae," I squeeze out.

He dips his chin and releases my hand, then turns his attention to Sloane, giving him a slapping bro hug.

My shoulders slump in relief, and I take a big mouthful of my drink.

Atticus' low chuckle vibrates through me. He dips down and kisses behind my ear. "Should I be worried about Phin?"

"What?" I turn my head to him. "No. He's...intense."

"Give it thirty minutes. It wears off."

I nod, but even I know it's not convincing.

Atticus steals a quick kiss. "You're doing fine."

"This is...a lot."

"We'll slip out after my parents meet you," he declares.

"No, it's fine," I urge, smoothing down his lapel. "This is important."

He regards me for a moment and then nods, plucking my drink

from my hand and taking a mouthful, then hands it back to me.

"Stealing people's food and drink is a family trait, I see," I comment.

Atticus grins as he pulls me in front of him and presses his front to my back, his arm snaking around my waist.

"Where's Felix?" Phin asks the group. "I saw Cam when I came in, but he hasn't seen him yet."

Sloane checks his flashy watch. "He should be here just before dinner starts."

If I weren't flush against Atticus, I wouldn't have noticed that this information makes him stiffen a touch.

"Who's Felix?" I ask.

"Felix Shaw," Constance supplies with a soft smile. "He's our first cousin. Cam, Camden, is his brother."

"He works at Shaw Inc.," I say, remembering that information from a few weeks ago. Storming into Atticus' office feels like a lifetime ago.

"Oh, shit," Sloane mutters, downing the rest of his drink, looking toward the entrance. "Here we go, friends."

Atticus tenses a lot more now as he steps out from behind me and moves to my side, moving his hold to my hip, as we all angle toward the entrance.

"Paloma Ramos," I say idly as I watch her greet every person walking in.

In her early fifties, the Spanish actress is still beautifully youthful, with long, thick black hair that has grays streaking elegantly throughout, dressed in a glittering floor-length gown that showcases her trim figure.

My parents have always been foreign film enthusiasts, so I've seen a lot of her work.

"Ramos-Shaw, technically," Constance amends. "Mom never bothered to correct anyone over the years."

My eyes tear from Paloma to Atticus and Constance. "That's your *mom*?"

Now, it makes sense why there are so many film stars here tonight.

"Your research wasn't very thorough, Lilac," Atticus says with a tight grin.

"Not everyone has Wade doing FBI-level background checks on people like you do," Constance teases, making Atticus roll his eyes. She bats her lashes up at him. "We appreciate it, though."

"Wade, the Shaw Inc. security guy?" I ask in confusion.

"*Atticus'* security guy," Constance clarifies. "He used to be my security, but big bro insisted I needed a whole team."

"And I was right," Atticus points out.

Constance sighs, lifting her glass to her lips. "Yeah."

There's a lot to unpack in that single word, but I divert my attention back to the current predicament.

"Does she prefer Mrs. Shaw, or Ramos-Shaw, or just Ramos?" I ask.

"Ramos," all four of them say in unison.

Add another item to the unpack list.

"Most likely, she'll tell you to call her Paloma," Constance adds.

I nod and look back at their mom as she moves through the room, now accompanied by a man that is *definitely* Atticus' father.

The senior Shaw is a giant of a man with short-cropped, black textured hair and sharp angular facial features made sharper by his stoic expression.

"You look like him," I comment softly to Atticus. The only major difference is that Atticus' father's skin tone is darker and Atticus inherited his mother's curls and slightly softer eye shape and cheeks.

"Unfortunately," he comments under his breath, his arm around me tense. I lean further into his side, and his muscles loosen slightly. The senior Shaw is another sore spot, noted.

"You ready for this, Phae?" Sloane says from Constance's side.

Constance elbows him in the ribs. "Shut up."

I sneer at Sloane, but when I glance up at Atticus, I'm feeling anything but ready.

"Don't let Frederic see you fold," Phin says randomly as he's straightening his posture and adjusting his suit jacket sleeves.

Christ, if one of the biggest names in the world is nervous about seeing a man he's known presumably his whole life, then this is about to be a disaster for me.

I quickly drink the rest of my drink and sneak it onto a table nearby, then smooth down my long, blown-out hair—mentally thanking Atticus' forethought about Diego's expertise—and steel my spine as the Shaws draw closer.

Showtime.

29
PHAEDRA

PALOMA REACHES OUR GROUP first. Her face lights up when she sees Phin.

"Séraphin," she coos, as he grabs both her hands and kisses each of them.

"*Tía,*" Phin says warmly.

She reaches up and pats his cheek, then moves on to Sloane. He kisses her cheek and she comments on his apparent new muscle, squeezing his biceps and both of them laughing about it.

Next, she bundles Constance in a hug, but the interaction looks more cordial than the last two with men that aren't her children.

They have a hushed conversation I can't hear as Paloma pushes Constance's hair off her shoulders and her eyes cast over her whole outfit. Constance looks like she's biting her tongue. The interaction ends with a kiss on each cheek, and then Paloma turns to Atticus.

"*Mi hijo,*" Paloma offers, holding her arms out in invitation for a hug.

"Mamá," he says, leaning down to kiss her on the cheek and accept her embrace. His hand slides from my hip and grabs my hand. *"Feliz aniversario."*

"Gracias, mi amor," she says, pulling back. Keeping him in her hold, she looks him over and notices our fingers laced together.

Her eyes rise to mine, and she gives me a soft smile.

"Quién es?" she asks Atticus.

Atticus steps out of her hold to my side, wrapping his arm around me again. "My wife, Phaedra Shaw."

"Oh! We finally meet," she says, pulling me from Atticus into an embrace. She smells like expensive perfume, the floral scent getting stuck in my throat.

"Lovely to meet you, Mrs. Ramos," I say as she pulls back.

She squeezes my elbows gently. "Call me Paloma."

She gives me the same once-over she did her children.

"Que hermosa," she croons to Atticus. Despite the number of foreign films I've watched over the years, my Spanish is limited, but I know that means beautiful. But the tone in the way she says it makes dread twist my gut.

That feeling deepens when her brow twitches as she releases me and steps back, saying a string of Spanish that I don't understand. Her tone says everything—she's found something about me disappointing.

Atticus responds in fluent Spanish, which makes Paloma huff indignantly and say something else in return.

"Ma," Constance chastises from Atticus' side at whatever comment she made.

Paloma sighs, her face smoothing out. "Let's not do this tonight."

"We won't be doing it at all," Atticus declares.

Paloma doesn't answer because Frederic appears beside her.

"This is her," he says, completely unimpressed at the sight of me.

Remembering Phin's advice, I hold out my hand, thanking the universe it isn't trembling. "Phaedra."

He looks at my hand like it's covered in shit. "I know."

"Frederic," Atticus says in greeting with just as much animosity in his tone as his father had for me.

Frederic turns from us without a second glance to Constance—to my surprise, he hugs her, even if it looks like a chore. He shakes the hands of Sloane and Phin, then continues with his greetings with the other guests.

"Dinner starts in thirty minutes," Paloma tells all of us and then floats off.

We all let out a collective breath.

"I need a drink," Sloane complains and Phin nods. They set off toward the bar.

"What did she say?" I ask Atticus and Constance.

"Nothing good," Atticus comments, looking around the room. "Constance?"

She winces. "Our mom is not the nicest person."

I cross my arms over my chest and wait for an answer.

She sighs. "She didn't..."

"She thinks you're below my caliber," Atticus finishes. "Undeserving of the Shaw name."

This marriage isn't even real, but her brutal disapproval still stings. I don't let it show on my face, using the practiced neutral expression from my minimal days in the spotlight.

"Rich, coming from someone who isn't publicly a Shaw." I turn to Constance. "We should go get a drink."

"Please," she breathes, and hooks her arm with Atticus. "Come on, At."

He pulls me to his side, and we head in Sloane's and Phin's direction. At the entrance of the bar, we're stopped by someone who looks like he might be hotel personnel.

"Mr. Shaw?" he asks.

"One of them," Atticus replies.

He gives Atticus a polite smile. "I'm the hotel manager. We've had an *unusual* request at the front desk this evening."

Atticus looks at Constance, and she takes the hint, excusing herself, but he pulls me in closer.

"This is my wife," he informs the manager.

"Uh, yes, I know," he says carefully, looking between us. "The request is actually for your wife, Mr. Shaw."

I frown. "Excuse me?"

"There is a man, a detective actually, requesting a meeting with you," he tells me.

"The police?" I blink, confused. "What for?"

"He wouldn't say. Just informed me it was police business."

"Who is the detective?" Atticus asks.

"Detective Ryan Wendell."

My eyes widen. Dylan's brother? I met him a few times during my relationship with Dylan, and we were friendly. He was serious about his job and his family, so this must be important.

"Is he still here?" I ask.

"In my office. I'm afraid he wouldn't leave the premise until I requested an audience with Mrs. Shaw," the hotel manager says apologetically.

I nod. "Let's make this quick."

"Absolutely not," Atticus barks, his hold on my waist tightening.

I turn and look up at his furious gaze. "I don't want him to come up here and make a scene. Because he will if he feels like he has to."

Atticus' jaw works, and then his angry gaze whips to the hotel manager. "Do you have cameras in your office?"

"Yes, sir."

"You *will* allow my head of security, Wade, to watch the entire interaction."

The manager nods.

Atticus turns back to me. "He'll meet you in the lobby."

I straighten his tie, then smooth my hands over the shoulders of his black suit jacket. "I'll be fine."

He catches my hand, pressing it into his chest over his heart. "You're back in fifteen minutes."

I nod. "I'll be back soon."

30
ATTICUS

I **SHOULD KILL HIM.** Eviscerate the entire Wendell line. They're making my wife literally walk away from me right now, and that's unacceptable.

I start thinking of all the ways I can wipe their name from history, but it would take more time and energy away from Phaedra, and they don't deserve more than the fifteen minutes I've granted them of our attention.

I breathe through the rage coursing through my veins and pull out my phone, messaging Wade about meeting the hotel manager and Phaedra downstairs, then pocket the device again and head straight for the bar, ordering a gin on the rocks.

"I hear your wife is being detained for questioning by the police?" my father asks as he appears at my side.

"A friend's brother, who happens to be a detective, is asking her about the welfare of his sibling," I correct, accepting my drink from the bartender, avoiding Frederic's glare. "Not in a professional capacity."

"You mean her ex-boyfriend," he retorts.

I force myself to take a sip of the liquor. I don't know who gave him that information, but it pisses me off how much he knows.

"What are you doing?" Frederic asks, disappointment dripping in every word.

I shake my glass. "Having a drink."

"If you need charity work, ask your mother for a project."

I frown, finally turning to the hateful man. "Excuse me?"

The firm set of his brows and the disgusted scowl scream disapproval. "She's a washed-up ballerina who grew up in a place that's a step up from the slums. Her father is a *janitor*."

I laugh at the irony as I take another sip of my drink. "The apple doesn't fall far from the tree, hm?"

Old money Frederic Shaw doesn't like to be reminded that Paloma was a nobody struggling actress working as a housekeeper before he plucked her from obscurity on a trip to Spain and made her a star.

"Yes," he agrees with disdain. "Unfortunately."

I place my half-drunk gin on the bar before I slam the crystal into his skull, knowing whatever he's about to say will give me the immediate urge to do so.

"You're just another Shaw that's fallen prey to low-life society-climbing pussy after their money."

Hands curling into fists, I stand to full height, my body vibrating with rage as I take a step toward Frederic. "Say whatever you want about the mother of your offspring, but disrespect my wife again, and you'll regret ever letting me breathe."

He scoffs. "You don't think I already do?"

A hand claps over my shoulder, holding me in place.

"Gentleman," Sloane greets.

"You marry a degenerate that brings the police into *my* celebration," he admonishes, ignoring Sloane's presence. "And you don't secure our family legacy and money with an ironclad prenup. How much more disappointing can you be?"

"Let's do this some *other* time," Sloane implores firmly. In my periphery, I can see the crowd inching closer to the scene we're creating.

"Hope for your sake there isn't another time, Frederic," I hiss.

His glare boils with outrage at my threat for a few tense moments, and then his face softens—if you can call it that—into its usual blank, harsh lines as he turns on his heel and storms off.

"You step between me and Frederic again, and you *will* be caught in the crossfire," I warn Sloane.

He releases my shoulder and steps up to the bar in front of me. "Yeah, yeah. You can thank me later."

I snatch up my drink and walk off before I wring his neck. I've known Sloane since elementary school, so he's stepped between me and my father before, but Frederic blatantly disrespected my Phaedra, and people die for less.

Finding a dark spot in the back of the room, I use the cover of shadows to breathe through the thoughts of patricide before I commit a felony in front of many, many witnesses.

My phone vibrates against my chest, and I pull it from the inner pocket of my suit jacket, accepting the call. "Wade."

"Mrs. Shaw is on her way back," he informs. "You might want to meet her in the lift lobby."

"How much does she know?" I ask, already moving through the crowd toward the exit.

"Enough."

31

PHAEDRA

WADE IS WAITING FOR us by the front desk when we enter the lobby.

"Mrs. Shaw," he greets with a dip of his chin, then turns his attention to the manager. "Where's the security room?"

He sweeps out his hand, gesturing to a closed door beside the front desk. "Near my office. Follow me, please."

We both follow the manager through the door and into a hallway in the staff area. The manager points to the end of the hall. "Last door on the right is the control room."

Wade nods and faces me. "I'll be watching the whole time."

I frown. "I'll be fine."

Something flashes over his face for a second that makes me uneasy. I'm assuming this meeting is Ryan justifying his brother's shitty behavior at the club last week, but with Wade and Atticus' reactions, I feel like I'm missing something.

Wade nods stiffly and heads toward the control room.

"I'm terribly sorry to disrupt your evening, Mrs. Shaw," the manager frets beside me.

"It's really okay," I reassure him. "Let's just get this done."

He still looks pained as he continues down the hall and stops at a door. I open it myself and step in, closing it behind me.

Perched at the end of the manager's desk, Ryan looks up from his phone and I'm reminded of how much he looks like an older Dylan. Tall, slim frame, and the Wendell light hazel eyes, but his hair is a much darker brown, and he carries a scowl from years on the job compared to his brother's carefree smirk.

There's something off about Ryan tonight, though. Dylan would call him "government-issue" because his appearance was always meticulous, but tonight, he's disheveled.

He's not in his usual suit that he wears on the job, instead in loose-fitting jeans, a gray T-shirt and a beat-up leather jacket. He also hasn't shaved in maybe three or four days and his hair looks like he's been trying to pull it out all day.

"Ryan, what—"

He jerks forward, making me immediately step back.

"Where is he?" he demands.

"Dylan?" I ask, confused.

"We haven't been able to reach him for almost a week."

I frown. "What's that got to do with me? We aren't dating anymore."

Ryan lets out a humorless laugh. "Yeah, I know, *Mrs. Shaw*. But you're the last person to see him."

I cross my arms over my chest. "Who said that?"

He lifts his phone into view. "Your phone did."

"What gives you the right to track my phone?" I accuse.

"Since I had to file a missing person's report on my brother," he bites out.

"Isn't it a conflict of interest to work your own brother's case?"

He paces back and forth in front of the desk. "Both of your phones pinged at that club last week," he says, ignoring my question. "He was probably there to ask you to forgive him."

"He knew I was there?" I ask.

"He saw a social media post from your friend and left my house, saying he had to get you back." Ryan stops and looks at me, a mixture of accusation and distress across his face. "That's the last time I saw him."

"I saw him," I say carefully.

Ryan steps toward me, and I move back immediately. There's something really off about this whole conversation.

"What happened?" he demands.

"Why have the police not called me for an interview?" I ask.

"I *am* the police," he points out forcefully. "This is the interview."

"I'm not doing this without legal—"

"Tell me what happened to Dylan," he barks.

"I don't know, Ryan. After he trapped me in a hallway, *against my will*, I left."

He shakes his head in disbelief. "No, you left with him. You had to."

"I'm married," I reiterate. "I'm not a cheater."

"No, no, *no*," he breathes as he paces again, raking his hands through his hair. "Both phones go dark at the club. You turned them off to sneak off together. He wouldn't have *left*."

He's talking to himself as he paces, but what he's saying doesn't make any sense.

"But your phone pinged *here*," he says, now addressing me. "You're still in New York, and he's not. They told me he left, but he wouldn't *do* that."

"What do you mean, left?" I ask.

Ryan stops pacing, rubbing his forehead with a sigh. "There's a one-way plane ticket purchase, a singular vague message to my parents and some really shitty airport CCTV footage of someone who looks like him leaving for South America."

"To Brazil?" I ask, remembering conversations we had about travel.

He frowns at me. "Yes."

I nod slowly. "He's... He's always wanted to go."

He throws his hands up in frustration. "No, he wouldn't go like this! He had responsibilities, had people, a good job."

"I don't know what to say, Ryan. I don't know anything else."

He paces again, muttering things I can't understand. Ryan isn't wrong; Dylan wouldn't leave randomly. He was really close to his family. That's why Connecticut was only ever temporary for him, and New York was his endgame. He had gotten all that he strived for, so it really doesn't make sense that he left.

"What did the message say?" I ask, curious.

"Something about not wanting to bother anyone ever again, or some bullshit like that."

An ominous promise whispered across my skin slams into me.

He won't bother you again. He's gone.
I have a few things to take care of.

I don't take kindly to other men having my wife's attention.

My heart hammers as I keep my revelation off my face. I know to my very bones this was Atticus. He's made Dylan disappear. I don't know how, but it can't be anything good.

I swallow. *Was* it blood that I saw in the mirror that night?

"I can see you're worried," I say, straining to keep my voice even. "And I don't know what Dylan was going through, but...it sounds like he really did leave." I take a breath and double down. "He wasn't himself when I saw him. He was physically aggressive with me. He'd never been like that before. And he was irrational about me moving on. It was...scary."

Ryan lets out a shaky breath, raking his fingers through his hair again.

"He probably left to get his head right," I reason. "He'll be back when he's ready."

Lie. An absolute fucking lie. From what I've gathered about Atticus, Dylan's vacation is *permanent.*

"I have to go," I inform Ryan, who's still staring blankly at the ground. "Take care of yourself, Ryan."

He doesn't acknowledge me as I back up and leave the room.

The manager is still standing in the hallway.

"He needs a minute, then he'll go," I say, then spin toward the exit.

Footsteps follow me as I enter the main foyer of the hotel.

"I'm going to kill him," I say low as I storm to the elevators.

"Are you okay, Mrs. Shaw?" Wade asks as I bash the call button.

"Can you get the car ready?" I ask, glaring at the elevator doors. "I'm grabbing my coat from upstairs and I'll be back down."

I don't hear his response as the elevator opens and I rush in, pressing the button of the floor I need.

Questions tear through me as I travel the few short floors. What happened to Dylan after I left the club? I saw Atticus immediately after, but I know he's behind his disappearance. How did he do it? Why did he do it? *What* did he do?

The doors slide open on my floor. No one's in the foyer area except Atticus.

"Everything okay?" Atticus asks as I approach him.

"No, everything is not *okay*."

"Phae—"

I spin on him. "It's not okay that I didn't know your mom is a famous actress who seems to like everyone else more than her own children. It's not okay that your father looks at me like he'd rather chew glass than know I exist. I didn't know you speak Spanish, or that you love your sister but hate your father, and the friends you grew up with are more family than your own. I don't *know* you, and I'm married to you. That's not *okay*."

I step closer to him until our chests are almost brushing. "And it's not fucking *okay* that the stranger I'm married to probably has something to do with my ex-boyfriend disappearing and I just had to lie to his cop brother about it."

His non-reaction speaks volumes, but I have to ask anyway.

"What did you do?" I demand.

He pauses for a long, long moment, his dark eyes devoid of any emotion.

"Do you really want to know?" he asks.

"*Yes.*"

He steps forward until we're touching, but I don't back up.

"He shouldn't have come back. I warned him what would happen if he did." He reaches up and plays with a strand of my hair. "He touched you; I shattered his limbs. He looked at you; I plucked out his eyes." His emotionless eyes return to mine. "He spoke to you, said your name; I slit this throat."

It *was* blood.

"He's dead," I reiterate.

"Yes."

I stop breathing; panic, confusion, and a bunch of other indiscernible emotions ravage my system. I'm not sure what to do with this information. I don't know how I'm supposed to react. Do I go after Ryan and tell him, do I ask more questions, do I run? Why am I not *already* running? Atticus literally just confessed to murder.

"What do you mean, you warned him?" I ask, because apparently that's what my brain is stuck on. "*When* did you warn him?"

"Three and a half months ago," he confirms.

"You're the reason we broke up."

"Yes."

"Were you the reason for other things?" I accuse.

"Yes."

Years. He's been manipulating the trajectory of my life for years.

As I'm about to demand answers, the elevators behind Atticus open, drawing my attention.

Two people step out, and my heart stops.

32
PHAEDRA

CUTTING WORDS AND VICIOUS laughter roar like phantom demons in my ears as memories play over and over in my head.

The words swirl together completely indiscernibly from one another, but the feelings of inadequacy, the nerves, the *pain,* from that time in my life floods my system, freezing me on the spot, staring at the woman who instigated my demise.

Tesia Kozak.

How is she here? And why?

A broad torso suddenly obscures my view of her, allowing the pressure in my chest to loosen slightly. I look up at Atticus—his hard stare watches every inch of my face.

"Who—" I clear my suddenly dry throat. "Who is that?"

His eyes narrow slightly. "My cousin, Felix."

I didn't even notice him. *"And?"*

His hard expression never changes, but his Adam's apple bobs as he swallows. The pressure in my chest returns. Fuck, he knows her. Like *"knows"* knows her. His background checks would have *definitely* told him who Tesia is to me, but who she is to *him* is the question, and something tells me I won't like the answer.

"You already know," he says simply.

"Mhm." This time my eyes narrow. "But who is she to *you*?"

"Atticus," a deep male voice says behind us, interrupting our standoff.

Stepping to my side, Atticus reaches around me and grips my hip hard enough that I can't flee, facing us to the newcomers.

Felix is another tall, attractive Shaw, with a leaner build compared to Atticus, medium-brown short curls instead of black, and a much lighter complexion. But he has a similar facial structure—strong jaw and high cheekbones—the same dark brown eyes as Atticus, and about the same age.

Dressed in a simple navy suit with a white shirt, he has his arm around Tesia at his side. As much as I want to forget she's even here, I can't, so I turn my attention to her.

She's dressed in a floor-length champagne-gold dress that fits her slim figure like a second skin. Her long black hair cascades down one shoulder in beautiful shiny waves, her plump lips are cherry red, and long dark lashes surround her light blue, feline-like eyes.

She's just as captivating as she was the last time I saw her, but instead of a vindictive victory grin on her face, there's a polite smile that quietly burns with anger and accusation. But not just at me; it seems directed at Atticus.

Yeah, Atticus and Tesia *definitely* know each other.

"Felix, Tesia, this is my wife, Phaedra." He says it so formally, like this isn't the one woman I never wanted to see again in my lifetime.

"Wife?" Tesia asks, surprised, her eyes dropping to my left hand.

"This is Felix, my cousin," Atticus directs at me. "And his girlfriend, Tesia."

"Fiancée," Felix corrects.

His cousin's fiancée? I wouldn't have expected that with the way she's shooting daggers at us right now.

"When did that happen?" Atticus asks, clearly surprised by this news.

"Last week," Tesia answers quickly, then points between me and Atticus. "When did *this* happen?"

"Almost three months ago," Atticus answers, squeezing my hip and pulling me further into his side. Tesia tracks every movement.

"Congratulations," Felix says to the both of us, finally dragging my attention from Tesia.

Now focusing on him, I realize he seems...uncomfortable. It doesn't look like it—Tesia fits at his side like someone he's intimate with would be—but there's something in his dark brown eyes that's detached to what's occurring right now.

"There you are." Constance's voice echoes around the foyer. We all turn toward her and she notices the new guests. "Oh, Felix, Tesia. You're just in time. Dinner is about to start."

Thankfully, the round dinner tables are so large that I don't have to interact with Tesia sitting on the opposite side. I do, however, have a clear view of her, which means I've watched her throw vicious looks across the table at both me and Atticus in between playing perfect socialite on her side of the table.

This being the "family" table, the seating arrangement projects the hierarchy of the Shaw clan, if you're paying attention. The people closest to Frederic and Paloma, like Cam and his wife, are people they seem to tolerate the most, Atticus and Constance are as far away as it is socially acceptable being their children, and then the rest of the table is filled with extended family or select friends of importance.

Tesia seems to be one of Paloma's favorites since she's seated close to her and has been chatting and laughing with her all night, with Felix on her other side mostly distracted by his phone.

"Are you okay?" Constance asks softly next to me.

"Oh, yeah," I breathe, picking up my glass of champagne and taking a sip. "Why?"

"You look like you've seen a ghost."

"Well..." I peek at Atticus on my left. He's deep in conversation with Sloane on his other side, so I lean closer to Constance. "What's the deal with Tesia?"

"Felix's girlfriend?" she asks, matching my low tone.

"Apparently they're engaged," I tell her.

She blinks at me in shock. "Wait, what?"

"They told us in the foyer."

"Wow, that's..." she breathes, glancing over at them with a confused frown. She clears her throat and turns back to me. "I'm surprised you don't know her. She's a ballet dancer." She looks back at them, her brow furrowing further. "I didn't think Felix was serious about their relationship. They've been on and off the entire time."

"How long have they been dating?" I ask.

"Nobody really knows," she muses. "At minimum, a year and a half. But if you go by the rumors, they started seeing each other before Atticus broke it off."

I still. Before *Atticus* broke it off?

"Those rumors, though, are very unsubstantiated, especially since..." Constance continues, but I don't hear what she's saying because I'm still stuck on the breaking thing.

"Atticus broke what off exactly?" I ask even lower than before.

Constance's brow furrows in confusion again. "He didn't tell you?"

I give her a pointed look.

"He and Tesia dated for a while," she practically whispers. "We thought it was going to be permanent, but then he broke it off suddenly."

"When?"

"I'm not sure exactly. A short while before Felix brought her to a family event on his arm." Constance shrugs, and reaches for her drink. "Atticus was totally fine with it."

Phin steals Constance's attention on her other side, so I sit back, resting the rim of the champagne flute on my bottom lip and stare at my half-eaten plate of food, reeling from the new information.

I was right about Tesia and Atticus. Has she been playing a long con for *this* long? Surely not. Her goal was to force me out of the company, and she did that. I'm completely inconsequential to her life now. Well, she might think I'm a problem *now* that I'm married to her ex, who she's *clearly* not over, but I'm gone soon. Knowing how easily you can bruise Tesia's ego, though, she still might try some bullshit.

But I was also right about Dylan.

That ominous word returns. *Years.*

Has all of this been Atticus? My chest burns as panic and anger sets in. A warm hand lands on my bare thigh, tucking under my dress.

"Take your hand off me," I sneer softly behind my champagne glass.

Atticus squeezes my thigh firmer and leans into my side like he's whispering sweet nothings. "What happened?"

I put down the glass and face him slowly, looking directly into his dark eyes. "Your *girlfriend* is watching."

His eyes narrow, flicking over my head, then back to me. "What did Constance say?"

"Has it been you the entire time?" I ask, discreetly pushing his hand off my lap. "Did you ruin my life?"

"Lilac—"

"Phaedra," I grit out. "Answer the question."

His jaw muscle works. "Not here."

I look back at my dinner plate, take my napkin from the side, and dab at my mouth, then place it down and grab my small clutch.

"Excuse me," I say to the people around me as I push out of my chair and stand.

I keep my head held high as I step away from the table, heading toward the restrooms. I hold it together, ignoring the beautiful bathroom around me, until I lock myself in a cubicle.

"Fuck!" I shout into the space, and slam the closed door with an open palm a few times, then rest my forehead on it as I struggle to breathe.

I need to get out of here, out of this city. I never should have come back. I hate to admit that I was getting comfortable. For a microsecond, I thought maybe, *maybe*, me and Atticus...

Stupid, stupid, Phae.

It's time to look at moving further away. After I finish this next week and get my annulment, I'm going to look for studio space in other states. Zahra always said she wanted to move to California. Maybe we could go together?

Sucking in a deep breath, letting it out closely, then repeating the process again, I pull my shit together. I need to have my shit together to get out of this disaster with most of my sanity intact. Once my heart rate and breathing have slowed, I push back from the door, smooth down my hair and leave the cubicle.

The restroom is thankfully still empty as I step up to a basin and wash my hands. The door opens as I'm drying my hands with a towelette. Tesia glides in on her expensive heels, stopping a few feet behind me with a vicious grin I know all too well.

"Phaedra Mills," she practically hisses.

I place the towelette into the waste hamper and turn to face her.

"It's Phaedra *Shaw*."

There's no way in fuck I'm giving Tesia the satisfaction of knowing that I'm not permanently a Shaw. I only have this role for another week, so I might as well play it to its fullest potential.

She screws up her face. "I don't believe for a second—"

"Believe it, babe." I lift my left hand and wiggle the giant rock on it. "Registered and consummated."

I fucking wink at her.

I can see the fury blazing in her eyes, but her face doesn't twitch from its smooth expression. She lifts a shoulder in a shrug. "He needs a plaything for the interim."

I grin. "You know, it was really smart."

"What?"

"You know," I say conspiratorially. "Marrying his cousin so you can stay in the family. Gives you the opportunity to see and talk to Atticus without looking like a crazy ex-girlfriend."

"That's not—"

"I don't give a shit," I cut her off. "I'm his *wife*, and you're nothing." I step into her space. "Stay away from Atticus."

She scoffs. "You couldn't hold on to ballet. What makes you think you'll be able to keep him?"

I laugh, the sound haunting. "I *beg* you to test that theory."

She stumbles half a step back, fear finally crossing her features.

Not bothering to wait for a response, I walk out of the bathroom, adrenaline from that interaction making my hands tremble. I need to find Atticus so we can get the fuck out of here. I have a lot of questions that require immediate answers.

Entering the bar area again, I scan the room with no luck, but as I'm about to go into the main area, a deep male voice calls my name.

I turn to see Frederic leaning against the wall by the door, holding a glass of brown liquor. Surprisingly, he's alone, and the look in his dark eyes is a summons with no room for discussion.

"Mr. Shaw," I greet as I walk up to stand a couple feet from him.

"If you're pregnant, I will arrange a doctor's appointment," he says instead of a greeting.

Great, so we're doing this right now. This night can't get any better. "I'm not pregnant."

He pushes off the wall and places his drink on a table nearby. "Have you filmed your relations with Atticus?"

Seriously? "No."

He nods and reaches into his back pocket, pulling out a rectangular leather item and a pen.

A fucking checkbook.

"We'll cover the legal fees for the annulment," he says as he opens the checkbook and scribbles across it, then rips off the check and holds it out to me.

"What is this?" I ask.

"More than someone like *you* deserves," he says with every inch of disdain in the universe.

"Someone like *me*?"

He grabs my wrist painfully and yanks, making me stumble forward, almost bumping into his chest.

"You're just another common whore," he hisses into my face. He shoves the check into my palm. "You're paid for your services. Now get out of my sight."

Bergamot and sandalwood wrap around me at the same time a familiar arm hooks around my waist and pulls me away from Frederic.

"You disrespect my wife, and now you touch her?" Atticus' low tone promises death.

"She will not carry the Shaw name," Frederic spits.

"This *common whore* already does, Freddy," I say. I glance down at the hundred thousand dollar check and laugh. "Oh, you think this would be enough?"

"Take it and leave," he sneers.

"I'm not a gold digger, Freddy, I'm a diamond miner. And not just any diamonds, *red* diamonds." I wave the check between us. "This is missing at least three zeroes."

He scoffs. "Go back to the slums you crawled out of."

I tilt my head. "Why would I do that when I can drain your son dry? Or I could just do you a favor and make myself a widow."

Atticus chuckles next to me. "If you want to drain my bank accounts and then cut out my heart, I'll give you the codes and the knife."

I smile sweetly up at him. "So considerate."

"Anything for you, my beloved."

I step up to Frederic and slap the check into his chest. "As the patriarch of the Shaw clan, it's really embarrassing that you can't afford me."

"Stupid bitch," he hisses.

I laugh as I step back to Atticus' side and take his hand.

"You're making a big mistake," Frederic tries again, the warning for both of us.

"Never speak to my wife again," Atticus warns.

"We're going to go make that film you suggested," I announce. "I'll send you a copy."

33

PHAEDRA

I'M PRACTICALLY VIBRATING WITH a mixture of emotions as Atticus and I head out of the party. We don't say goodbye to anyone, but I make a mental note to ask Atticus for Constance's number so I can thank her for being so wonderful tonight.

When we approach the elevators, Atticus presses up instead of down.

"What are you doing?" I ask.

"We have to talk," he says, reaching into his pants pocket and producing a keycard.

"We can do that at—"

"It can't wait that long," he cuts me off. A dark energy pulses off him as he glares straight ahead.

I inhale deeply, keeping my volatile annoyance in check as the elevator doors open and we step in. Atticus presses one of the high floors and we ride up in silence. The tension is so thick in here I can't take a full breath until we're walking down the hallway to a hotel room.

Atticus scans the card and lets me in first. The room is a blur of luxury as I head straight to the minibar and pull out the first alcoholic beverage my hand lands on, which is a small bottle of white wine. I unscrew the top and drink directly from the bottle, ignoring Atticus moving behind me.

"Did you eat enough?" he asks. "I can order something."

I take another large mouthful of wine, then turn to face him. "You can have dessert with your girlfriend."

Atticus is across the room near the armchair by the windows. He's perched on the edge with his jacket off and his arms crossed over his chest.

"Tesia isn't my girlfriend," he says, frowning.

"But she *was*."

He pauses a beat. "Yes."

My fingers tighten around the bottle. "How long?"

"Be specific, Phaedra."

I take a step forward. "How long ago were you fucking her?"

"Two years ago," he answers, face completely blank of emotion.

"And that's when you broke up?"

"Yes." He was with her when she was a vindictive harpy at the East Ballet Company.

"Is she how we met?" I ask.

"In a way."

His rudimentary answers are really pissing me off. "Why are you being so fucking cryptic?"

He scoffs. "I'm answering your questions."

"Do you know who she is *to me?*" I ask.

Another pause. "Yes."

That answer makes my blood boil.

"You knew this *whole* time. And you didn't think you had to tell me?"

"Yes."

An incredulous laugh falls out of me as I set down the wine bottle and pace. "I knew it. It's all a big joke." More laughter bubbles up. I feel and sound like I'm losing my mind. "You and Tesia are in on it. How did you get Dylan and Ryan to play along to?"

"This isn't a ruse."

I shake my head. "It has to be. This is fucking *insane*. I'll give you credit. You've been incredibly convincing about this fake marriage and had me there for a second about the murder thing. Real committed to the bit."

"It's not—"

I hold up my hand to stop him. "Look, I don't know what I did to you, but I'm sorry, okay?"

"Lilac—"

"No, no, you got me, you all did." My chest is tight. It's hard to breathe. I close my eyes so I don't cry. "I would like to stop playing this game now."

"Phaedra," Atticus says with more force, his tone sending a shiver down my spine. "Look at me."

I take a shaky breath and peek at him through my lashes.

"We. Are *not*. A game." Atticus annunciates each word with intention.

He could be lying, but there's something about his demeanor, the way he looks angry that I'd even considered this to be fake.

My gut says he's telling the truth, but can I even trust it anymore?

Would he have introduced me to his family if this was all some sick game? Or are they part of it too? Is this what the stupidly rich do for entertainment?

"This isn't a trick?" I ask, disbelieving.

"Far from it."

"You... Me..." I can't formulate the question.

"Real," Atticus declares.

Real.

"Tesia?"

"Inconsequential."

The tightness in my chest worsens. "You murdered Dylan."

"Yes." He doesn't hesitate this time.

My heart explodes into a gallop in my chest. For the first time in this entire arrangement, true fear courses through my veins.

"No, no, no, no," I whisper over and over, backing up to the minibar again, my lungs struggling to get enough oxygen. He really did it. And for what? Ryan is a *cop*. He's going to find out, and then we're *both* going to be so fucked.

In my periphery, Atticus moves closer. One minute the wine bottle is back in my hand, and the next it's flying across the room at Atticus. He slides out of the way and it smashes into the floor-length mirror behind him, shattering the glass.

"Stay away from me."

Atticus holds out his hands placatingly. "I won't hurt you."

I reach out and pick up the first thing I touch, which is a wine glass, and throw it in his direction. He dodges easily. "Why would I believe you?"

"Will you stop throwing things?" he asks calmly. "You'll hurt yourself."

I toss two more glasses in his direction; each of them he dodges and moves closer to me. "Why do you even care?"

"I care a great deal."

Fury drives me forward and I shove at his chest, but he barely moves. "You're a fucking liar."

Anger burns in his dark eyes. "I've never lied to you, Lilac."

"It was *you*," I cry, shoving at him again. "You took ballet from me."

"I didn't—" When I try to push him again, he catches both my wrists.

"Why?" I ask, voice thick with unshed tears as I try to pull out of his blazing touch. "Why did you ruin my life?"

"You ruined *mine*," Atticus snaps in my face.

That makes me pause.

He leans forward, eyes somehow darker and more lethal. "You've consumed every fucking second from the moment you fell into my life. All that has happened since then is all for *you*."

"Me. *Me?*" I shout, fighting his hold again. "You're a fucking murderer."

He laughs, the sound deep, rich, *terrifying*. "Yes, but it doesn't *really* bother you, does it, my beloved?" He tilts his head in that predatory way.

I spit in his face. "Fuck you."

Atticus wrenches me forward, his mouth crushing to mine. My body instantly wants to melt under him, but I resist, instead sucking in his bottom lip and biting down hard. Surprised, he jerks back. I use the distraction to wrench out of his hold and stumble backward, landing on the bed.

Atticus wipes the blood on his lip and turns in my direction, but I slide onto the floor before he gets to me. I frantically crawl towards the door as fast as I can, but have to pause when a piece of glass lodges in my palm.

Warm fingers wrap around my ankle. I scream, twisting in his hold and kick out as Atticus drags me across the room over the mess of broken glass, some of it sticking into the bare skin of my back. His hold disappears from my ankle and I immediately lift off the ground, but my chest is shoved back down hard, my head thudding on the floor, blurring my vision.

Something heavy on my sternum restricts my ability to breathe. I blink rapidly, my vision clearing, and look down. Atticus has me pinned under his shiny, expensive Italian shoe.

I look up at the predator looming over me. He looks so calm, his clothes pristine, not a hair out of place, but his eyes *burn*.

"Get. Off. Me," I squeeze out as I grip his ankle and try to move him.

He steps down harder with a wicked grin. I watch as he reaches down to his belt, pulling the tongue out of the loops slowly.

"You think I'd let you go that easy, Lilac?" he asks, as he unbuckles the leather. "The fun has barely begun."

"You're fucking crazy," I wheeze.

He chuckles, pulling the rest of the belt from the loops with a quick snap. "For you, my beloved? Absolutely."

I continue to struggle under him as he unbuttons his slacks and pulls the zipper down, opening his pants just enough so he can pull out his hard cock. From this angle, it looks way more intimidating as he strokes it lazily, watching me with those wild eyes.

"This is all for you," he says, stroking harder. "Every depraved act, every broken law, every life gone. All for you."

The hold I had on my tears disintegrates and they pour out of me in heaving sobs that are garbled by the pressure on my chest.

"Look at you," he breathes. "Unable to move, unable to breathe, scrapes across your skin, makeup ruined, glass in your hair." He moans, his eyes rolling back. "Oh, it's a fucking beautiful tragedy."

"Let me go," I sob, choking on saliva.

His attention returns to me. "You know I can't do that. And I know you don't want me to, either."

I shake my head.

He chuckles softly. "I know your secret. The one you won't even admit to yourself." He pauses, making sure he has my full attention. "This is the most you've felt alive since you left the stage. You don't want this to end."

I shut my eyes tight and shake my head vigorously. No, it's not true. It *can't* be true.

"Oh yes, baby," Atticus breathes. "You love all of this. The fear, the pain, the confusion. It gives you the same rush as it did to dance in front of thousands of people. You probably love it *more* than dancing." He makes a rough sound in the back of his throat. "You're probably *soaked* right now. Should we find out?"

I open my eyes as the pressure disappears from my chest, but is quickly replaced as he sinks down and sits on my torso, over my waist, using his knees to pin my elbows to the floor.

Hand still wrapped around his cock, he reaches behind himself with his free hand and slides his fingers down my thighs and under my dress. I didn't wear underwear tonight.

I clamp my legs together, but he easily wedges between them and slides a finger over my clit.

"So fucking wet," he groans, his finger travelling further down, and sinking knuckle deep, joined by a second digit.

My legs tremble around his hand at the sudden lust bursting through my body.

"It's okay, baby," he coos above me. "Let go. Scream, cry, fight, fuck. Work through it all, because you're not leaving this room until you're just as insane as I am."

He suddenly pulls his hand away and stands, tucking himself haphazardly in his pants. Instinctually, I pull myself out from under him and get to my feet, ignoring that for some fucked-up reason, I miss his touch.

I take one step back; Atticus stays where he is, but he's tracking every step.

"Even if you get out of this room, this hotel, no matter how far you run, I will *always* find you."

My body is frozen on the spot. The logical thing to do *is* to run. Run far, far away, and get out of this fucked-up situation. I should *want* to leave, go out into the world and find some kind of normal.

That thought immediately feels...*wrong*.

I've had a taste of this adrenaline-spiked insanity, its decadent intensity that makes me act in ways that I never considered letting uncaged, and yet, Atticus seems to have the key.

I should run.

But, I *hate* running.

I launch forward, wrapping my arms around his neck and my legs around his waist, slamming my lips over his. He tastes like everything right and everything wrong in my life as our lips and teeth war, my fingers sinking into his hair, reveling in the silky strands.

We're moving and then my back presses against something cool that crunches. I pull away from his lips and drop my legs from his waist, then turn us and shove Atticus into the mirror, shattering it further.

"Down," I huff, pulling on his shoulders.

He obliges, sinking to his knees, his eyes never leaving mine. Staring into those dark pools of depravity, I pull my dress higher so the split is almost at my pelvic bone, and then hook my knee over his shoulder.

Atticus doesn't waste a second—he rips the dress at the split, exposing my lower half, then grips my hips and jerks me forward, burying his face in my cunt.

The momentum forces me to catch myself by slamming my hands into the broken mirror. The sting of a jagged edge slicing into my palm quickly mixes into the jolt of pleasure from Atticus' tongue laving over my clit.

Pain and pleasure, pleasure and pain, the epitome of me and Atticus.

Keeping one hand gripped tight on my hip, Atticus leans back slightly and lifts my other leg onto his shoulder, then spears two fingers into me, making my whole body shudder and my eyes roll closed. Tongue and fingers in tandem, he works my body to a higher fucking plane as I roll my hips, riding his face, racing with him there.

He was right—I feel *alive.* I never want this to end.

The orgasm that bursts through my body is hard and messy, my arousal soaking Atticus' face as I pant and my legs shake. I force my eyes open and I catch my distorted reflection.

My hair is a mess, but somehow my makeup is relatively intact. The top section of my dress is in place, but the bottom is destroyed. Most of my skin is fine, but I also have superficial cuts scattered about that are dribbling blood.

Fragments of beauty and destruction.

I climb off Atticus' shoulders and sink onto his lap. It's barely a breath before he's pitching forward and cradling the back of my head as we crash onto the floor.

He catches my lips in his teeth as he reaches between us, pulling his cock out and thrusting into me. I shout at the burn of the stretch, but it quickly turns to molten heat as Atticus fucks me hard and fast.

He scrapes his teeth off my lip, then presses his forehead to mine.

"Look at me," he demands.

My eyes pop open and my breath hitches. It's like the veil is gone and all that's left fucking me is a predator determined to consume *everything.*

His hand moves from under my head to wrap around my throat, and he squeezes hard. That light feeling spreads over me from the pressure in my head, and my eyelids are heavy, but I keep them open as I snake my hand between us. I press my fingers into my clit, circling over the sensitive spot firmly, making my hips buck.

I'm already so close to ecstasy again.

"Is this *real* enough?" he growls in my face.

"Y...Yes," I barely croak out.

"This is all you need," he says, softer than I've ever heard him. "All *we* need. Just us. You and me."

I choke out some sort of sound in response, but I'm now at the precipice of another devastating orgasm and it's scrambling my brain.

Atticus' strokes get harder and almost desperate, like a man fucking his will into me, the rhythm turning frenzied. My fingers on my clit match him, and just as I crest, Atticus releases my throat, and I detonate.

Absolute static.

I see nothing, hear nothing.

My body feels as if I'm suspended in pleasure, in a place that's truly free.

Then I'm wrenched back to reality. Sound comes back in stereo. Heavy breathing in my ear, my own breathing labored. I blink, my eyes surprisingly wet, and open them to a white ceiling. A heavy body presses me into the plush carpet and shards of glass that poke in various places.

Comfort and danger. Is it possible to find that in one circumstance, or are they destined to remain opposing teams?

34

ATTICUS

EYES OF GOLDEN TOPAZ, usually so full of fire, are now nothing but dying embers.

My chest squeezes painfully.

She's going to leave me.

No. I won't let it happen.

She'll have to kill me before I let her go.

She breaks eye contact by turning her face away.

"I need to shower," she whispers.

I pull out gently, tucking myself back in my pants, and lift off Phaedra, carefully scooping her off the destruction on the floor and walking to the bathroom. I put her on her feet in front of the vanity, then look in the drawers at the amenities. Luckily, there's a box with "tweezers" printed on the front.

"Show me your palms," I instruct softly, opening the box.

She lifts both to me, but her eyes remain trained on my torso. Avoiding eye contact, shoulders hunched in. Is she afraid of me? No—if she was, she would have told Ryan I murdered his brother.

Is she *ashamed?*

Ashamed of what I've done, or what she's done? Of what we are? Preposterous.

Pushing aside my roiling emotions, I concentrate on the current task: inspecting the wounds on her hands, and picking out small shards of glass. Once those are clear, I turn her around and check her back. There are only half a dozen knicks and some smeared blood, but no glass.

I still wet a face towel with warm water and wipe at her skin, making sure none of the wounds are actively bleeding or need stitches. Satisfied they're all superficial, I turn her back around.

She still won't look at me.

I grip her chin gently and lift her face up to mine. Those beautiful golden irises, so cool and distant.

I hate it.

"I'll get you some clothes," I tell her.

Phaedra steps back and drops her gaze back to the floor, the only response a meek nod.

We stand there for a few more stagnant moments before she turns and walks to the shower, turning it on and stripping out of her ruined dress.

I squash the urge to follow, knowing I'll just make whatever this is worse. Instead, I retreat out of the bathroom, cross to my jacket still on the armchair, and pull out my phone.

I call Wade; he answers on the second ring.

"Have Rose pack Phaedra a bag, and bring it here," I instruct.

"Yes, sir."

"When you arrive, pay the hotel manager. There are damages

in the room."

"Done."

I glance at the open bathroom door. "I also have another task for you."

She wants to leave.

I'll make sure she can't.

35

PHAEDRA

*E*N BAS, EN AVANT, *tendu, rond de jambe, plié in fourth, turn. En bas, en avant, tendu, rond de jambe, plié in fourth, turn, turn, turn.*

I execute another pirouette and then relax out of position, taking slow, controlled breaths as I close my eyes.

A chestnut gaze flashes through my mind. So warm and inviting. Somewhere to hide, to rest.

The warmth suddenly turns cold and menacing, the brown now almost black. Eyes of a predator, a *murderer*. Eyes I'm drawn to on an inexplicable level that's...unnatural.

Or is it? I shake my head. I don't fucking know anymore.

Maybe if I do more pirouettes, I can disorient my brain enough so it's quiet for one fucking second.

I stand in first position, facing the mirrors. *En bas, en avant, tendu, rond de jambe, plié in fourth, turn.*

"Add a *fouetté*," a familiar voice says across the studio. Zahra. I could cry with relief; she's just the person I need right now.

I spy her in the mirrors near the entrance. She's dressed in a figure-hugging black pencil skirt and matching blazer with an ivory blouse and cute red heels, her long braids down over one shoulder and a red lip to match her shoes. I'm assuming she's just come from the office since it's almost six in the evening.

I reset and, as requested, perform a number of *fouettés* and pirouettes in a row, and end facing her.

"*Magnifique*," Zahra praises as she glides over with her arms stretched out like our first ballet teacher used to do.

"*Merci*," I say, as I sink into a graceful bow, then back up to the mirrors. "What are you doing here?"

"You've been avoiding me since Saturday," she admonishes. "It's *Thursday*."

I sit on the floor by my duffle bag and undo my pointe shoes. "I know, I'm sorry."

Zah kicks her heels off and sinks down next to me. "You owe me all the juicy Shaw gossip from that dinner."

As I put my shoes away and stretch out my leg muscles, I give Zahra exactly that.

"You *really* told Frederic Shaw, one of the most powerful people in New York, you were going to send him your sex tape?" Zahra asks between laughter.

"Is that all you heard?" I ask lightly as I dig out a hooded sweatshirt from my bag and put it over the gray leotard I'm wearing.

"Oh, I heard the rest," she says. "Tesia is the worst, but she's one of those bullies that scuttles away the moment you show teeth. Proud of you for that, by the way. And Paloma seems rude, too.

Not the vibe at all."

"An understatement."

"I can't believe you met Séraphin Baptiste!" she practically squeaks. "I wonder if he'll still be friends with us after you leave."

I give her a half-ass shrug as I pull out sweatpants.

"Phae?" Zahra asks.

"Hmm?"

"Oh, shit," she breathes. "You want to stay."

"No," I answer immediately. "I... Fuck, I don't know."

"Lay it out for me, babe."

I lay down, pop my legs up so I can slide my pants on over my tights, then stay horizontal, staring at the ceiling as I fasten the waist. "What happened after the dinner was... intense."

"Did you film the sex tape?" Zah asks.

"No filming."

"But yes to the sex," she surmises.

"It was more than that."

"Ooo," Zah drawls. "Did it get *freaky*?"

I look at her.

Her expression is both surprised and impressed. "Oh shit, you finally found a guy you trust enough to get messy with."

I sit up, hugging my knees to my chest. "It isn't the sex, it's the circumstances around it that are on my mind."

"Tell me more." She sits straighter, her expression more serious.

"Have you heard anything about Dylan?"

She frowns. "Weird diversion."

"Do you remember Ryan, his brother?"

"Yeah..." She pulls out her phone, tapping the screen a few

times. "Pretty sure he messaged me. I must have deleted it. Something about him leaving?"

"Yeah. Ryan came to see me at the dinner."

Zahra's eyes widen. "Whoa, what?"

"Dylan's left the country...allegedly."

"Allegedly?" I can see the wheels turning in her dark eyes. Her mouth drops open. "*Allegedly*. Like, 'I won't tell you because I have spousal privilege, and you don't' kind of allegedly?"

"Yeah," I breathe.

She blows out a breath. "Damn. Okay."

I sigh, resting my cheek on my knees. "It's so complicated. I have so many questions that either don't have answers or answers that I can't decipher." I pause. "Atticus. He...he scares me."

"Are you safe?" Zah asks immediately.

"Yes. Well, I'm pretty sure."

"Do we need to get 'Kevin' involved?" she asks, not convinced.

"No, no." I let out a deep breath. "There are just other parts of me he's bound to break in ways that aren't repairable."

Zahra sits with that, regarding me, her brow slightly creased.

"There are so many reasons to leave," I whisper after a while of comfortable silence. "Any other person would have run *well* before now."

"But...you don't want to?" she asks softly.

"I *have* to," I say, a little firmer, more to myself than to Zahra. "I should have taken your advice and gotten a lawyer the second that certificate was authenticated."

"But you didn't."

"Yeah, and now I'm in too deep. I know *way* too much."

"But you're not trapped," she reasons.

"No," I agree lightly. "But..."

"You want to be?"

I sigh. "It's complicated."

We sit again in silence, *"complicated"* swirling around me like an all-too-familiar phantom that has been haunting me since this whole thing started.

"Do you know why my parents didn't hesitate to keep you in ballet all those years ago when I asked?" Zahra asks.

I lift my head from my knees, interest piqued, but very confused about this sudden pivot.

She smiles warmly. "Because the moment you enter a studio, you come alive. Ballet is a spark that lights the fire within you. You're the truest version of yourself when you dance." Her eyes glitter with emotion. "And when you were on stage? You were a blinding fucking inferno."

"The stage fed that energy into me." My tone conveys my melancholy. "And then I lost it."

"You never lost that fire," Zahra corrects. "You still light up a room when you dance. But that big, blinding part of you changed when you got injured, and so did the spark to ignite it."

She gives me a knowing look, waiting for me to make the connection.

"You think *he's* the spark?" I ask.

She barks a laugh. "Atticus is more like the kerosene that started this new, slightly out-of-control wildfire in you, but it's *you*. This is the most life I've seen from you for a long time."

"I feel *insane*," I confess. "Is that what fuels me?"

Zahra laughs. "Yeah, kind of. We're all insane. You just have to find people who're on the same wavelength. Think about our whole friendship. We've been fueling each other's crazy the whole time."

"True."

"And from the state of your back, I would say Mr. Shaw *scratches that itch,* too?"

I hide my face in my hands as I laugh, Zahra joining me. My laughter turns into short, heaving breaths as I fight the sudden tears building in my eyes.

"Why are you so okay with this?" I ask, dropping my hands to my lap. "He's literally—"

"No, no, don't tell me. You know what my dad says..."

"Plausible deniability," we say together.

"You remember why he tells us that?"

I comb through my memories. "Something about that uncle we never talk about?"

Zahra nods. "All I know is that he got my dad into a lot of shit that should have ended *very* badly."

"Before he married your mom and they had you, right?" I knew Zahra's dad didn't exactly have the cleanest past. He doesn't really talk about it, but he seems to have been nothing but an upstanding citizen since he married Zahra's mom.

"Right, and look at them. They have all kinds of 'spousal privilege' between them and they're the best."

"That's very true," I muse.

Zahra pulls my hands from my lap, clutching them tightly. "Just do what feels right, Phae. Even if it's a little insane."

"It's probably going to be *a lot* insane."

Zahra smirks, releasing my hands. "That's my girl."

I pull on my sneakers and close up my bag, as Zahra stands and slides back into her heels, then we head out of the studio.

"By the way," Zahra says as I'm locking the doors. "If that man steps a foot out of the lines you draw, you tell me and I'll 'spousal privilege' his ass."

I laugh and pull her into a tight hug. "You're crazy."

She beams. "You know it."

— 𝔖 —

It's past ten when I walk into the penthouse, and I'm starving, so I head directly to the kitchen. I pause at the threshold: dressed in nothing but sweatpants, Atticus sits at the island bench in the low light, typing furiously on his laptop.

Not only have I been avoiding Zahra since the dinner, I've also been avoiding Atticus. I've only seen him in passing in the penthouse or the gym, and in bed, where we sleep on opposite sides of the massive mattress.

I take a moment to watch him. He's been different lately. Withdrawn, like he's remembered what boundaries were and took three giant steps away from them. It's weird, and I'm not sure I like it.

Observing him now with his brows furrowed and hair mussed up, he seems...tired. I don't know why seeing anything but the perfect business mogul surprises me so much.

Stepping into the space, it's like he feels my presence and stops typing immediately, his whole body turning toward me.

"Hi," I murmur, approaching the kitchen tentatively, suddenly feeling like I'm invading his space.

His eyes track from my hair piled in a messy bun atop my head, all the way to the sneakers on my feet, then back to my face.

"You hungry?" he asks, standing.

"Uh...yeah."

"Take a seat," he says, crossing to the fridge.

I put my duffle down on the floor and take the stool next to his original spot, watching as he pulls a pile of containers out of the fridge, placing them next to the stove. Moving with preternatural grace, he goes back and forth from various cupboards and the pantry, emerging with a loaf of bread and a pan. He takes it to his growing pile, then slides out one of the chopping boards and places it in front of him.

Watching Atticus' sculpted back muscles move as he cooks is a sight to behold. Hell, his whole body is carved stone, moving with magnificent fluidity; it's incredible. My eyes catch on the lines of strange symbols on his side again. I frown. I think there are more of them.

He suddenly turns around with a full plate and I jerk up straight and clear my throat, my cheeks warm.

He places the food in front of me and my mouth waters. "Grilled prosciutto and gruyere, with fresh pear, arugula and fig jam on sourdough."

Fuuuck. All my favorite things. With Atticus watching intently, I pick up one half of the huge grilled sandwich with both hands and take a bite.

Salty, creamy, sweet, peppery. The sound that comes out of me is completely unseemly.

That reaction must be what he wanted, because as I dig into the delicious sandwich, Atticus slides over a glass of a mystery green juice, a bottle of water and then cleans up the kitchen. I've practically inhaled the whole half of the sandwich by the time he takes his seat next to me with his own juice.

"Good?" he asks, regarding me neutrally.

"Incredible," I sigh, as I pick up the second half.

He nods and angles toward his laptop.

That's it? I wait for it. Another second. He's bound to lean over and—

He starts typing.

What?

I've decided I hate withdrawn Atticus.

I hold out the last sandwich half to him.

When he pauses his work, staring at the screen for a beat before finally turning to me, his face gives nothing away.

We're suspended in a moment that's heavy with words unspoken and emotions never expressed. I'm on bated breath as that assessing gaze tracks over every inch of my face, analyzing every twitch and blink, looking for *something*.

Then slowly he leans forward, his eyes glued to mine as he takes a bite of the sandwich.

Tension melts from my body as I take my own bite and Atticus returns to his work.

Something shifted, a truce, or maybe an understanding of sorts, forged in this simple moment. It feels familiar, but new and fragile, something that needs a tentative touch. Something I'm now willing to try.

I finish my food and pick up the juice, three seconds away from a food coma. My eyes wander back to Atticus, to the tattoos again.

"Are there more of those?" I ask, gesturing at his side.

"Yes," he answers without looking up from his laptop.

"What are they?"

"Morse code."

I frown. "What does it mean? Or rather, say?"

"Do you have plans on Saturday night?" Atticus asks, like I asked nothing.

Not wanting to break our truce in the first ten minutes of its existence, I let my curiosity go, and stand with my dishes, walking around to the dishwasher. "Nothing after work."

"I would like to take you to a performance."

The tension comes back with vengeance, my muscles locking up, hand frozen on the dishwasher. "What kind of performance?"

"Ballet," he says easily, eyes not leaving his laptop.

Shit, just what I feared.

"It's a work thing," he adds conversationally.

I haven't been in a theatre since my injury. I tried once to go to a performance to support one of my last choreographers, but as I pulled up in the cab, anxiety, anger, and shame choked me. I couldn't even reach for the handle. I just begged the cab driver to take me back to the hotel and cried myself to sleep.

That was one of the last times I came to New York, too.

I've been silent for too long, so Atticus looks up from his laptop.

"Seven o'clock curtain call?" I ask lightly, focusing on opening the dishwasher and stacking my plate.

"And the party after."

"Perfect," I force out with a smile.

I can feel him watching me as I close up the dishwasher, then skate around and pick up my bag. "I'm heading to bed. Early morning."

"I'll join you in a moment," Atticus calls after me as I'm already moving.

I get through my night routine quickly—brushing my teeth and hair, washing my face and then changing—and tuck myself into bed before Atticus arrives. The whole time, my chest feels like a boulder of emotions suffocating me.

I shut my eyes, trying to breathe around the discomfort, but my mind keeps spinning.

It'll be fine. Most people probably won't know who I am. They'll write me off as Atticus' new purple-haired wife. Maybe it'll be nice to see some familiar faces? Or maybe horribly mortifying.

I don't realize I have company until I hear my phone charger clicking into my phone next to me. I open my eyes with a jolt.

Atticus smiles softly down at me. "You left it in the kitchen."

"Thank you," I whisper as he rounds the bed and slides in, the magical cloud mattress barely dipping at his weight.

I watch him plug his own phone in and then settle on his back, closing his eyes.

Brain frazzled, I don't fight my craving for his warmth as I shuffle across the bed and curl against his body.

Atticus doesn't even open his eyes as he moves his arm and

scoops me forward, pressing me flush to his side. I throw an arm over his torso, rest my head on his chest, wedge one of my legs between his and sigh in relief.

The war of emotions in my mind and body finally stops, and I take a deep breath in, filling my lungs with bergamot, sandalwood, and Atticus.

With the steady rhythm of his heart under my ear and his body heat seeping into me, I sleep.

36
PHAEDRA

WHY IS IT SO goddamn hard to pick shoes?

I look over the rows of heels before me, completely lost. I can't call Zahra *again*; I've already called her three times and I can't keep bothering her at her work event for something so ridiculous.

She helped me pick out a strapless dress in black velvet that's floor-length and fits like a glove, my make-up is simple, just a subtle winged liner and a glossy nude lip, and Diego made another house call to blow dry my hair straight, the smooth length laying down my back, so I could literally choose *anything* for shoes, but I'm stuck.

"Phaedra," I hear Atticus call. "Are you—"

He stops talking abruptly, and I turn. Holy hell. Dressed in a black tuxedo and bowtie, expertly tailored as usual, his hair and beard cleaned up and professionally styled by Diego, he looks downright sinful.

"...ready?" he finishes absently as his dark eyes track down my body and burn a hot path across my skin, the cufflink he was adjusting forgotten.

"Almost." It comes out all breathy. I clear my throat and turn back around. "Just need to pick shoes."

I don't hear him, but I feel him moving around behind me. A drawer slides open and quickly closes before he appears at my side. He steps forward and picks up a black pointy pair of high heels with ankle straps, then turns and sinks to his knees in front of me. He lifts one foot—unbalancing me, so I use his shoulders as support—slides the heel on, and secures the strap surprisingly quickly, then does the second one.

"Thank you," I whisper, crossing to the large floor-length mirror to check my outfit and makeup one more time.

Atticus appears behind me in the mirror, his arms coming around me, and then something cool slides across my bare chest. My eyes drop to it and I stop breathing.

Atticus fastens a necklace made up of two strands of pearls around my throat, the pearls all perfectly round and gorgeous ivory. The bottom row also has a huge pear-shaped diamond hanging in the center, glittering between my clavicles at the base of my throat.

Goosebumps raise in the wake of his fingers skating across my skin, and then he leans down and kisses the top of my shoulder. "Now you're ready."

—— § ——

My knee bounces as we inch closer to Lincoln Center, my chest tight with panic. I don't want to do this, but I also do. I've watched ballet performances on the internet, but it's a whole different feeling when you're in the theater.

I didn't go more than two months without attending a show as a patron since I was six, and I hate that my experience and injury took that away from me.

I shut my eyes. *I want this. I want this. I want this.*

A warm, large hand rests over my wringing ones in my lap, drawing my attention.

"Are you okay?" Atticus asks.

"I... I haven't entered a theater since I got injured." I huff a laugh and shake my head. "It's stupid."

He grabs my chin softly and pulls me to face him.

Warm brown eyes regard me. "We don't have to go."

"No, I want to," I say quickly. "I *need* to."

He looks at me for a moment more, then nods once and releases my chin, sitting back. He doesn't move his hands from mine in my lap, and I anchor myself to that touch.

Wade pulls the car over, and my stomach dips at seeing the softly lit fountain of Lincoln Square.

Okay, you got this. I take off my seatbelt with shaky hands and try to breathe through the tightness in my chest. My heart pounds loudly in my ears as I fiddle with the small clutch in my hand and pull the faux fur jacket around me tighter, struggling to move on to the next part—getting out of the car.

My door suddenly opens and the frigid November air rushes in. A hand appears in the opening, and I follow the jacketed arm to Atticus' perfect face.

"I've got you," he says encouragingly.

"Fuck," I breathe, as I slap my hand in his and let him help me out of the car.

He pulls me to his side while Wade closes the car door and places my hand in the crook of his elbow as we walk closer to the theater. My whole body is locked up and I'm wobbly on my heels as we cross the pavement, so I hold on to Atticus for dear life as we head toward the doors, merging with the stream of people going the same way.

I vaguely hear voices greeting Atticus as we cross the threshold into the building, but I'm too busy concentrating on not falling over or passing out from the lack of oxygen there seems to be.

Atticus leads us through the growing crowd, up some stairs, and then we enter the main theater. We're on one of the upper levels, but all I see is a sea of red as we walk down the rows until we get to the very front. Atticus gestures for me to enter the first row, and I use the banister as support to pass a couple of patrons until Atticus tells me to stop.

I sit stiffly, and try to look around and register what's around me. We're on the first level of the theater, front and center, with an incredible view of the stage and orchestra pit. The stalls below are very full, but there aren't many people up on this level. Actually, no, there are, but there aren't many people around *us*.

I sit back, turning to Atticus. "Did you buy the surrounding tickets?"

He shrugs, looking over the programme he acquired at some point. "They make exceptions for investors."

"An investor?" I ask, surprised. "Since when?"

"The Shaw's have invested in just about everything for almost a century." He lowers the programme, turning to me. "But performing arts, ballet specifically, is a *newer* interest."

His dark gaze carries heavy meaning, the effect this close intense. That tricky word between us whispers in my head. *Years.*

"So, it was a business interest?" I ask.

"No."

"A personal one?"

His eyes drop to my lips. "Very."

At this moment, the lights dim. I turn forward before *I'm* the one giving a performance and focus on the orchestra pit.

The boisterous melody of Tschaikovsky's *Sleeping Beauty* begins, and I feel my whole body go light. The music seeps into my bones and as the dancers come on stage, the world falls away. My body remembers every position and turn, every hand movement and lift, as I absorb the beautiful work of the moving art developing before me.

The performance holds me in its grasp from curtain open to close for intermission. The breaks go by quickly, and then I'm caught up in the performance again, my eyes never leaving the stage.

Part of me misses all of this, but as I'm watching the dancers leap and bound across the stage, I realize I don't yearn to be them anymore. The opposite, in fact.

Ballet is part of my soul, and once upon a time, I wanted to share that part of me with as many people as possible so they could experience this beautiful art form, too.

Now, I just want it to be solely mine.

As the curtain closes and the orchestra performs their final notes, I'm rising from my seat and applauding with the rest of the audience. I feel invigorated with this lustrous energy that only comes with experiencing the magic of a full ballet production.

The dancers take their well-deserved bows, and then the house lights brighten, and the theater starts to empty.

I sink back into my seat next to Atticus and turn to him. He's already watching me with those disarmingly warm chestnut eyes and a rare soft smile.

We're suspended in time, unspoken *somethings* wrapping around us.

Warmth spreads in my chest, and for just a breath, I let myself think that this could be more. That no matter the fucked-up way this began, that we might be able to make something of whatever this is between us.

I don't even know *why* I want it. Maybe I'm just shallow and vain, and he's a good-looking rich guy that can give me a life of dumb luxury I don't have to work hard for. Eventually, he'll get bored, I'll get paid, and I can live the rest of my life comfortably.

But a part of me wishes, *hopes*, it's something more. Is it because he sees beyond the pleasant, pretty veil at the imperfection underneath and doesn't recoil? Is it because he's made of the same imperfection, and those blackened parts of us call to each other?

Whatever it is, I live in the fantasy for another second, and then pull myself back to reality, breaking our eye contact.

"Thank you," I whisper, staring at the emptying orchestra pit.

He stands, holding his hand out to me. I accept it, allowing him to pull me from my seat. He leads me out of our theater and into the hallway, then down the stairs, but instead of heading toward the exit, he takes me through the building until we're entering a small function space teeming with people.

Well-dressed men and women stand in small clusters through the space, drinking champagne and eating canapes while the faintest classical music plays. As we step further into the room, a server approaches with a tray of champagne, so I take two flutes and pass one to Atticus.

"We won't be long," he reassures as he clinks my glass with his.

I nod and take a sip of the bubbling liquid.

"Phaedra Mills," a male voice calls from our side.

I frown and turn to see a familiar face coming toward us. "Jacques?"

"Mon amour," he coos as he grasps my biceps and pulls me in to kiss both cheeks, then holds me an arm's length away.

Dressed in a black suit and white shirt, his long hair still a rich brown, Jacques was the ballet master in Boston who perfected my technique, which landed my spot at the East Ballet Company.

"You look fantastic," he comments in his thick French accent as he releases my arms.

My smile deepens. "Thank you."

"Which company do I need to talk to so I can steal you back?"

I laugh. "I'm not at any companies."

He frowns, confused. "You are dancing, no?"

"I'm teaching." I clarify. "In Connecticut."

Jacques scoffs, waving off my statement. "Teaching is for old people. Come, meet the art director."

Before I can protest, Jacques has my arm hooked around his and we're moving away from Atticus. I turn back and he lifts his drink to me before a suited man approaches him and they shake hands.

Jacques pulls me to a small huddle of people, one of those people being the art director of the New York City Ballet and their resident choreographer. He introduces me to them both, and we strike up a conversation about NYCB and my dancing career.

"Getting into EBT is impressive," the art director comments. "It might be small, but they create quality dancers. We have many of their alum join us."

"I learned a lot when I was with them."

"Why did you leave?" the choreographer asks.

"I got injured."

"And you never returned?"

I shake my head with a smile. "I'm enjoying teaching now."

The art director reaches into her purse and then holds out a card. "You survived Jacques' mastery and come back from an injury, let's talk about you joining us."

I reach for the card, but my brain is scrambling to understand what is happening right now. The art director smiles and excuses herself, telling me to call her next week for a meeting, and then moves away with the choreographer in toe.

"She'll want you to perform again," Jacques comments.

I look up from staring at the card. "I don't want to perform."

He shrugs. "Either way, *ma belle*, she knows talent when she sees it." He steps to my side and gestures with his empty champagne flute. "And it looks like you have a patron already."

I look in the direction he pointed to find Atticus watching us from across the room. He's in the same place I left him but now has a small huddle of people around him.

"That was Atticus Shaw you walked in with?" Jacques asks, pulling my attention back to him.

"Yes," I breathe, then finish my glass of champagne and place it on a table nearby. "It's not like that."

"Then make it like that." He steps closer to me, looking around to see who's listening. "He made a large donation to sponsor a dancer for the whole season on behalf of his wife."

"Oh?"

"*Oui.* He hasn't told us who he's sponsoring yet, which has the company in a buzz."

I guess he's finalizing the terms of our agreement. Even though I know this ends in two days, it still stings to think about.

"Any idea who he'll pick?" I ask, pushing through the unease in my stomach.

Jacques shrugs. "I guess that's up to his mystery wife."

I'm surprised he has yet to notice the massive rocks on my hand, but now I'm glad he's standing on my right. Someone comes to Jacques' side and starts a conversation, and I take the moment to survey the room again. There are more people now, the company dancers intermingling with their patrons.

I definitely don't miss the party obligations of being in a company. Having to uphold whatever image management wants to display to get funding is utterly exhausting.

The person Jacques was speaking to leaves as a server approaches us with more champagne and we both take a glass, clink them together and take a sip.

"Mon Dieu," Jacques splutters. "Is that Tesia Kozak?"

The hairs on the back of my neck stand straight up at the mention of her name. My stomach twists more in knots as I turn to the entrance and see Tesia standing in the doorway.

As usual, she's dressed beautifully—in a sapphire-blue dress that fits like a glove—and has the attention of most of the room.

"Does she dance with NYCB now?" I ask as we watch her move through the crowd.

"Non..." Jacques confirms.

We both watch as she slides up to Atticus' side like she belongs there, hooking her arm into his. I hold my breath as he pulls away from her touch...but then he puts his arm around her, never once stopping his conversation, his hand resting between her bare shoulder blades. He's *touching* her. My blood fucking boils.

"That must be his wife," Jacques comments.

I don't correct him because I can't speak, can't think, past my heart pounding in my ears. He's fucking lied to me over and over.

Tesia leans in and whispers into Atticus' ear, her whole body pressing further into his side as she does. He pulls back slightly to look at her, nods once, then turns to the people he was speaking to, seemingly making excuses to leave. With his hand still on her back, they walk toward the exit.

Jacques chuckles, turning back to me. "Maybe not his wife, but *definitely* up to her old tricks with the patrons."

I let out a breathy laugh, and then take a healthy mouthful of my champagne, trying to mentally delete images of Tesia's "old tricks" with Atticus.

I'm so fucking stupid. They're probably laughing about my naivety in a back room. I need to go.

"Oh!" Jacques grabs my arm and pulls me through the crowd. We end up at a small bar I didn't know was in here, and approaching a familiar face.

"Felix," Jacques calls as we stop at his side.

The other Shaw's face softens in familiarity. "Jacques."

He's dressed similarly to the first time we met: this time a black suit and white shirt with no tie, his curls neat, and a hint of facial hair this time. He turns to me, his brown eyes narrowing slightly.

"Phaedra Mills," I say, holding out my right hand.

Thankfully, he plays along by grasping my hand and shaking it. "Felix Shaw."

"Phaedra is thinking about joining the company," Jacques announces. "Maybe you can convince her with your checkbook?"

We're both surprised at Jacques' boldness, but he doesn't seem to care as he kisses both my cheeks and flutters away.

"Mills?" Felix asks.

I rip my hand out of his and steal the drink in front of him, downing the amber liquid in one mouthful. Scotch, gross.

I set the glass down a little roughly and glare up at Felix. "Do you know your *fiancée* is fucking my *husband* in another room right now?"

He stares at me. The accusation doesn't even faze him.

"Another drink?" he asks.

I blink. Blink again. He's serious.

"Another drink?" I repeat, dumbfounded.

He sighs, turns and holds two fingers up to the bartender.

"Don't bother," I declare, fishing my phone out in my small clutch bag. "You and your cousin and your fiancée can enjoy whatever bullshit Shaw game this is."

"For what it's worth, he's probably not doing what you think he is," Felix says, making me pause, but I don't turn back to him.

"It's worth nothing," I say over my shoulder.

"Atticus doesn't make a move unless it gets him something he wants."

I twist slightly back to Felix. He's leaning lazily against the bar, drink in hand. "And her?"

Felix shrugs, not one ounce of emotion in his dark gaze. "Tesia is the same."

I let out an incredulous laugh. "So they're made for each other? Great to know."

He lifts his glass closer to his mouth. "She has nothing of value to him."

"Neither do I."

He scoffs into his glass. "I doubt that."

Sudden exhaustion washes over me. I'm tired. So unbelievably tired of this whole farce. My lip wobbles and my eyes sting with tears, but I refuse to cry here.

"It doesn't matter," I say dejectedly, turning back toward the exit. "I'm done."

37
ATTICUS

EVERY STEP AWAY FROM Phaedra is agony, but this must be done.

Tesia pulls me into a random office nearby and closes the door behind us.

"That little wife of yours didn't hold your interest for long," Tesia comments as she presses me into the nearest wall, her body sliding against mine. "I'm not surprised her pathetic whoring routine was disappointing."

Her hands travel up my arms and over my shoulders, heading toward my neck. "I forgive you for your lapse in judgement. We all have them from time to time."

I grin down at her as I reach out and brush my fingers down the front of her throat. "If you don't get your hands off me, I will break every one of your fingers."

She freezes, blinking at me in confusion.

"Atticus," she admonishes. "What—"

"Being the Shaw pass-around is not why I asked you here

tonight."

Her touch finally leaves me as she moves back enough to fold her arms over her chest, irritation crossing her features. "You can't be serious. You're choosing *her* over me? That useless bottom-feeder is—"

"If you say one more thing about my wife, you won't see another sunrise."

The warning in my tone finally cuts through, and fear flashes in her eyes.

"Atticus..."

I take a step forward, away from the wall. Tesia stumbles back a step. "I will only tell you this once. Stay away from my wife. You won't speak to her or about her until your last breath." I take another step. "I don't give a shit what you do with Felix, but interfere any further with me or my wife, and Paloma will find out about your relationship with Frederic."

I wasn't surprised at all when Wade found out that Tesia was fucking my father on the side. My parents aren't faithful to each other—they both have an abundance of lovers worldwide, buried under layers of ironclad nondisclosure agreements—but there's an unspoken rule about fucking someone from their so-called "inner circle."

Not only is Tesia the closest she can be to Paloma, but she's one of her favorites, and this is the ultimate betrayal.

"I don't know what you're talking about." She keeps her face neutral and her stance the same, but the slight dilation of her pupils screams of the lie.

I narrow my eyes. "His standing meeting almost every Thursday for almost a year doesn't ring a bell?"

She looks irritated, but that nervous swallow nearly makes me laugh. She's not as subtle as she thinks.

"Last week must have been a celebration since he even took you out to lunch first," I muse. "I hear the duck is superb at that bistro. What's your review?"

"You have no proof," she concedes, a touch of panic in her tone.

I pull out my phone, find the video Wade emailed me and play it, angling it toward her.

"I'm sure you recognize Frederic's West Side apartment," I comment, reveling in the terror dawning across Tesia's face as the sounds of her fucking my father echo between us. "He has a proclivity for filming his mistresses as an insurance policy."

Tesia's tear-filled blue eyes flick up to me. "This can't get out. She'll *ruin* me."

"That all rests on your actions," I point out.

She nods, taking a shaky breath. "Consider yourself and your wife strangers to me."

I stop the video and pocket the phone. "Excellent. Now, get out of my sight."

Tesia pats at the corner of her eyes and sniffs softly, then rolls her shoulder back and heads for the door.

"Oh, and Miss Kozak," I call as her hand lands on the doorknob. She turns to look at me. "If you continue this tryst, you might want to choose the locations more carefully."

Saying nothing, she turns and slips out of the room. It feels as if a weight has lifted as the door clicks closed and my shoulders drop. That's one more thing out of our way.

Now to tackle the hardest obstacle that's impeding our happy marriage—my wife.

I smooth down my suit jacket and adjust my cufflinks as I cross to the door and exit the room. Turning toward the direction of the party, I pause.

A vision in black and lilac stands in the hall, frozen in place, looking at me. The same listless, empty look from last week plagues Phaedra's beautiful face as she regards me. Without turning, she takes a step back.

This time, she's *actually* running.

Absolutely not.

"Where are you going, Lilac?"

38
PHAEDRA

EVEN FROM THIS DISTANCE, Atticus' warning tone carries clearly. The hairs on the back of my neck stand straight up, alarm bells lighting up in my mind, but the idiotic, dark side of me craves one last injection of chaos.

"Did you enjoy yourself in there?" I sneer as he closes the gap between us. "Tesia seemed like she did." Actually, Tesia looked hollow, and brushed past me coming out of the party like I wasn't even there.

Taking unrushed steps toward me, his hands tucked into his pants pocket and his posture completely relaxed. "Enjoyable, but nowhere near satisfying."

Rage boils hotter in my veins; he's *really* admitting he just fucked Tesia when we're supposed to be married?

"You're disgusting," I spit.

"Am I?" he purrs, still lazily strolling forward.

The glint in his dark eyes has those incessant alarms blaring louder in my head, but *fuck*, are my legs trembling in anticipation at whatever that look *means*.

"I hope you both have the lives you deserve," I say, backing up the hall, shoving my phone back in my bag. I was going to call a rideshare service, but I'll just get a cab.

"You still haven't told me where you're going, Phaedra," he commands, his tone deceptively light.

"Away from you," I seethe. "Away from all of this. I'm done."

Atticus chuckles, the sound *deadly*. "Oh, my beloved, but I'm not done with you."

Heart pounding wildly, my whole body breaks out in goosebumps at those words, everything I ache to hear, and everything that's wrong with this whole situation.

"You will be," I admit, still backing up. "I'm an infatuation to you, Atticus, nothing more."

He frowns, pausing his approach. "An...infatuation."

"I don't know what this is between us anymore, or why you pursued it in the first place, but our arrangement is finished and I'm leaving."

He jolts a step forward. "No."

I throw my hand out to stop him. "Stop. I don't care."

Turning swiftly, I open the nearest door and slip through. I continue unseeing, nothing but my heavy breathing echoing back at me in the dark hall. I have no idea where I'm going, but I just need to *go*.

The smack of a door closing behind me makes me jump, and I look back. A tall, wide figure advances toward me in the darkness. Atticus.

"You think I'd let you go so easily?" His voice, so deep and *angry*, echoes against the walls along with my pounding heart in my ears as I continue forward, moving faster, fear's lethal claws skittering across my skin.

"I warned you, Phaedra." *Fuck, is he closer?* "No matter how far you run, I will find you."

I scramble around a corner into another hall, opening the first door on my right to a narrow stairwell. I climb the stairs as quickly as I can, almost whimpering when I hear the door below open and close. Emerging into another dark hallway, I race past door after door, until the hall opens into a space that feels familiar.

Ropes and fabric hang every which way, random pieces of stage furniture dot the room. A portable barre sits in a corner, a tray with remnants of rosin next to it. I've never been here before, but every backstage is relatively the same.

Knowing how close Atticus is, I dart over to a stairway stage structure on wheels, and squeeze myself between it and the wall, then climb into a hollow space in the back. I can hear my labored breathing echoing in the structure, so I close my eyes and try to control it.

Heavy footsteps make my heart beat wildly and I squeeze my eyes closed harder.

"Oh, Phaedra," Atticus sing-songs, drawing out my name.

Tears stream down my face as I cover my mouth with both my hands, swallowing a whimper, my whole body trembling.

"Come out, come out, wherever you are." His footsteps move about the space, followed by the swoosh of curtains being moved.

"Do you really believe you're just an *infatuation?*" he asks, the words biting, his voice bouncing around as he moves. "Something so frivolous and fleeting?"

His steps fall a little harder and faster, curtains sound like they're thrown open, and other furniture moves.

Then everything stops.

"I will find you, Phaedra," Atticus promises. He sounds far away. "For you, my *'infatuation'*, I'm a very patient man."

Footsteps recede, a door opens and closes, and then it's quiet.

I wait, then wait some more, listening for a whisper of movement. But there's nothing but my short breaths, so I slowly crawl out of my hiding place and squeeze out from behind the stairs. I need to get out of here. There should be some sort of side stage exit to the stalls and then hopefully the main doors aren't locked.

I head for stage left when deep, rumbling, *familiar* laughter comes from behind me. *Fuck.*

Adrenaline explodes through my veins, and without turning back, I run.

There's no exit here. I turn—there's one on the other side.

I get a third of the way across the stage when a heavy body slams into me. I shriek as I fall face-first to the floor. At the last second before impact, the world spins, and I land hard on a warm body.

I'm stunned for a millisecond before I kick and elbow out of Atticus' hold and roll to my hands and knees, trying to get to my feet. Why the fuck did I choose to wear heels with straps? No, *he* chose them. Did he plan this?

A firm grip on my ankle startles me, and I let out another scream as I'm dragged back and flipped onto my back.

"No!" I shout, bucking side to side as Atticus straddles me, sitting over my hips.

He captures both of my wrists, then advances forward, pressing them into the floor above my head. I cry freely, his face hovering above me, slightly distorted by the tears.

"Now, now, my beloved, quieten those tears before you choke."

I shake my head, crying a little harder.

He presses his free hand to the center of my chest. "Slow your breathing."

I don't want to do anything he says, but self-preservation kicks in and I take a deep breath, then another, until my sobs quieten and my breathing calms.

"There you go," he praises, rubbing my chest slowly. I blink up to a soft smile across his face. "You're a fucking mess, Mrs. Shaw."

"Let me go," I plead, tears stinging my eyes again. *"Please."*

He *tsks*. "Not until we talk."

"Talk?" I croak out.

"Mhmm." His smile broadens. "There was no need for all these theatrics, but I admit, I *very* much enjoyed it."

"I didn't," I rush out.

He does that head-tilting thing, regarding me. "What did I say about lying to me, Lilac?"

"I'm not."

He arches a brow, his gaze hardening.

I open my mouth to say something, but he claps his hand over it, silencing me.

"I don't want to hear any more fucking lies, Phaedra," he growls.

An errant tear rolls down my temple as I nod vigorously.

He waits a beat, then moves his hand from my mouth back to

my chest.

"W-What do you want to talk about?" I ask, changing tactics. If I play along, maybe he'll let me go.

"Us," he whispers reverently. His eyes follow the path of his hand as he moves it across my chest, his fingers caressing my skin, skating the base of my throat. I swallow; his eyes flick to the motion, then back up to my face. "Have you figured out how we met yet?"

I shake my head.

"You may not remember," he muses. "It was a *painful* day."

I frown. Painful? For me? The only day that comes to mind is... My eyes widen.

Atticus nods. "Yes, *that* day."

The injury. He was there. But... "I don't remember."

"I noticed the incremental fault in your leap," he says. "So did the art director. She thought you were going to collapse in the middle of the production. But then you kept going, without a crease of pain on your beautiful face."

All I remember after that leap *was* pain. And then nothing until I woke up in the hospital.

"A broken little thing still spinning," Atticus sighs. "The rest of the performance was perfect. Mesmerizing. *Haunting*." His eyes blaze with a wicked fire. "From that last turn, you had my attention. Thoroughly piqued my interest. I needed to know the stunning broken creature before me. But then *you* chose *me*."

"What?"

"You sealed our fates the moment you pranced off that stage and collapsed in *my* arms. *Mine*." He chuckles deeply, the sound vibrating through me. "Those golden eyes looked up at me with so much terror and hurt. And then you spoke two words. 'Help me.'" His eyes close for a moment as if he can hear them again. "Those two words, the misery in those glittering eyes hooked into me and wouldn't let go. God, it pissed me off how a beautiful stranger had pierced through to my dark soul, stirring every wicked desire I kept caged, so *easily*."

He brushes an errant piece of hair out of my face, his fingers lingering on my cheek. "That's when I knew I wanted to own your misery, to *be* your misery. But you asked for my help."

My mind is spinning. "A-And?"

"I looked after you," he supplies. "Got you the best medical team and physiotherapists. Massages and acupuncture. Whatever you needed."

I shake my head. "That was—"

"Insurance?" Atticus scoffs. "They would've covered practically nothing. Besides, you needed that money for an apartment."

"Did you..."

He shakes his head. "That was all you, my beloved. Until I paid it off recently. And the studio building purchase. But before you decided you weren't returning to East Ballet, I purchased them, too."

I blink at him, confused. He shrugs like it's not a big fucking deal he bought an entire private ballet company.

"I sold it back to them when you decided on teaching," he informs me nonchalantly. "With interest, of course. That sent them bankrupt. They had to downsize substantially. Most of the dancers *mysteriously* never got jobs in New York again."

"Why?" I whisper. "Why would you do any of that?"

"Because you chose *me*," he stresses. "Asked for *my* help. And I did, gave you anything you needed for you to feel whole again."

"All so you could just break me again? Be my *misery*?" I ask.

"Yes," he practically purrs, a wicked grin lighting his face. "*You* called to the sick and twisted part of me that raged through me until it got to taste that jagged little heart that never beat the same after that fateful day."

I did this. I didn't know I did it, but I started all of this. I brought this certifiable man into my life, and he's been playing puppet master all this time.

Years.

My chest constricts painfully. I don't know what to do with all of this information.

"Now you know," Atticus concludes, his voice muffled slightly by the static buzzing in my head. "And now I need an answer."

39

PHAEDRA

I FROWN, SEARCHING ATTICUS' face above me. "Answer to what?"

"What do you want?" he asks.

I shake my head, not understanding.

"What do you *want?*" he asks again.

What do I want...from *this*. From him.

"I... I don't..." My rapid breathing makes it hard to speak, to think. I feel my eyes rolling closed. I'm going to pass out.

Atticus taps my cheek a few times, rousing me. My gaze refocuses on him, my throat burning from hyperventilating. "I don't know."

"You do, Lilac," he argues gently. "What do you want?"

"Please," I sob.

He leans down, pressing his cheek to mine, his hot breath on the shell of my ear.

"Tell me, baby," he coaxes into my ear, his beard tickling my sensitive skin. "Tell me what you want."

Too many emotions, questions, *accusations*, wrap around me. I'm drowning. I start pulling at his hold on my wrists. "I...I can't. I can't breathe."

Surprisingly, he lets go. He also lifts off my hips. I immediately scramble out from under him and stand on shaky legs.

"What else?" I demand. "What else did you do? To *'help'* me?"

"Many, many things."

I pace, my mind scrolling through the last two years. "So, all the healing, the growth, the strides in my career...was *you?*"

"It was *us*," he corrects. "You wanted it; I opened the door. If there was an obstacle, I removed it *for us*."

I pause. "Obstacles. Like Dylan?"

He nods. "And your other useless boyfriend... That asshole art director—"

"Tesia?" I can't help but ask.

"I never touched her again from the day you chose me. Broke up with her within the week. She was already fucking Felix by that point, anyway, but the second you became my life, she was obsolete."

His words from the hotel room come back to me. "You said I ruined your life."

"Yes," he confirms.

"But you still 'helped' me," I point out.

"Of course."

"And yet, you want to be my misery?"

He just smirks, saying nothing.

I shake my head, confused, *frustrated*. I don't understand what any of this *means*.

This is too much. I can't do this. Panic seizes my chest painfully as I spin toward the exit and take a couple of steps to freedom.

"What do you want, Phaedra?" he demands, making me halt in my escape. "All I ask is that you answer before you leave."

Him. My brain, my fucking soul, starts an incessant chant. *Him, him, him.*

I try to shake it out of my head, but it just gets louder. Why? Why do I want him? He's manipulative and stubborn and a literal *murderer.*

That didn't bother you before, that stupid dark side of me whispers.

It's true, and for some fucked up reason, it *still* doesn't bother me. None of it does. He's been scheming and manipulating in my shadow for years, all for whatever diabolical reasons of his, and it invokes many strong emotions in me. But not the *right* ones for this situation. And *that's* a problem.

If it was anyone else, I would run for the hills and Atticus would be in jail by now. But he's not, because he's...Atticus.

It makes no sense, and it's eating away at my sanity.

"I need to go," I say, refusing to look at him.

"You could," Atticus muses. "But you'll have nowhere to go."

I lift my head to look at him. "What do you mean?"

"Your house has sold," he informs me simply. "And Will has detailed instructions on what to look for in a teaching replacement."

My heart stops, my ears pounding with static.

"Say that again?" I ask slowly, taking measured steps toward him.

A self-satisfied grin breaks out across his face. "Your belongings are packed and on the way to the penthouse. Will is honored you promoted him to studio manager. He looks forward to visiting you in your New York studio when you decide on a space. And of course, when he's interning for Shaw Incorporated, he'll make sure he finds an adequate replacement."

"You sold my house," I say carefully. "Removed me from my own business."

"You still own the Connecticut studio. The New York location will be a secondary location. The one *you* teach at."

I'm boiling with fury. "You better be fucking lying, Shaw."

"I don't lie to you, Lilac." He moves closer, matching me step for step. "Your life is here now. With me."

I launch forward and shove him in the chest. He doesn't move. I do it twice more before he catches my wrists and holds my hands against him.

"Why?" I shout. "Why do you keep doing this to me?"

"Because you're my madness, Phaedra," he bites back. "You're the festering madness under my skin, slowly infecting every part of me. You're already in my bones, my organs, my fucking head. If I cut you out, I'm dead. So, *you. Are not.* Leaving."

His words resonate with me more than I want them to. Because he's *my* madness, *my* disease. So expertly designed specifically just for me that I didn't know I was infected until it was too late.

And I'm beyond repair.

I pull my hands roughly out of his grasp, and slap him hard across the face.

He laughs. *Laughs.*

I grab a fistful of his shirt and yank, bringing his face down and crushing my lips to his. The buzzing in my head stops, and I feel like I can breathe again. This, us, is wrong and right and everything in between. But I don't fucking care anymore.

If this is what "misery" is, then I want it. All of it.

I release his shirt and shove at him again, breaking the kiss, breathing hard.

Irritation flashes through his eyes as his hand shoots out, grabbing a fistful of hair at the nape of my neck and pulling me back, his mouth possessing mine once more.

I reach between us and palm his crotch, his hard cock straining against the fabric. I slide my hand further down and then squeeze firmly. Atticus jolts back, looking at me, confused.

I squeeze slightly harder and he winces. "Let. Go."

He releases my hair immediately, his hands out contemplatively.

I smirk. "Good boy."

Lust burns hotter in those dark eyes I can't seem to escape.

"So we're playing like that, hmm?" Atticus purrs. "You want me to submit?"

I nod, my hold still firm on his balls, but then it slips, sliding up the center of his body as Atticus lowers to the floor on his knees in front of me, his captivating gaze never leaving mine.

"Is this what you want, my beloved?" His hands trail down my side, over my hips and lower, the fabric of my dress doing nothing to dampen the electricity in his touch. "Me on my knees before you?"

My fingers coast over his Adam's apple and beard, then traces his perfect lips. "It's a good start."

His eyes spark in challenge. "Am I not to your satisfaction, Mrs. Shaw?"

I pull my hand from his face and reach for the side of my dress, unzipping it and letting it drop to the floor along with my bag I somehow haven't lost. Still dressed in my fur coat, I stand before him in a black lace bustier, matching panties, and heels.

Using his shoulder for support, I step out of the dress, nudging it to the side with my foot. My touch lingers on his shoulders, relishing in the strength under my fingertips.

"Magnificent," Atticus sighs, his electrifying touch returning, starting at my ankles and slowly creeping upward.

"Now you," I say softly, tugging at the shoulder of his tuxedo jacket.

I miss his touch immediately as he pulls off his jacket, discarding it to the side. I reach for the tongue of his bowtie and tug, unraveling the silk, and dropping it to our growing pile of clothes as he pulls off his cufflinks. Seeing them this close, I realize they're a single letter in platinum: P.

I unbutton the top two buttons of his shirt as he pockets the cufflinks and slips off the straps of the black suspenders I didn't know he was wearing underneath his jacket.

My fingers linger at his throat, tracing over those symbols, the morse code, on his neck.

"What do they mean?" I ask softly.

"They're dates," he answers. "All of them are dates."

"Dates for what?"

He places my fingers on the lowest one at the base of his throat.

"The day you fell into my arms." He moves my fingers to the next one. "Our wedding day three months ago." He moves them to the top one, the freshest one. "The hotel when you first put me on my knees. When you saw us as *real*."

"And the others?" I ask, my voice thick as a tirade of emotions swirls around me.

"All of your healing, your triumph, the success we've achieved *together*. It's branded into my skin. Everything."

My everything. That's what he called them when I first discovered them. His everything.

His touch returns to my skin, sliding up the sides of my knees and curving toward the back of my thighs, distracting me from the newest revelation. My hands fall to my side, my coat slipping off in the process, as my eyes droop closed and my legs tremble while he caresses my thighs, my body already pulsing with pleasure at just his touch.

"There's just one thing," Atticus muses softly, and then suddenly my knees buckle and I'm falling.

I land with a yelp, straddling Atticus' lap, my hands gripping his shoulders and my knees slamming into the stage floor. Atticus' hold returns to my hair, his fists wrapping the length around twice. He tugs hard, craning my neck so I'm forced to look at him in his angry gaze.

"You haven't apologized," he says.

"For what?" I huff.

Atticus leans forward, our noses almost touching. "You have a lot to apologize for."

I scoff, which makes him tug on my hair again, making me

wince. I dig my nails into his shoulders. He groans.

His free hand slips between us and into my panties, his fingers sliding over my clit and through my arousal.

"Soaking," he groans, inserting two fingers into me. "I knew it."

My eyes close again as he pumps his fingers in me, curling them forward to hit that spot that sends me to oblivion while his thumb rubs firm circles over my clit. My body responds so quickly, rushing up the hill to an orgasm that will turn off my brain.

My grip tightens on Atticus' shoulders, as I hit the peak and then—

He stops moving, his thumb disappearing.

My eyes fly open as the orgasm dissolves.

"What—"

"Apologize," he demands, face as hard as stone.

"What?" I say again, my mind a pile of confused goop.

"Say you're sorry," he articulates slowly.

"For?"

"Apologize for leaving."

I huff out an incredulous laugh. He can't be serious. "Your fingers are literally *inside* me."

"You tried to leave before," he argues.

"But I didn't."

"You left the party," he clarifies, anger burning hotter in his eyes. "You assumed the worst, and you were leaving me."

"Att—*Fuck*." His name transforms into a curse as he starts his ministrations again, his fingers pumping harder, his thumb circling with intention.

He tugs my hair again, my neck arching back, the pain pulsing in symphony with the pleasure. He licks a hot path up my exposed throat as I race to the peak once more, faster this time.

And then he stops *again*.

"Apologize," he growls into my neck.

"No," I spit.

He repeats the glorious torture, working my body like the puppet master he is, stopping before I can come and demanding I apologize.

After the fourth round, my body is wound tight to the point of unwanted pain, tears streak down my face, and my brain is fragmented.

"You want this to stop, Lilac?" Atticus asks softly.

"Yes," I sob. "*Please*."

"All you have to do is apologize."

"I'm sorry," I rush out.

"And what are you sorry for?"

"All of it," I wail. "I'm sorry, Atticus. Please, *please*, I'm sorry. I'm sorry."

He untangles his hand from my hair and wipes the tears from my face.

"It's okay, my beloved. I forgive you," he coos comfortingly. "And I apologize, too, for giving you the wrong impression. Nothing happened in that room, I promise. I'll show you the video later. First, let me make it up to you."

He cups the back of my head as he tilts forward, laying me flat on the floor. Slipping his fingers out of me, he makes quick work of his pants zipper, pulling out his gloriously hard cock and then leaning down over me.

He sinks into me smoothly, bottoming out, and I swear I can feel it in my throat. I relish in the burn of the stretch to accommodate his girth, the fullness. I will never get enough of it. Of *him*.

He hooks one of my knees into the crook of his arm, sliding the other one between us, his thumb finding my clit. He starts moving then, leaning further down, stretching my legs open and I'm already seeing stars.

"Fuck," I choke out, my eyes rolling, both my hands sliding into his hair, gripping the short curls tight.

"All I want is you, Phaedra," Atticus grunts, without breaking his rhythm. "Just us. You and me."

Last time I heard those words, I didn't know what to do with them. This time, it's the only thing that makes sense.

"Yes," I breathe. "You and me."

"Tell me," he demands, thrusting harder. "Tell me you'll never leave me."

"Never," I barely squeeze out around the feelings choking me.

"Say it," he growls.

"I won't leave." My eyes roll. "Never leave you."

Atticus shoves into me hard, the pain making me shout as he grabs my throat and pulls my head up, my eyes opening to a burning black gaze. "You're mine, Mrs. Shaw."

"Yours," I agree in a rush. "Only yours."

He pants, still buried in me, not moving. "Say it again."

"Yours, Atticus. I'm yours."

His whole body seems to loosen the slightest, his eyes shuttering in relief. "All mine."

"Yes," I whisper. "And you're *mine*."

Suddenly, we're turning and I'm straddling Atticus.

His grip flexes on my hips. "Take it, Phaedra. Take it all."

Using his chest as support, I sit straighter and whimper, feeling impossibly more full at this angle. I roll my hips and both of us moan. Digging my nails into his chest, I ride him hard and fast, grinding down with every roll of my hips.

I take what I want, which is Atticus. It will always be him.

Atticus moves one of his hands to my clit, applying the right pressure and pattern of the sensitive flesh until I'm panting.

I'm rocketing to the peak again, not sure my body could be stopped at this point. Atticus now meets me thrust for thrust, following me to ecstasy.

To forever.

I come so hard it feels like I transcend space and time. Every atom of my body burns as hot as an inferno, the flames consuming everything around them, consuming Atticus, using his fire to create something new, something everlasting.

Fates entwined.

I come down from the biggest high of my life and collapse onto Atticus. Both of us breathing heavily, absolutely spent. I don't have the capacity to do anything but tuck myself under his chin and just exist.

So I do.

And so does he.

Then reality comes trickling in and I huff a laugh.

"We're in public," I mumble into Atticus' chest.

He makes an agreeing sound in the back of his throat.

"On a *stage*," I wheeze out.

"Your best performance yet," he mumbles.

I grin, reveling in the heat of Atticus' body, his comforting bergamot and sandalwood scent, and let my mind wander into thoughts of what tomorrow will bring. And the day after, and all the days after that.

Which reminds me...

"Atticus?"

"Yes, my beloved?" he mumbles into my hair.

"If this marriage is going to last, I have terms."

ACKNOWLEDGEMENTS

To my Readers: Thank you again for letting me take you on this chaotic journey. Without you, I wouldn't be doing what I love, so I am grateful you take a chance on me every time.

Ash: The spice to my chaos. You're incredible. I love you. Never change. This life is easier with you by my side.

EJ: My goth girlie. My emotional support travel buddy. The other Mrs. Shaw. I'm so glad we found each other. I love you. Thank you for fuelling the gremlin behaviour.

Callista: You have the patience of a saint. I'm honoured to know you.

My betas: Huge shout out to my beta readers because this one was a doozy. You're all so patient, and I'm beyond grateful for staying with me on this journey.

My little internet writer community, my people: I love seeing all of your faces daily. Thank you for joining me no matter how many changes we go through. You make me feel seen and I can never thank you all enough.

ALSO BY CASSANDRA B. ANDREUCCI

Betrayer of Blood *(Other Side Book One)*
Wrath of Darkness *(Other Side Book Two)*
Dark Siren *(Vicious Games Book One)*
Broken Songbird *(Vicious Games Book Two)*
Lie for Me

WANT MORE?

ENTER THE WORLD OF CHAOS
SCAN THE QR CODE BELOW